THE HEDGE FUND

Where Blood Meets Money

by
Burton Hersh

Best Wishes,

Burton Hersh

BY BURTON HERSH

Nonfiction

Edward Kennedy: An Intimate Biography (2010)

Bobby and J. Edgar (2007)

The Shadow President (1997)

The Old Boys (1992, 2002)

The Mellon Family (1978)

The Education of Edward Kennedy (1972)

Fiction

The Nature of the Beast (2002)

The Ski People (1968)

TREE FARM BOOKS/CREATESPACE
2014

U.S. Copyright Registration Number: TXu 1-868-357

www.treefarmbooks.com

CHAPTER I

I think I first caught on that something was roiling Dad up Christmas afternoon of 2007. By three o'clock the carnage of wrapping paper and discarded ribbons had already been swept out of the Music Room and we were starting to wake up after gorging on Anastasia's super-succulent free-range turkey and key lime pie. The brothers-in-law had headed home. Our Dad and I were settled into Dad's Jacuzzi. Beyond the lichen-covered timbers of the sea wall some kind of makeshift regatta was trailing into the yacht basin.

Dad repositioned the base of his spine against one of the surging jets and slumped into the cascading bubbles. "For what it's worth," he opened up, "the accountants have been all over my vulnerable old ass all week. They're starting to break the tax year down." Steam started Dad squinting, heavy beads erupted across his tonsure. Dad was a stocky sixty-plus-year-old, still muscular from fighting it out most mornings with his elliptical machine followed by laps in the regulation-Olympic pool that overlooked the Bay. "Stillman says he needs a lot more paperwork than he's got. Especially regarding your hedge fund."

"*My* hedge fund?"

"You drew up the contracts."

"I reviewed the contracts. Kicking and screaming every minute, if you remember."

"Could that be true, Michael? At my age the memory is very selective."

I knew Dad was giving me the business, but it was hard

not to overreact. I was still dumbfounded at how skillfully our recently acquired brother-in-law, Ricky's glamorous Cuban-emigre father, the financier Ramon Perez y Cruz, had played Dad over the months since his son Enrique married our sister Wendy.

Looking back I now think Dad had been doing so well moving in on the exploding local real estate market that nothing seemed out of the question. Highly regarded professor and writer in economics that he was, Dad understood the multipliers immediately when Ramon showed us how – once the embargo got lifted – his ascendant Sunrise Capital Partners hedge fund could cut us in on *miles* of choice Cuban beaches picked up for pennies on the dollar.

We had to pledge to Ramon's hedge fund most of Dad's choicer up-market acquisitions. Following up the trust negotiations as Dad's personal lawyer, I had squeezed whatever protections I could into the paperwork. A real-estate boom was raging from Tokyo to Dublin; Citigroup and AIG seemed positioned to gobble up the known world

Then the panic started, months before that fateful Christmas of 2007. Pumped up with subprime mortgages, on the line for billions in unsustainable credit default swaps, Lehman Brothers had burst like a giant piñata. Soaking in his Jacuzzi I realized that even a romantic optimist like Dad was terrified.

Dad regarded me balefully over the heavy brine of bubbles and attempted to confess, in his way. "I suppose every great man makes one big-time blunder. With Churchill it was the Dardanelles."

"Churchill? Why settle for Churchill? Didn't Jesus ever do

anything wrong?"

"Right. How about Moses? Mustn't look too grandiose, Michael. I want you to remember that."

"Modesty. You're pushing modesty now?"

This exchange was wearing thin. Even through the steam I could see that Dad's attention was drifting off. "If this goes bad it will be mine to sweat, we can agree on that," he grunted finally in a subdued voice. "Taken to the cleaners by greaseball economics."

The moment he said that I could tell Dad regretted it. It was the first racist dig I'd ever heard come out of him. "Don't tell your mother I said that," Dad muttered. "You know how she is. I'm convinced that if some coked-up paisano were slicing off her pearls with one hand and hiking up the hem of her nightie with the other she'd find some elaborate sociological justification." Dad swabbed his flushed face with one stubby hand. "I think that's guilt, too many generations on trust-funds."

"It's going to get more complicated than I thought," Dad rumbled on. "Stillman says a couple of the properties had already been earmarked for the charitable endowment. We could get buried in retroactive penalty and interest payments."

Just then we both became aware, through the steam, of Cybil. The folks were putting Cybil up for the holiday. She was the pert, divorced sister of one of our newly acquired brothers-in-law, Buckley Glickman. An impudent ectomorph in a string bikini, Cybil's hipbones now yawned like jaws as she squatted behind the tray of gin and tonics she had trotted out from the main house.

"Whose endowment are we talking about here, Sylvan?" Cybil giggled, peering over her long nose into the maelstrom of bubbles. She had a baseball cap on backwards.

"Mine," Dad said. He all but growled; Cybil had crossed a line. Mostly friends his own age addressed Dad as Sylvan.

"I should have guessed that." Cybil tittered. "Well, you *are* a special case."

"Nothing that out of the ordinary." When Dad felt condescended to he could get outrageous. "If you're hung like a rhinoceros."

Cybil stepped back, still carrying the tray.

"Keeps the womenfolk on edge," Dad acknowledged, grinning up. "But I *have* got quite a following in the rhinoceros population."

We have come into a time when great wealth is all we take very seriously. The infatuated young public relations trainee you pick up in an East Side club is much more likely to permit you a run at the back door than show you her bank book. Within families of well-established means, once outsiders start marrying in, the rule remains: Kiss, but don't tell. Checks from remote brokerage offices turn up in the mail every month, there is some indication on the basis of which outsiders can attempt to guess how the investments are allocated among sectors and specialty funds. From time to time the still-intimidated newcomers are presented with papers to sign.

Things weren't that different in our family until the dog days of the Reagan Administration. Even as a kid I thought Dad took our finances over by way of a fatigue duty, as if he'd come upon a waterlogged manatee on one of our beaches here and performed mouth-to-mouth resuscitation to keep the ugly old mother heaving and snorting. Until 1987 he'd seemed to like life well enough throwing his intellectual weight around, publishing books and teaching the post-graduate economics seminar at Temple. There was a lot of gratification in posturing for the coeds, and Dad obviously enjoyed his role as The Iconoclastic Hebrew at Main Line dinner parties.

My parents originally ran into each other at Yale. Dad had stayed home for college to study economics at the University of Minnesota. He was a precocious student and moved on after graduation by winning a Fulbright Grant to the State University of Styria in Graz to pick over the archive notes of the dandified young Josef Schumpeter. There Dad's draft board cornered him, on semester break skiing the Obertauern.

The Viet Nam war was boiling, Lyndon Johnson was scrounging for bodies, and Dad's stratospheric General Technical score had doomed him to eighteen months as a radio operator. By early 1968 Dad was one more grunt in 'Nam nursing hopes of getting through his hitch alive. He wound up a lackadaisical staff sergeant presiding over a perimeter communications trailer the night the North Vietnamese went for Tan Son Nhut Air Base, hours into the Tet Offensive. The breech and trigger housing of the 50-caliber machine gun he grabbed got so hot from the thousands of rounds of suppressive fire Dad poured into the attacking Viet Cong that both Dad's forearms got scorched, repeatedly, and never again grew hair. All that scar tissue was especially fascinating to my nosy little sisters growing up. Dad won the Silver Star.

Dad was a stand-up guy – everybody depended on that. I think at some level he was never completely at home in what our mother would teasingly refer to as the "Evil East." For Dad his Minnesota origins were bedrock – he'd toughened up dealing with his starchy Episcopalian prep school and the brutal YMCA canoe camps and fist fights with freckle-faced Mick youngsters in empty lots visible from the cornfields. That was the real America. The Philadelphia Society he'd married into was nervous, held-in, mannered. And as for Florida? Florida was built on sand. On slime.

But I'm definitely getting ahead of myself. The father I remember first was on the make in academia. His break-in book, *Josef Schumpeter and the Paradox of Creative Destruction*, would lead directly to a tenure-track offer at Temple University in 1980, where he was just settling in when I was born. By then he had been married a matter of months. Our mother, Louisa Winant, had wandered into his life late in the seventies at Yale while he was still attempting to put the emotional convulsions of too much combat behind him and break in as a section man.

Mother had been bored too long at Wellesley and transferred to New Haven to explore her fascination with the Weimar-era expressionists. This tempted her into Dad's seminar in Twentieth-Century Central-European economic thinking. Yale during the seventies struck her as pretentious but sterile, and Mother – never too outspoken, even then, but devoted to nursing her appetites – was on the prowl for something authentic with a sperm count. She absorbed Dad effortlessly, casually – like a Jewish hors d'oeuvre. I doubt he noticed at first. He was uninhibitedly ribald, emphatic, all shoulders with a dark torrid gleam in his bulging eyes and a big head of bristling coal-black hair that my sisters later giggled over as Dad's Afro.

Our mother – Louisa – Weezee – came from the oldest money around Greater Philadelphia. There had been a seventeenth-century interlude of discreet trafficking in slaves, but the prerevolutionary fortune came largely from tanneries and, throughout the nineteenth century, Western land speculation. By World War II the bulk of the Winant capital was locked up in what was still referred to as merchant banking.

A speculation in Nazi bonds had cost the Quaker branch of the family the bulk of what they'd inherited. My mother's grandfather had been astute enough to pool up at the last minute with Joe Kennedy and the notorious Ben – "Sell 'em Ben!" – Smith when the economic tremors started in 1929 and speculate under a bogus name against the collapsing markets. When his sons – "The Uncles," in Winant family parlance – resigned their Navy commissions in 1945 and returned to their chilly Dutch Colonial mansions along the Main Line the important capital was intact.

The first time my father ever saw the inside of one of those mausoleums was the November weekend in 1979 when my mother took him home to meet her parents. My mother could see at once that they did not approve. She really hadn't thought they would. In any case, Weezee was already pregnant with me.

That weekend was the first time Dad ever watched our mother ride. Horses are a passion most young women manage to outgrow. Mother never did. She was a lissome, understated

7

young debutante with short, sculpted chestnut hair and a quick response to the idiocy of the passing world – her deep, snuffled laugh told all of us immediately what was going on. She had a profile like the goddess Minerva – strong chin, powerful brow, a nose with definition and character. The presence of a horse enlisted something ancient in her. Her favorite horse, Monument, travelled on the train with mother to Foxcroft and he was still alive during my childhood.

She rode that weekend when Dad met her family, if carefully. She and my father were married on April Fools' Day in a private civil ceremony. There was some sort of hotel reception afterwards during which Dad's new father-in-law, normally as austere as the headmaster of a third-rate boarding school, knocked back his fourth Scotch and blurted his deepest feelings to a pair of well oiled cronies. It just might develop, Edward Winant IV pontificated just before he passed out, that a dose of Hottentot blood would wake up this goddamned flea circus of a family. When this got back to Dad he was more amused than offended. Black, white, niggers, Jews – everybody else was third-world to Weezie's lovable father. That was Big Eddie, he assured me many years afterwards. You could always depend on that tight-assed old cocksucker to improve on garden-variety anti-Semitism.

I was pushing one when Dad and Weezee relocated to Philadelphia. My sisters arrived promptly. Mother found a skinny bowfront on Society Hill within walking distance of The Philadelphia College of Art. She limbered up Monument on weekends. Dad had wangled an associate professorship at Temple. Big Eddie died unexpectedly of cirrhosis of the liver, and a couple of the Winant trust funds became irrevocable. Mother had been named as a trustee, along with one of the Quaker uncles and a Philadelphia bank. Every couple of months she was expected to stop by the bank and rubberstamp the investment decisions. She started taking Dad along.

So we were bona-fide trust-fund bambinos. For several years Dad wasn't really paying attention – his second book, *Adam Smith and the Advent of Zombie Capitalism*, got a lot of press as a leading-edge refutation of Reaganomics. He was in and out, lecturing. Then one late afternoon the two of them came in from one of those conferences at the bank and Mother was close to tears. I was six.

"Nobody wants any trouble," Dad said. He banged down into the Queen Anne armchair. "Why do you drag me into those things, Weez?"

"It's not what you said, Sylvan. It was your tone of voice. Almost...snarling. Didn't you see Lionel's face?"

"Just emphatic. Just trying to make a point."

"But wasn't there some other way–?" The kettle had started whistling; Mother crossed over into the kitchen and poured two cups of green tea. On her way back she noticed the sisters and me through the door to the study, playing pick-up-sticks but listening. She put Dad's tea down on a candle-stand. "Lionel is very fragile. First they lose what little he had left on those disappointing German securities, and now he told me the other day he's worried about his position at Fahnestock."

"So where does that leave us?" Dad yawned and wove his fingers and turned his palms inside out and stretched. "Did you see your list of holdings?"

Mother didn't say anything. She started to rub the butter-fly-shaped discoloration on her left cheek.

"A debt issue by some godforsaken Louisiana parish as likely as not below flood level. Nicaraguan railroad bonds! Have you looked at the papers this week? This administration is this close to taking out every foot of trackage down there before the end of the month. They've already mined the harbor."

"But isn't that why the interest payments are so high? To compensate for the risk? Wasn't that Lionel's point?"

"It won't matter what they pay if they stop paying it."

Mother looked beseechingly at Dad. She hated fights.

"Yours is a trusting nature, sweetie pie" Dad said, lowering his voice. "Angelic. That's why people like you are attracted to pit bulls like me. Enough of a mujik not to roll over just to keep the peace in the family." Dad grinned up into her face, that notorious grin. "I'm merely an economist, what do I know from life on the Street? I'd give you odds that Fahnestock is either underwriting directly or at the very least loaded to the gills with a hell of a lot of the garbage in your portfolio. Saintly old Uncle Lionel is no doubt dragging down a pisser of a commission dumping it on you."

"I really don't care for sweetie pie," Mother said. Her lovely face darkened. "You actually think he's doing that intentionally?"

"With the best of intentions. He intends to keep his job."

Mother looked at Dad. "That's really disturbing," she said after a long moment. "Awful. Really, really awful. Just thinking about it that way makes me sick to my stomach." Mother looked up and breathed heavily through her mouth. "I'm tired. Everything makes me tired these days," she stated, idly. Dad set his teacup aside and put his arms around Mother.

CHAPTER II

By 1987 Dad was committing more and more of his time to looking after Mother and the complications of her inheritance. His nerves depleted, Uncle Lionel had reconciled himself to rubber-stamping Dad's recommendations rather than push back and jeopardize his honorarium. Dad socked away most of Mother's capital in high-yield triple-A municipals, which threw off a lot of interest. The financial community was still spooked by the Carter era.

Mother really wasn't well. She was headache-prone in any case, and increasingly her ankles swelled and the joints of her beautiful hands turned blue and ached in the dank Mid-Atlantic cold. Putting threadbare old Monument through his paces, she coughed for minutes at a time and her lungs hurt. Mother's rheumatologist ascribed many of her symptoms to horses, they looked great but they were as often as not galloping depositories for *the most nefarious* of the protein allergens. But it was more than that. Mother had lupus.

But not to worry. These days lupus was a manageable condition.

My parents were stunned.

What would help, the rheumatologist offered, was a change of climate. Out of the chilly weather. Some sunny place. South of the Mason-Dixon line, if they followed his reasoning.

Dad let it be known that he was willing to relocate if he got an offer he liked. Meanwhile, the rejuvenated stock market was beginning to feed on its own momentum. Hit-and-run arbitragers and underfunded portfolio insurance strategists had panicked the deacons of Wall Street into gambles Dad felt made no sense. He put up Mother's securities against cash loans and shorted the averages. On October 19, 1987, "Black Monday," the Dow Jones Industrial Average collapsed, giving up almost a quarter of its valuation in one sickening session. Just before the closing bell, on heavy margin, Dad locked in naked calls on a dozen oversold Blue Chips they'd acquired that bounced back within a week and left Mother very nearly five million dollars richer.

The same week Dad got the job offer he wanted. SFUTB, Southern Florida University of Tampa Bay, was looking for a department head in economics for its newly established satellite in downtown St. Petersburg. Somebody with a name, published. Dad flew down the next morning.

A month later we relocated. After the duty-ridden, white-collar ethos of Philadelphia there was a backwash of unembarrassed self-indulgence about St. Petersburg. Give everything a try, the humidity excuses anything.

This was a place mostly to enjoy yourself furtively. There was a rumor around the Bay Area that whenever the mob in Tampa knocked off anybody over fifty they trucked the corpse over the Howard Frankland Causeway at night and propped the remains up on a bench in a St. Petersburg park. It might take months before the local authorities realized this wasn't just another retiree napping in the sun.

I think Dad liked the fundamental earthiness of the place, the Caribbean languors. Termites owned the real estate ultimately, humidity was rotting every timber. I suspect we settled into our big Mediterranean Revival palazzo on Snell Isle in good part because Dad expected that so much hewn stone might stand up. The house was basically Morocco as Addison Mizner must have envisioned Morocco – towering doorways with molded concrete frames embossed with floral designs, a portico of Moorish arches backing up a new travertine patio that extended to the sea wall. That went in last – Dad had his pool and the Jacuzzi grotto installed before the travertine went down.

Upstairs, along the loggia wing, Mother and Father each had a suite with a very large office and a private library and a sitting room. Mother had been picking up prints and a few water colors by the expressionists she loved, and displayed them all around her office. I remember several unabashed nudes and a café scene by Georg Grosz and corpses in a trench during the Great War by Otto Dix and a pencil drawing, by Klimt, I believe it was, of a teenage boy sprawled over the edge of a Viennese four-poster receiving head from a naked matron whose heavy, fanning hair almost covered her ample backside. Both my little sisters liked to sneak in there when Mother was out and peep at her art collection.

They were growing up. Virtually every summer, to ground us in the real America, Dad arranged for all of us to take a month's lease on one of the guest units in his parents' condominium, adjacent to the Jewish golf club on the outskirts of Minneapolis. Dad's father, Barney Landau, came up from nothing and put together a substantial estate jobbing caps and scarves. Mini – Miriam, our grandmother from an old Rhenish family – was one of the outstanding mah jongg players in her Hadassah chapter. By then Grandpa Barney was permanently retired, and grumpy from inactivity. He had an annoying propensity to lecture the young, so Mother saw to it that both my mouthy sisters stayed out of his way.

With Wendy, the oldest girl, that was easier. She had a round face and snapping black-coffee eyes and bristling eyebrows and coarse, heavy hair like Dad's, but she was taller, like Mother, with smooth, extended muscles and a boisterous intensity all her own. She tended to be something of a wiseass. By the summer of 1997, when I was about to enter my last full year at Exeter and Wendy was starting her sophomore year at Choate, she was already emerging as a star on the private school tennis circuit. Barney's club had a well developed tennis ladder, so Wendy tramped over there every morning to hit balls with the pro.

I got back to the unit one broiling afternoon when the rest of them were shopping downtown. Something moved in the girls' bedroom, and so I barged in unthinking and confronted Wendy bare-ass on her bed, pink from the shower with her knees spread and a joint in her back teeth pluming blue smoke while her right hand was poised to introduce a chattering vibrator between those long, hollow thighs. I was too stunned to say anything. I'd groped a date or two but I had never before come face to face with the meat-market rawness of unprotected cunt.

Wendy examined me between half-closed lids. "Getting an eyeful, Mikey?" she muttered huskily. "It's a Choate thing." I could not move. "You ought to fill your pockets." She eased the vibrator in and reached around to fondle her emerging clitoris. "Not stopping now," she got out. "Not this high."

The wryness of the marijuana was making me start to tear. My heart was hammering.

"Go ahead and watch if you're *that* weird," Wendy mumbled. Her pelvis was heaving.

I still felt rooted, but somehow I backed up and slid out into the hall.

Even that, I suppose, qualified as one of those primordial Minnesota experiences for which Dad insisted we go back every summer. Both of our parents detested the pre-packaged, market-tested emptiness Americans mistook for vacations. Every summer our Dad and I would take a week out of our layover with Grandpa Barney and Mini and push off by canoe into northern Minnesota's Boundary Waters. Throughout his own adolescence Dad had explored this gigantic preserve, from the Gunflint all through the Canadian fastness of Hunter's Island. Even pontoon planes were precluded from overflying this wilderness of low granite outcroppings and blueberries and hundreds upon hundreds of miles of lake chains. Anybody stricken with an attack of appendicitis four days in could kiss his butt goodbye.

Normally Dad was voluble, wisecracking. But once we had picked up the beef jerky and the freeze-dried vegetables and the canoe and all the gear the outfitter in Ely bounced into our rented station wagon Dad began to throttle down. The scenery absorbed him. Certain days we paddled the major lakes all afternoon without a word, silent enough to glide in next to the astonished loons. Dad's paddle barely raised a ripple, he never seemed to rudder much even to change direction or shoot the rapids of the hardscrabble rivers along our route.

One night, after we had pissed all over the embers of our campfire, a black bear arrived to forage among the cooking scraps and caught us in our half-crumpled Rocky Mountain tent. We stood up – Dad unsheathed a Bowie knife – but the bear decided merely to hug us inside the canvas and wheeze its asthmatic wheeze, inches from our faces, and lumber back into the brambles. "We stank too bad to think about eating," Dad confided.

After we made camp we stripped down and swam and soaped up and swam and smeared on fresh mosquito repellent, and then Dad liked to go out alone in the canoe and cast dry flies to pick up some kind of bass for dinner. Usually he got something. Once a considerable walleye hit. Dad carved its gullet out and kept it moist and for the rest of the week we trolled all day with that and dragged along anything we caught on a stringer, still flipping and churning.

On long portages Dad always slid into the food pack and slung up the canoe and eased the yoke around his thick farmer's neck. This left me with the much lighter equipment pack and the paddles as we stumbled forward, sometimes for miles, up stony paths and across still-flowing creek beds to where we could put the canoe in again and start up the next lake chain.

Sometimes – rarely – we ran into other parties. I remember a pair of very brawny girls who had been on the trail for a month. The taller one was menstruating and they had long since run out of rags. She was bleeding openly down the inside of her thigh; the heavy-duty smell of iron she gave off was attracting flies, which clustered. She didn't really seem to care, or notice. Everybody was fighting too hard merely to keep going.

By the middle of the week we were invariably sunburned, and Dad's sensitive bald spot had started to peel. He was always burly if never fat, but by the end of a week in the woods he started looking carved, much younger.

Everybody seemed happy enough to see us once we got back to Minneapolis. They'd all been busy. Only Carol, our baby sister, ever seemed to care much either way whether we were around or gone. This came up later, during her therapy. She'd secretly felt excluded, that induced her anorexia. We were somehow responsible. She'd wanted to go too, she told her analyst. We'd refused to take her.

I'm not that sure that I looked like a much better prospect than Carol to either of my parents at that stage. I think they sent me to prep in New England in hopes the small classes and ice-water showers would wake me up in time. Phillips Exeter was the real world – unforgiving. I was acceptably tall – taller than both parents – but closer to gangling than particularly well-knit. By really putting out I ultimately made second string on the soccer team and a few times got to swim the third lap during swimming meets. I was best at debating. My boards were good enough to get me into Amherst.

At Amherst I joined one of the off-campus fraternities, the Dekes. At Dad's behest I majored in government. I think Dad felt we could use a lawyer in the family. Cautiously, Dad had begun diverting some of Mother's capital into picking up the big, palatial three and four bedroom condominium units in the high rises behind the yacht club along with the occasional antebellum manse headed toward rooming-house status and vest-pocket Tierra Verde estates and the retail outlets. Once the market cooled, Dad started to acquire plainer properties.

They translated into rentals. Rentals are a slippery slope. What begins as an immaculate arms-length operation, with brokers and syndicates of genteel investors and ironclad rental agreements, degenerates into a rolling fiasco of jumped leases and rump-sprung couches teetering out the back windows of shabby two-deckers above rusty vans idling in the night alley and headed for the Carolinas. This sort of property management provides the most graphic example in Christendom of ground-level vulture capitalism, with lawyers flapping day and night above the sordid proceedings

Dad preferred to see this side of his investments as conducive to social betterment. Providing for Joe Sixpack, the well-intentioned goofus unlucky enough not to have married Mother. Once I was out of law school and slaved through a stultifying summer and part of a fall in smog-bound Philadelphia as an associate at Humper, Fardle and Wrath – Great-Uncle Lionel's connections brought that beauty off – I succumbed to Dad's half-joking blandishments and relocated – along with my then-wife Janice – in gradually awakening St. Petersburg. By then enough third-generation trust fund income had kicked in so I could afford to lease a modest law office on sleepy Central Avenue. My penance was to run Dad's slumlord acquisitions.

Before the year was out I had a partner. Buckley Glickman had been a fellow Deke in college. We weren't that close at the time. Buckley claimed some shirt-tail relationship on his mother's side to the oil-rich Buckley family in Connecticut. I had always regarded William F. Buckley, Jr. as a pundit whose stammered condescension masked a lot of air space where preparation should have been. As it turned out, bad judgment and too much sailing resulted in a late-life bankruptcy, so not much in a financial way was to be expected from that side of Buckley's family. On the Glickman side there was a spate of marriages and a lopsided investment in non-performing Las Vegas casinos.

I began to notice while we were both in law school that Buckley made a point of sitting with me and Janice at college reunion events. We'd both been recognizably out-group, besides which Buckley came over as little too Society and more than a little flighty. But I was loosening up – sometimes after a couple of drinks what Buckley would blurt out could get amusing as hell. We began to exchange e-mails.

To start with, it had been my expectation that, as a lawyer helping my father out, I might get pulled in occasionally to witness somebody's signature or – rarely – round up the sheriff and serve an eviction notice. The first years I seemed to be on call every day, for everything from co-signing leases to fencing with my ambulance-chasing colleagues who advertised enthusiastically on television that they could keep you in your house indefinitely, whether you made your payments or not. Too often, they could.

Meanwhile, Buckley Glickman had been putting in his time as one among a dozen or so trainees in the legal bullpen of a New York publisher of high-gloss gardening magazines.

His salary was barely enough to rent one fifth of a bedroom floor in mid-Manhattan. In hopes of upgrading his resume with an eye toward something on Wall Street he'd signed up for night courses in international finance at The New School, jammed, he tweeted me, with sallow aspirants to overnight billions from every blowhole around the planet from the tent cities of Mongolia to the meandering cesspools of Bangladesh. Exchanges on the internet led to a telephone call we both laughed through. Before I hung up I'd offered Buckley a job.

Physically, Buckley reminded me a little of my sister Carol, so why was I surprised when they seemed to hit it off? They both had rumpled sandy-blond hair, both smoked – furtively –, they were both nail-biters. Buckley's high-speed takeouts seemed to reassure Carol, to hint there *was* a world in which she might be appreciated.

That world wasn't us. Carol's psychologist had been lamenting that our family standards were so high she'd batter herself to pieces pretending to keep up. Competition anxieties supposedly triggered sieges of anorexia. That, and the ambivalence the psychologist ascribed to our helter-skelter approach to sexuality.

Family life. The psychologist obviously came from a different social universe. We weren't exhibitionists, exactly, and while the women were a little careful about towels and how they moved in the surging water nobody really bothered with bathing suits once they were immersed in Dad's steaming Jacuzzi. Mornings, Dad himself liked to swim a few laps starkers before he pulled himself together before classes.

Mother definitely went along. She savored his bohemian

21

impulses, which she would refer to with a wink as the Last-Train-For-Istanbul, or Balkan, side of his complex personality. I remember one cocktail hour when she turned around as she was lowering herself into the Jacuzzi and he exclaimed "What a tush! I could make a meal out of something like that." The sisters were just getting into the age when a crack like that could paint a very rich picture, and Wendy laughed and Carol threw a towel around herself and scampered toward the main house.

I suppose our parents were influenced by their exploits in Europe. Dad was under contract at Random House to write a frank, all-encompassing critique and biography of John Maynard Keynes. Sabbaticals took them again and again to England. Over country weekends exchanges got heated – not Cliveden-level restraint at all, shouting matches at times – and after things broke up bedroom doors would open and close until dawn.

Several times they ended their stretches abroad in Berlin. Mother developed contacts. Her patrician good looks and Dad's genius for effrontery amused people in the reawakened capital. One couple invited them several times to uninhibited holidays on the nudist beaches adjoining Sylt.

Her doctor had been right – the wet oceanside air off Tampa Bay and the prevailing Southern culture were what it took to relieve mother. Her hands looked better. The slow-moving, indulgent Florida mannerisms resonated to her energy levels. A suspicion was starting to find its way around town that Dad wasn't merely another college professor, that he was running money north of eight figures. Dad heard about that, and stepped up his contributions to the Free Clinic and the Florida Symphony.

Money, as economists like to say, is fungible. But expectations are also fungible. There is Mercedes 300 rich, but there is also Gulfstream IV rich, and I suppose even a dedicated academic with a character as solid as Dad's wasn't above occasional fantasies of opulence. The Clinton years had turned out to be very slow. By now Dad understood that fortunes were not built dubbing around with blue chips. The big money – the insider money – came from special situations. That kind of information was not lying around in the streets of St. Petersburg, Florida. You needed contacts, well connected friends. Then Ramon showed up.

I myself had relocated to St. Pete in 2005. Janice and I had met while I was still buried in paperwork in the tomblike research library on the top floor of Humper, Fardle and Wrath. She was just out of junior college by then and had signed on as an intern. She was an extremely clean girl, almost always chipper, and – like her parents in Chappaqua – a dedicated, churchgoing Congregationalist. It seems to me, in retrospect, she never actually cast a shadow.

When we moved to St. Petersburg Dad helped me find an inexpensive brick-faced bungalow in the Pink Streets, on the Oval Crescent Annex to Serpentine Drive, a few blocks shy of Pinellas Point. During our early months Janice kept taking me aside to reassure me that our snug little bungalow was definitely *cute,* if maybe a little cramped.

I could see that the whole scene terrified her. A resourceful cockroach crawled up out of her bran flakes and skittered as far as her elbow and launched itself into her closely trimmed curls. Worse, one stifling afternoon a week later one of the fruit rats dropped out of the calamondin tree and found itself trapped between her firm if modest breasts. It scratched her up pretty badly before, shrieking, she succeeded in shaking it out into the utility toilet.

She flushed it cheeping and milling in the converging flush. That evening Janice literally burned her bra on the outside grill. The next weekend she flew back to Chappaqua for a few days and didn't come back for almost a month. I suppose I missed her, to a certain extent. What romance had flared among the file cabinets at Humper, Fardle had pretty largely dissipated. Long before we separated I'd realized that sex, for Janice, was in the end a mildly distasteful responsibility, like aspirating her sinuses. I suppose I blamed myself for never having aroused her temperament; afterwards I found myself dealing with a recurrent hopelessness, the fear that in me something was blocked, not capable of really making contact. There was a municipal warning sign posted at the turnoff into the Oval Crescent Annex that read: NO OUTLET. Afterwards it occurred to me we both should have taken that as a warning.

Carol had seemed to like Janice, but Wendy, being Wendy, never made the attempt. At the mention of Janice's name Wendy would usually roll those delicately protrusive mahogany eyes of hers and clap her big sinewy hands together, as if in prayer. Lord Save Us! At that point Wendy had transferred down from Wheaton and was finishing up her undergraduate semesters at the University of Miami. She had been recruited on a tennis scholarship and was spending a lot more time on the collegiate tour than worrying about the soft-core sociology that was her alleged major. I believe she met Enrique Perez y Cruz in class, and before too long he started showing up at matches to applaud the big, perfectly timed overhead that petrified her opponents.

Neither of them had a chance.

CHAPTER III

Once Wendy's infatuation with Rick got serious, Dad tapped the features specialist at *The Miami Post-Dispatch*, Freddy Wilmot, who had done a three-part profile of him when his Adam Smith broadside turned into such a blockbuster. Wilmot specialized in the local Cuban community. Taking on a son-in-law was a serious business. Dad thought it might be productive if I went down there and sounded out Wilmot personally.

Rounding out his fifties, Freddy Wilmot certainly looked his age, and more. He was very petite, and shriveled to the point of undernourished. A few token strands of hair were thrown back over his wrinkled scalp. His decades on the phone with the butt of one cheap cigarette after another burning down at one corner of his mouth had cured the tip of his long, twisted nose to something bordering on amber. "Fucking management is out this morning with today's idiot brainstorm. Anything to demoralize the troops," he greeted me. "No more water cooler. We buy the water, two dollars a bottle. And in that motherfucking crinkly plastic. Jesus!"

"Look, we appreciate whatever backgrounding you can come up with," I said. "If there are any expenses—"

"There won't be any expenses. Your dad helped me out."

Before I got there Wilmot had scrounged around in the newspaper's back files and surfaced a lot more detail than any of us expected. Most of the archive contained material that had never been published and was designated *Sensitive, Awaits Further Attribution*.

Because Ramon Perez y Cruz was turning into such a magnate all up and down Florida's East Coast, the arrival of his son on the scene got picked up by several of the paper's stringers, and ultimately merited a separate file. It had developed that Enrique – Ricky – had been brought into America after a State-Department-mandated six months in Canada late in the heyday of Bush I. He was barely a teenager, a big tawny muscular Cubano kid of thirteen who seemed to be watching everything and everybody, starting with the influential father who had pulled strings to get him in.

Rick's father, the shadowy Ramon Perez y Cruz, had already justified a mention or two in the early Post-Dispatch reporting the month he first showed up in the States in 1963, at the time Castro traded off the survivors of Brigade 2506 for medicine and tractors in the aftermath of the Bay of Pigs. There was a background file on the Cruz forebears in Cuba; Ramon found his way into one reporter's notes as a physician's son with English enough to interview, on leave from his pre-medical semesters at the Universidad when he joined the resistance. He had been rescued from a dungeon outside Havana by John Kennedy's negotiators. Of primarily Spanish antecedents, in Miami Ramon caught the eye of that emerging telephone cable tycoon and godfather of the Cuban contingent in South Florida, the podgy, explosive Jorge Mas Canosa.

Even as a flunky the watchful Ramon quickly came to understand that the underground wiring in the Cuban community ran in unexpected directions. "With those pricks, it was one hundred percent catch- as-catch-can, and keep your good hand on your balls," Wilmot told me. "They arrived hungry. The place was in turmoil anyhow with Bobby Kennedy and those goombahs of his from Operation Mongoose tearing the absolute living shit out of the Cuban sugar refineries around The Island. The Mafia heavy hitters, starting with the sainted Santos Trafficante, worked out some kind of back-alley deal with Castro to lock up the cocaine traffic. Mas Canosa was somewhere in the middle of that, although we couldn't prove a fucking thing."

"And Ramon was involved?"

A tall, rather delicately built youngster in his early twenties, with long black hair like wire and huge Latin eyes full of insinuation, drifted into Wilmot's cubicle, stepping carefully around a ficus plant. The boy had a powdered, hothouse look. The last couple of inches of a very dark tattoo emerged from his collar and narrowed out just below the lobe of one ear.

"Thiz Humberto Jiminez," Wilmot said. "My intern. We like to pretend he's learning the business. We hope he gets it right before the paper folds."

We shook hands. Humberto's palm was disturbingly moist.

"The story is, Mike here's sister is going to marry the son of Ramon Cruz. That SEAL we did a feature about. I'm filling Mike in. He's only around today."

"Until tomorrow." I said.

"Oh, yeah? Where you staying?"

"The Marriott downtown. On Bayshore Boulevard."

"Used to be, the place wasn't that bad," Wilmot said. "Bit of a dump, these days."

"Beats sleeping on the street."

"So they tell me." Wilmot's gaze was following Humberto

as he wandered out. "Kid's got possibilities. But Christ, those tattoos! From asshole to appetite, if you know where I'm headed with that." Wilmot looked down; he'd said too much. "Why don't we take a walk? We just landed ourselves this dandy new executive editor who's got a fucking goddamn Komodo *Dragon* up his ass about smoking inside the goddamned building."

It was much hotter outside, strolling underneath the Royal Palms. "What I didn't want to get into in there, a lot of what went down around here got done for people from the Agency. The CIA. They had some under-the table arrangement with Trafficante so they could skim running-around money off every sizeable cocaine deal that went down, even inside Cuba. Off the books, definitely off the books."

"Castro looked the other way," Wilmot went on, "and the frigging Comandants cut up the payoffs. By then Ramon had brown-nosed his way up the pecking order and he was very, very tight still with Canosa and his hotshots. Except that at some point early in the Reagan administration a jurisdictional dispute among the Comandants who looked after the retail cocaine deals kicked up and Ramon had to sneak back into Havana by way of Mexico. Their deal needed reworking.

"I'm informed that Castro – trusting nobody, needless to say – assigned one of the huskier female case officers in that very efficient spy shop he had, the Direccion General de Inteligensia, to stick with Ramon and keep the dictator up to speed on Ramon's every maneuver. But Ramon outfoxed el Lider. He seduced Teresita his first night on the Island. He fucked her senseless, and when she drifted off he snuck out and put together some deal with his compadres down there. He also left her pregnant. With Enrique."

According to Wilmot, it took almost thirteen years for Ramon to persuade Enrique's doctrinaire mother to give Enrique up. Officials in both countries had to be bribed. When Rick finally turned up in Miami, Ramon expunged his son's maternal surname and enrolled him as a boarder in Gulliver Academy a few miles from his business in Coral Gables. Ramon dropped by whenever he was out on the circuit extorting remittances for the Cuban-American National Foundation, Mas Canosa's pressure group. Ramon prodded Ricky about his fitful English and even sported him to the occasional jai alai match. "I think he thought of himself as basically the kid's father, but only when it occurred to him," Wilmot explained to me, and ground out the last of a butt under his heel.

By the time Rick made it out of Gulliver his English was much improved, he showed something of a knack for mathematics – statistics especially – and he was a black belt in the Japanese combat discipline Goju-Ryu. He was beginning to dominate local martial arts competitions.

At that point Wilmot heard that Ramon was alarmed about Mas Canosa's heedlessness, his susceptibility to his CIA handlers, the great man's gullibility when it came to putting his own name on checks for limpet mines that made their way into the hands of terrorists like Luis Posada Carriles and wound up sinking Soviet and Cuban freighters and blowing out of the sky an Air Cubana jet liner. Mas Canosa had no scruples when it came to utilizing Ramon as a cutout on the riskier operations, a courier of money and instructions to psychos willing to demolish Castro's suppliers.

Scrutinizing his irrational boss, an increasingly prudent Ramon was emerging from behind the scenes. He joined the Knights of Columbus. This provided legitimate associations once Ramon began merchandising *himself,* utilizing his important-family-in-Havana credentials with the Cuban exile shopkeepers and petit-bourgeois boat people and poverty clinic managers who had grumbled for years as they anted up to support Mas Canosa's perilous brainstorms. Ramon started by tapping them modestly, selling them once-a-week custodial services.

What began as maintenance turned into unacknowledged protection, then property and casualty insurance. Ramon weighed in as a conspicuous contributor to the unsuccessful gubernatorial campaign of Jeb Bush in 1994; at that point Ramon's corporation had started writing premiums on hospitals all the way up the East Coast to Daytona. He became a Third-Degree Knight of Columbus.

His financing became more imaginative. Under the expansive Bill Clinton the SEC was predisposed to look with favor even on Republicans like Ramon. His Sunrise Medical Ventures Corporation got green-lighted to issue an initial $5,000,000 of promissory notes. The notes paid better than 10% interest. A surprising proportion of the notes were absorbed by Ramon's shoe-leather following in the tight-knit exile community.

The second Bush presidency found Ramon breaking in a young wife and two very young children in a gated residence in Coral Gables. Rick had become something of an afterthought. At his father's urging, Enrique signed on for a hitch in the SEALS the day he graduated from Gulliver. Himself laid back, patient and calculating, Ramon continued to dismiss the burly and sometimes bumptious teenager as quick when it came to numbers but hopelessly in need of seasoning. "You'd see them together at the big Cuban rallies and political events once in a while," Wilmot remembered. "It was like – Christ, what's this? Fernando Llamas meets The Incredible Hulk?"

Rick survived the killer dropout rate at boot camp in Coronado and participated in the post 9/11 ramp-up in Afghanistan. He'd emerged unscratched after one fire fight with an unidentified Zodiac boat smuggling AK-47s into an Iraqi port. He ground through several exhausting weeks early in Operation Enduring Freedom scrounging with his squad among the caves of Zawar Kili for Taliban ammunition caches. Surprising several Al Qaeda asleep just before dawn one morning, Rick took a bullet in the thigh. Except for a barely discernable limp he seemed to come out of it all right. With that Rick qualified for a disability, which ruled out another hitch.

Paradoxically, the impact appeared to loosen him up. He could be gruff at moments still, but now you couldn't miss a sort of precocious, hard-won fatalism about this strapping Cuban-American *joven* with his premature widow's peak and his GI buzz cut. Battle-hardened, nothing fazed him. He enrolled at the University of Miami the same semester Wendy transferred in. They met in a quantitative analysis workshop – Rick was a business major – and there must have been so much obvious physicality coming off of both of them that they were a pair almost before they contrived to bump into each other.

I got a lot of the background for all of this from Wilmot while he was walking and talking and making up for lost time going through a pack of cigarettes as we circumvented Dispatch Plaza. As I was leaving I took a couple of Manila mailers Wilmot sent Humberto to fetch for me, plump with copies of everything the paper had on Ramon.

I carted Wilmot's handout back to my room at the Marriott and spread everything out on the coffee table in front of the TV set. This kind of reporting took money and man hours. Somebody at the Post-Dispatch was biding his time. Most of the details about Ricky's combat performance came out of Department of the Navy p.r. releases.

By seven that evening I had worked my way no better than halfway through the pile. I was taking notes – I am, after all, a lawyer. I decided to go downstairs to the Coffee Shop for a quick bite. As I was letting myself back into my room I sensed movement inside more than actually seeing anybody. The floor lamp above the coffee table snapped off just as I was letting myself in; I think I sensed more than I actually saw whoever it was rushing by me in the dark and out the half-open door. Whoever it was seemed agile, inexperienced, gasping in panic; I could smell talc. I was too stunned to move for three or four seconds. Then I edged back into the corridor just in time to catch a glimpse of a blue-black mane of hair as whoever that was scrambled through a fire door next to the bank of elevators and disappeared down the fire stairs.

My hoard of clips and awaits-further-attribution memos had been thoroughly culled. Anything at all startling or likely to upset Ramon was gone. I had my notes, and of course I remembered a lot of it. But that was largely hearsay.

Fortunately, just then, we really did not have a lawsuit in mind.

CHAPTER IV

The two got married in 2004 in what must have been one of the great cross-cultural blowoffs even in Florida history. Ramon had a raft of insurance clients he intended to include, and the bride and groom both wanted something accessible for their college friends, so Dad and Ramon agreed over the phone to split the costs. A staff woman in the headquarters of Ramon's investment syndicate staged this extravaganza on the side lawn at one of the nonsectarian country clubs outside Coral Gables. The vows were exchanged a couple of minutes before noon, beneath a tent; a Monsignor and a lesbian rabbi Dad found in Seminole traded off the speaking parts. Just before the ring ceremony Governor Jeb Bush and his entourage waded in from the back and everything stopped until his honor guard was seated.

Afterwards the restive mob trampled into the enormous dining room. Two bands alternated salsa and rhumba; the ballroom throbbed. Alongside the salty ambience of freshly boiled lobster the odor of pulled pork swamped the more delicate after-aroma of enchiladas and baked grouper and the side of beef turning over and sputtering on a spit just outside the kitchen. Blintzes were laid out next to the desert table.

"They're for our benefit," Dad said "I haven't even *seen* a blintz since your Aunt Lillian overindulged after my grandmother's funeral. They had to pump her out at Abbott Hospital. Lillian was a thrill-seeker. Mostly on the gastro-intestinal level."

Mother was escorting Great-Uncle Lionel toward the buffet tables. Unsure of his footing, Lionel had the nervous look of a Presbyterian at the zoo who is wandering among the larger predators and not at all sure the cages are locked. Animated Cuban Spanish rose on all sides. At Ramon's elbow a tall stripling I recognized with a start as Humberto Jiminez shouldered carefully by me without a word. Above the neck of his open shirt the tattoo of some kind of reptile with blazing emerald eyes had almost been whited out with powder.

A delegation including the governor advanced on our table. Everybody stood up. A small, monkey-faced aide with a slab of blond hair that looked molded onto his skull seized Dad's hand. "Larry," he said, "it is an honor for all of us, and I know I speak for the governor, to meet a genuine war hero like yourself."

Dad's full name was Lawrence Sylvan Landau. Everybody close in called him Sylvan.

"What we've got here is *two* war heroes," the aide pressed on. "A father and a son."

"Son-in-law," Dad said. Dad stood up, careful not to step on the loosely woven straw hat edging out from beneath his chair.

"Doesn't it amount to the same thing? I've always thought patriotism runs in families. You know the governor's father, the first President Bush, won the Congressional Medal of Honor—"

The governor spoke. "Distinguished Flying Cross," he corrected the aide. "He was the youngest airman in the Navy throughout the entire war in the Pacific." Bush was a sizeable, neatly combed presence, his pudgy face fixed at the verge of boredom.

"I'm sure you know the governor and your daughter's husband's father go way back," the aide said. "He worked with that incredible civic leader Mr. Mas Canosa. Like our irreplaceable Jorge, Ramon has been a reliable resource throughout both the philanthropic *and* the political crusades with which the Bush family has been identified for many, many years. We'd like to think that, going forward, we'll be able to say the same of you."

Dad was never easy to back into a corner. I was getting nervous.

"Especially now. With – you know – Iraq and the rest."

Dad didn't say anything.

"In many ways," the aide attempted, "your war and, and–"

"Rick," Dad said.

"Yes, right, Rick's war and the liberation of Iraq – they're all very much the same. Wouldn't you say?"

"Very much," Dad said. "They made no sense and they cost a lot of money and we wind up with the wretched of the earth handing our bloody nuts to us. Did you ever serve?"

"I haven't had the privilege." Frowning, the aide took a step back. "I'm sure you're disillusioned," he said after a moment. "Sometimes veterans get that way."

"I'm speaking as an economist. What's good for Kellogg, Brown and Root isn't necessarily a good idea for the federal budget, long term. Let alone the poor bastards who wind up splashing their brains all over some clay wall because the perimeter guard didn't spot a suicide vest in time."

"But that was always true."

"Maybe. It's just that these days our rulers are mopping up the empire with other people's children."

The aide forced a smile. "You are a very hard sell," he told Dad. "We'll keep trying."

"I'm confident of that," Dad said.

"What a shmegeggy!" Dad said once the governor's party was gone.

"I don't know that word."

"It's really a shame Yiddish is such a dying language. Sometimes it's very efficient. That means something between a sap and a professional suck-butt." Dad fanned himself with his hat. "That's my mission in life, Michael. Teaching you Yiddish. So you can express yourself with sufficient precision."

We all gathered on the margin of the parking lot to watch the bride and groom climb into Rick's Jeep Cherokee and set off for their honeymoon in Key West. Balloons bounced along the pavement behind them. Wendy had looked radiant, Amazonian. A late afternoon letdown was telling on Mother. In the open sunlight her skin looked scalier than usual. Fatigue was enriching the dark circles beneath her eyes.

"Glad it's over?" Dad said to her.

"I suppose so. He's really a very worthwhile boy, don't you think? And such a hunk!"

"I think he's a project under development. Smart, though. We got into a discussion of derivatives last night at the bridal party. That whole subject is a financial snake pit, but he seemed to have the handle. Which I'm sure I don't, quite. He's working part time for Ramon while he finishes up. I gather they're turning into some sort of feeder outlet for one of the big Manhattan underwriters. Speaking of which—"

Ramon Perez y Cruz sidled up. He was a fine-boned man but fairly tall, with a solid, professional smile and a head of very black crinkly hair. He may have been the only man in the Western Hemisphere who still used Brilliantine. A much younger Latin woman with her hair up in combs seemed to be bouncing in place at his side.

"It is really a pleasure for me to become acquainted with someone like you," Ramon said. He spoke very carefully. "I like how we cooperate to plan this very beautiful festival together. No problems. Still, I hope maybe we would have the good fortune and meet before this wedding. But they are young people. In a hurry."

"They are that."

"I read your book." Ramon said. "About Adam Smith. Which I of course admired. Adam Smith becomes like a hero to a lot of us at the university in Havana after Batista was no longer present. 'An Inquiry into the Nature and Causes of the Wealth of Nations,' correct? We admired the invisible hand. We have the hope the invisible hand would pinch off Castro."

"It certainly hasn't so far."

"That is coming. Castro is becoming *viejo*, pretty old."

"Who isn't?" Dad said. "I don't think you've met Wendy's mother. Louise Landau?"

Ramon took mother's hand and obviously fought the impulse to kiss it. "And my wife? Annilita?"

Annilita inclined her head, solemnly, and produced a child-like smirk.

"Ricky really is a lovely person," Mother said. "Sylvan

tells me he's actually very precocious in certain ways. On the economic side."

"He does some work for me, so maybe that helps a little bit," Ramon said. "He has the opportunity every six months to obtain a visa and visit his mother in Cuba, so when he goes down for a few days he is able to discharge obligations for us." Ramon was studying Dad. He went on. "I think Raul Castro is a little different, maybe a little more advance than his brother. Fidel has step back a little now, you see. Digestive disorders."

"I think I see where you're going."

Ramon was getting intense, his English was slipping. "We have establish what is call on Wall Street a little hedge fund. We go short sometimes, long sometimes. We try an' accumulate assets. Like Warren Buffet, only not so grand. There is a Canadian partner, and he is entitle to option properties in Cuba. Beachfront properties. Mineral rights. So Enrique goes down there, and everybody signs the papers, and reimbursement goes out from here to numbered accounts in the Cayman Islands for individuals in the regime. Everything perfectly legal."

"Unless somebody gets caught," Dad said. That seemed to go right by Ramon. "Then, when we recognize Cuba?" Dad prompted.

"On that day? Madre! Everybody adds a zero. Two zeros." Ramon's smile had turned itself up, high-voltage. "Right now the problem is naturally to generate enough cash. They will accept only cash. If it should happen you have some interest…"

"I can appreciate that," Dad said. "Our problem is, we're not particularly liquid."

"You have a great deal of real estate as I understand it, correct?"

"Jesus. And I thought the governor was well briefed. All that war hero bullshit."

"Information is extremely important." Ramon shrugged. "But – you know what is best for your case."

Dad's eyes rolled up, obliquely, toward the fronds of the surrounding palms. "I don't see how the real estate—"

"Real estate can be an asset. Something which you trade. You put together *his* falling-apart apartment house, and *her* vacation condominium, and produce a big bundle-type security. And that you sell. To us, maybe, for the hedge fund. We guarantee ten percent."

"A subprime mortgage package, don't they call that?" I finally put in.

"They call it a lot of things," Ramon said. "The rating agencies love those sonabitches. Buildings, something they can forcclose on."

Dad looked half convinced. "Mike here and I will talk this over," he said. "He runs that kind of stuff for us." There was a pause. "I like the Cuban possibilities, though."

"You let us know, OK? Maybe you be our guests at dinner?"

"Love to. But we've got to get on the road. We've got another wedding to start planning. Did you meet Carol and Buckley?"

My parents and I were about to settle into Dad's Lexus when the rabbi appeared with her partner. They were parked in the next space.

"Rabbi Ginsburg," Dad hailed her, "You did an inspired job." He pulled a hundred-dollar-bill out of his wallet. "Something extra for the collection box. Kind of a mixed congregation today."

The rabbi was a small, plump woman who looked as if she had dressed quickly in the back room of a thrift shop. She was still wearing her elaborate, gold-embroidered yamulkah. She accepted the money and pushed her perspired face up to confront his. "I think I earned my pittance today. I tell you something, it isn't that easy to upstage a Monsignor. Now, tell *me* something Mr. Landau. Except for you and me, were there any Jews present this morning?"

"Three. Not including my wife. Weezee is extraordinarily devout."

"She hides it well. Why did I think she fell asleep when I was attempting my remarks? And I wasn't speaking very long."

"Rapture. That's how Weezee expresses herself when she is genuinely moved."

"If you say so," the rabbi said. She gave Dad an amused look. "I haven't met a b.s. artist like you since I left Queens." Her face darkened. "One remark in passing, something I left out of my sermon. The father-in-law there, Raymond was that?"

"Ramon."

"Right. Look, for what it's worth, I don't know how well you are acquainted around these parts, but he isn't just another local businessman. They tell me he is..connected. Or whatever they say down here. My mother is retired to Boca, so I am down here a lot. Friends of mine tell me they saw Ramon at one point palling around with Orlando Bosch, who supposedly took out a lot of rolling stock all over the Caribbean. With dynamite. The mishugina Bushes supposedly got Bosch out of jail and even snagged him a post in the government. Ramon is no greenhorn. So—"

"What are you trying to tell me?"

"You haven't figured it out? Watch your ass! I've got to run, I've got a bris in Seminole at seven. I'm still stuffed, but my partner Angela called to say she's hungry. It's past her feeding time." The rabbi winked, a fat wink. "You know how ravenous these old mackerel-snappers get."

CHAPTER V

The nuptials joining Carol and Buckley were a whole lot quieter. They both preferred a nonsectarian ceremony. A blubbery, humorless Justice of the Peace trudged out to Dad's palazzo and tied the knot in front of a couple of dozen well-wishers. Buckley's widowed mother came down from Greenwich and one of the Cincinnati Glickmans, a cousin, showed up and stayed loaded for two days. Enrique represented the Cuban side of the family. I was the best man.

Carol seemed a little bit more glassy than usual and even a touch squeamish. "Her psychologist suggested tranquilizers," Mother confided to me while Carol was cutting the cake. "So apprehensive, this morning in particular. Such a sensitive, caring girl!" Buckley was visibly manic, jumping from guest to guest and talking up a client he had acquired the previous week who was going to spot him points in a movie under production outside Longboat Key.

"All three kids married already," I observed to Dad. He was nursing a tulip of champagne and contemplating the water. The tide was rising.

"At least for the moment," Dad said. My divorce was pending. He gave me a sharp look. "I liked the last wedding better. That fruitcake of a rabbi, Wow! She pounded my gong all afternoon. Traditional. Foul-mouthed. Zaftig. How could anybody improve on that? On the long road to spiritual awakening?"

I picked a crabmeat canapé off a tray by the window. Dad had returned to contemplating the horizon. "Nobody seems to want to leave you guys in peace," I said. "Did Ricky tell you that he and Wendy are both signing up for graduate courses in Tampa next semester?"

"I heard that. I have a feeling he's up here beating the bushes for that hedge fund Ramon was pitching at the lunch. Hide your wallet."

"You better hide yours. He wasn't making love to *me*."

"It's my distinguished hairline," Dad said. He rolled the champagne glass in his fingertips. "The truth is, Mike, that might not be too bad an idea. With real estate around here exploding the way it's doing, can you imagine what beachfront properties in Cuba will go for once el Bardito is out of the picture?"

"Wouldn't that be the time to buy?"

"If you could get any. You'd need an inside track. Ramon is obviously...."

"Connected? Wasn't that Rabbi Ginsburg's euphemism?"

"He knows people, OK?" Dad moistened his upper lip. "We probably ought to take a bite. A nibble."

Everything started with that. Ramon's subsidiary, Sunrise Capital Partners, had come into existence two years earlier. After weeks of negotiations on several levels – my accountant will be calling your accountant – Dad's people – me, mostly, breathing down our trust attorney Prescott Wallaye's neck – and Ramon's people came up with a strategy. Sunrise Capital Partners was structured as a hedge fund, a hot financial instrument at the moment because it permitted its managers to invest in just about anything – stocks, distressed debt, overseas currencies, pork bellies, gambling casinos in Macao – and go long, or short, or both at the same time if there was any percentage in arbitrage. There was little if any serious governmental supervision.

Outside investors would pay substantial management costs and give up a sizeable chunk of the trading profits to an insider "performance fee," sometimes as high as 30%. But in a good year the remaining 70% could turn into a lot of money. We would get a substantial allocation of shares in the partnership. What made the deal look irresistible to Dad was that Ramon wasn't asking for an out-of-pocket investment. The up-market condominiums and Tierra Verde palacios Dad had been picking up since the later eighties with the accumulated capital from Mother's 1987 stock market killing – the scattered real estate Dad had brought me down to Florida to supervise – would be repackaged into a unified mortgage bond.

Afterwards we became aware that Ramon and his braintrust presented themselves to their outside investors as sole owners of the bond itself. But in fact we – Dad and I – reserved the right for the first five years to take these assets back on thirty days' written notice if – in our judgment – circumstances in the marketplace deteriorated enough or the monthly payments on the bond flagged. By 2005 the appraised value of the real-estate package topped out at perhaps $30-40 million.

With our little cluster of very choice properties to anchor his expanding partnership, Ramon had already lined up a Miami banking syndicate, his mysterious if – we picked up on this little by little as the months unfolded – decidedly ominous *counterparties*. It would develop that a semi-retired consigliere from the Trafficante wing of the mob was the principal cash investor. When the whole deal went down Ramon's backers seemed to be absolutely clawing the earth to advance Sunrise Capital Partners assets they had been laundering, something north of thirty million dollars, against our very tangible properties. This charge of capital amounted to feed stock, seed money, for Ramon and his backroom plungers.

We found out later that all those voracious "counterparties" were kept in the dark by Ramon when it came to the encumbering provisos I had slipped into the documents. Ramon was focused entirely on this opportunity to capitalize himself, and on a major scale, and to hell with the fine print. Buckley and Rick took it on themselves to keep us pumped up by passing back word as Ramon's agents continued to acquire title, through a holding company in Toronto, to a wide range of beachside properties in Cuba.

We certainly didn't know it at then, but at the time almost all the fresh capital in Sunrise Capital Partners seemed to originate with us. Along with our annual 9% remuneration as stakeholders in the embargoed real estate and whatever we picked up in dividends from the overall fund, we – Dad – could look forward to 20% of the proceeds post-Castro when *that* bonanza hit. Billions, potentially.

Heady stuff for a lifelong academic. Meanwhile, in backwater St. Petersburg, I continued to collect the rents and pass them along to the syndicate in Miami. We wanted to keep our hand in. Dad made very sure that he, as well as his trust attorney, had tucked away copies of the original deeds and mortgages.

For me, at least, the day-to-day hedge fund maneuvering

could get maddening to follow. Ramon and his wizards were indulging in a lot of trades, overnight strategies to double up against the box and heavily margined placements on algorhythm-based computer programs that could rocket if the numbers lined up or permit us to bail out on some prearranged uptick or downtick.... I fought down skepticism at every stage. This seemed too easy.

By then I was beginning to generate a modest legal practice to supplement my hit-and-run property management for Dad. Buckley had a lot of unbilled time, and certainly a better preparation than I did when it came to tracking the gyrations of Ramon's high-powered hedge fund managers. That first year Buckley took the financial scud-work over, day to day. It seemed to fire his imagination – big numbers, exorbitant reported profits, a lot of action every minute. A couple of times a week he and Rick met in Tampa at one of the steak houses and strategized prospects for the exploding market.

I'd put it off since summer, but toward the middle of January in 2008 I reserved an afternoon to pop in on my short list of iffy tenants – iffy meant people who weren't bothering to pay their rents. Normally we sent a reminder note, then something stiffer on our legal letterhead. If that didn't produce at least a partial payment I'd hitch up my guts and drop by personally.

One of St. Petersburg's most respected slumlords had stroked out six months previously. Like the rest of the market, housing was starting to head down. We picked up several of the recently deceased's rather ramshackle multifamily tenancies just south of Central, adjacent to the giant hummock on Third Street called Thrill Hill because it cost so many drivers their mufflers. These odds and ends were definitely not the sort of acquisitions the Miami bankers were after, but they were cash-flow generators and no doubt good for a pop when we broke them up and turned them over down the road.

We understood well enough that our underpriced acquisitions bordered what white folks around town dismissed as the St. Petersburg Ghetto. The term remained applicable, God knows, although up-market black families had long since moved on to Lakewood Estates, or Clearwater, or even Pinellas Point. There they lived sedately, maintaining beautiful lawns and slipping in and out toward evening without a lot of fanfare.

I got to the last address on my list, #5 Muldavey Court, around five. It was still hot, close. The little efficiency apartment I wanted was three flights up and accessible from the back, off the parking area that adjoined a cul-de-sac. A railing of gray old pressure-treated two-by-four ascended to a tiny rear landing. A badly dented anodized aluminum door seemed to be the only entrance. The inside looked dark, vespertine.

There was no bell. I knocked, resoundingly, on one of the aluminum panels. Nothing. The heat of the afternoon was coming off the patched-up pavement below. I draped my jacket over one arm and knocked again, sweaty and a little out of breath from the climb.

I was about to start down when I heard the click of toenails scurrying across dried-up linoleum and sensed a form. The handle turned. The door opened outward and the muzzle of a half-grown boxer, as black and glistening as licorice, strained toward me with an expression so doleful yet full of inquiry that I stepped back on impulse, not wanting to provoke this high-strung animal. Behind the dog a short woman with searching, canted eyes was patting the boxer's neck.

"She won't bite you," the woman said. "She is a big pup."

The woman waited. Her heavy black hair was drawn back behind her neck in a tortoise-shell clasp. Something about her reminded me immediately of the woman in Mother's Klimt.

"I'm here," I started. But that seemed lame. "We sent you...letters?" I started again.

The woman nodded, resigned. "You are the representative of the landlord."

"I am the landlord. For all practical purposes."

"What purpose is not practical?" the woman said. "You look very warm. Come in."

She had a level, melodious voice. The woman and the dog backed up; as I went by her I inadvertently grazed one generous breast; a corner of her full mouth lifted, crimped: a smile. The room was clean but very nearly empty. A futon in the corner, several chairs and a table of woven raffia. There was a lighted parchment lamp with a fringe and a tattered geometric rug. I sat down in a chair by the table while the woman went over to the primitive sink and drew me a glass of water and handed it to me. As I was starting to drink the boxer sprang onto the table and inclined toward me, shuddered, and plastered my entire jaw with an extravagant lick.

"She is a pretty good judge of character," the woman said. "For an animal that is still so young."

"That, or I'm awfully salty."

That broke her up suddenly, a rilling, uninhibited laugh I'd seen no reason to expect. Her hollow cheeks seemed dark yet glowed with a pearlescent cast. She looked somewhere in her mid-twenties. I noticed a wall hanging behind her, intricate, entirely of beads.

"This is a guess," I said. "But are you..Native American?"

"You guessed that one. All Injun. Pure squaw."

I pulled the notebook that I carried instead of a briefcase out of my jacket pocket. The room was getting warmer as the evening settled in. "You must be...Alice Meadows."

"I wish I was. She went to Hawaii. I told her, you just go. Alice is my cousin. I told her, leave Penelope to me. Penelope is her dog here. That has a crush on you."

"I hate to start in on you like this, but did Alice Meadows mention anything else to you? Like her lease. No pets, no sublets, pay once a month, annoying details like that? I hate to come on like Simon Legree, but—" Abruptly my collar itched; I attempted to shrug it loose.

The woman stood up to help me off with my jacket. She hung it carefully over the back of the chair and went back and sat down. "Who is Simon Legree?"

"Another landlord."

"You work for him?"

"Sometimes it feels like that." There was a little water in the glass, which I drank carefully to buy time. "Maybe you should tell me your name."

"We have to be careful when we do that. Our medicine men say, when you give a stranger your name you endow him with the reflection of your soul." She sat a moment, looking into my eyes. "My true name is Dances-Like-Fire," she said. "For on the rez. People here call me Linda."

"Linda Meadows."

"Why not, if that is what you want it to be."

I felt stymied. Penelope sat unmoving next to me, her snubbed profile distinct against the waning afternoon.

"You want money," Linda finally announced.

"Isn't that the deal? You – or Alice, or somebody – gets to stay here and we get reimbursed in some way." I really didn't like the way that came out, and I could see by her frown that Linda didn't either.

"If you want money," she said, briskly, "I have a proposal." She produced a battered wallet and eased a dog-eared card out and leaned over to flip it onto the table. The square-cut bosom of her dark shift lapsed open for a moment; I endeavored not to look. The White Man's Burden. Penelope jumped off the table and I hoped she wasn't going to sniff my hard-on.

The card attested to Linda's racial purity. Certificate Degree of Indian Blood was printed across the top. Linda contained 4/4 degree of Indian blood, it said, and followed up with a registration code and her Social Security number.

"I am a full-blooded Comanche," Linda said. "We have a trust fund from the profits of the casinos and the hospital on the reservation in Oklahoma and the smoke shops and all the enterprises. Every six months the comptroller sends the check. And then you got the percentage Savage Owl – Charlie – has to send me from Big Cypress. You know that crazy resort? Outside Hollywood, before Miami? Charlie is mostly Seminole, but still he doesn't get all that much."

"You're an heiress?"

"I get a trickle. A tiny pitiful drop or two."

"Who's Charlie?"

"He was the husband. The tribal council there gave him the baby. Our sweet little papoose. And why? His uncle is the chief." Linda looked off into space. "You think I'm a deadbeat, right?"

"Just passing through," I said. "Not passing judgment."

"How much do you have to have? I lived in my smelly little Volkswagen before, you know."

"I didn't know. Would Penelope go too?" Penelope laid her snout on my knee, and I fondled the gristle behind her lapsed ears. "We ought to be able to work something out."

She shot me another very ambiguous look from under those glittering hooded eyes. "Three hundred a month?" she said finally. "Maybe they will take me back on at Pizza Hut." Linda exhaled, slowly. "And I will write Alice. Maybe she will come home sooner or later."

From a shadowy corner one of the ubiquitous local lizards, the anole, darted toward our table, dodged Penelope's marauding nose and all but levitated onto the back of Linda's hand. Very large, prehistoric-looking, it pumped its leathery torso five or six times, then reared back and inflated its slate-colored larynx, which ballooned out until it was almost transparent.

Linda regarded the lizard and blew on it, affectionately, which it seemed to like. "She is named Isabella-Yearns-For-Water," Linda confided. "She eats the cucarachas. This is my only friend here," she confessed, pinching up that one-sided smile. "Except for the dog. But Penelope is more, like, you know, my family now. She is a very old spirit."

CHAPTER VI

When I got back to the office that evening I juggled the books a little. If we could manage a five-figure donation to the Free Clinic every year we could carry Linda until her prospects improved. Dad would understand that, and certainly Mother would. Dad could get short with me that winter – his every intuition told him the stock market was in serious trouble. Real estate was losing altitude fast and growth-crazy outfits like Countrywide showed signs of public indigestion after gobbling up backwoods homeowners by the hundreds of thousands lured into adjustable-rate paper. The Federal Reserve was cheering the inevitable train-wreck on.

I brought up Linda's predicament to Dad toward the end of January, when I stopped by at Snell Isle to catch him up with what was happening with his real estate day to day. "Sure, why not?" he conceded right away, just as I anticipated. "Is there an alms category in your receipts book? The thing is, try to get something every month. Ween her into respectability. The dog sounds like an asset. Keeps an eye on the premises. Maybe we should pay *her.*"

At this point Dad was obviously feeling seller's remorse about entrusting to Sunrise Capital Partners our precarious little collection of overpriced condominiums and ocean-side villas. By then we would have long since doubled or in some cases tripled our original stake if we had gotten out perhaps a year earlier. At current prices, which were still high, we could have sold and come out with something like $25,000,000 on a capital investment not much more than half the size.

"Our problem," he reiterated to me directly a few days after my visit to Linda, "is the unfortunate fact that most of our choicer properties are locked up in Miami. I'm starting to develop a nasty case of investment *spilches*. The itch to make some changes, fast."

Dad was at his desk in his library in the loggia. Through the clerestory window you could glimpse the ocean.

"Don't look at me," I said. "What was all that about maybe a little nibble?"

"You're more than flesh should have to bear sometimes," Dad said. "A lawyer is bad enough. But a lawyer with a memory...?"

"How about the escape clause? We get to annul the entire arrangement and recover the constituent properties at any time during the first five years if Sunrise doesn't perform. I'm sure you remember how long they kept stalling us about the October payment, and January is almost over, and zilch. Also, it's been six months since we've seen any payout on our hedge fund participation. "

"Jesus," Dad said. "You do sound almost like a lawyer. What are you saying, you think they're sliding into Chapter Eleven or something? They might have liquidated our real estate?"

I inclined forward. "If Sunrise Capital Partners had sold any of our stuff they were required by contract to get our approval six weeks beforehand. Which they have not. Done. Could not do, because we're still the mortgage-holder. We kept the paper. So we're probably OK." I let myself back in the antique Barcalounger Dad reserved for visitors.

Dad minced his lips together. "This could get..personal, if you know what I mean. Family shootouts are always the nastiest, like incest without the home-cooked meal. The Bobbsey Twins are all about that goddamned hedge fund every time I run into either of them." Between us the Bobbsey Twins was code for the brothers-in-law.

"It's what they've got. If it puts together, they're made."

"I guess I understand that."

"Home-cooked meal! Christ, if that isn't far-fetched! You and your metaphors."

"That's what this editor says. I'm going over the galleys for the Keynes book before we jump over the pond next week to cross-check a couple of last-minute references she spotted in the notes. This punk kid they assigned me as an editor at Random House has taken it upon herself to demand verification for *everything*. After months of quibbling over *every Goddamned phrase*." Dad flashed one page, which was spider-webbed with crisscrossing red lines. "Editing software! It's the worst idea those merchandising chazirs have come up with since the English started promoting Enema Cruises."

Later in the week I stopped by for a supper with Carol and Buckley. They lived in Pass-a-Grille, a spur of beachfront that hung down into the Gulf of Mexico below the gigantic turreted pink landmark of a twenties hotel still called the Don Cesar. Their concrete walkup condominium had a balcony wide enough for a dining table; when I showed up, Rick and Wendy were there too.

"Sort of a family reunion," I said. "Jeez! When do we pass

around the pictures of the grandchildren?"

Wendy gave me her sultry, fuck-you look. "We'll get to that," she said. She planted her big right hand on Rick's knee. They were both in cargo pants. "At least we're working on it. We definitely never saw any indication that you and – what was her name, Janine? – got anywhere *near* pumpin' them bambinos out–"

"Her name was Janice," Carol broke in, and crushed out her cigarette. "Wendy, I think you're really out-of-bounds, bringing that up—"

"Too much time in Church," Wendy overrode her. "I heard the rumor she left her ovaries in the collection plate–"

Rick roared. "Jesus, Wendy," I said. "That's rough."

"I'm my father's daughter."

"Dad wouldn't have said that," Carol said. "You know he wouldn't have said that."

There was a very awkward moment. Buckley stood up. "Listen, boys and girls, Carol here has concocted these ab-solutely mind-boggling clam dip and mushroom hors d'oeu-vres, which I am about to rescue from a fiery afterlife and lay before you, pronto." He edged through the half-open sliding door and into the galley-like kitchen.

"Don't say a word!" Carol warned her sister. "Not a word!"

"What's to say?" Wendy arched those untended brows. "He's fucking perfect!"

The main course came off the outdoor grill, either skinless chicken breasts or bratwursts so packed with fat they threat-ened to burst into flame every time Buckley turned one over. The dining area was cramped, especially for Enrique, who kept arching his back and pushing out his heavy legs. The extended scar from his wound was visible on his left thigh just below the hem of his shorts. The no-see-ums were after him, and he was continually twitching his high temples and wiping down his arms and calves.

Out at the margin of the Gulf the sun was the exaggerated red of an inverted forest fire and tinted a layered banking of cloud that reached across the horizon. The wharf a few blocks to the south looked overpopulated from our balcony. Fishermen, many in rags, were pulling in mullets and bluefish and filleting them while they wriggled and tossing the guts to the hovering pelicans. Carol produced a tub of chocolate swirl ice cream and pried the top off and handed each of them a spoon.

"Saves dishes," she announced.

"Good thinking," Wendy said. "Keeps the germs in the family."

"I tried to invite the parents," Carol said. "But Mother said they were going to England early next week and she was worried about finishing up the packing. Her energy level is not outstanding these days. Did you know they were going away, Mikey?"

"Dad said something. They want him to run down some footnotes before they commit to the bound galleys on his Keynes book." The ice cream got around to me and I levered up a healthy mouthful. "He won't be gone long. I know he wants to get right back. He's teaching a seminar, and I know he wants to consolidate and switch around and sell just about everything he can get his hands on before this market hits the fan. Dad's worried about all that real estate we lent to the hedge fund. Time to liquidate that. The old guy is definitely in a high-speed panic." I was nervous, sounding like Buckley. Talking through the ice cream, I realized I hadn't made much sense.

Rick was examining me. "How realistic can it be, to reorganize at this time?" he wanted to know. "The hedge fund have a lot of these properties, an' we have to use them to provide principal for the investments. I think the counterparties don't like that, if no more we have the principal. Dangerous! Very difficult to make the unwindings...."

"Dad knows that." I said. "That said, it still may be necessary to exercise our repurchase option."

Rick sat up in his chair. Except for his frown he looked mostly stone-faced. Unreadable.

Buckley took some ice cream and glanced at Ricky and handed the tub to me. "You have to realize, Mike, any move your father or anybody else might make at this stage fiddle-fucking with the assets of the fund could throw off *every*body's timing. We don't want to spook the Canadians, let alone our confreres in Cuba. They are still hot to trot, and it is *essential* to keep them geared up...."

"Talk to Dad," I said. "He ought to be back in a little over a week."

The following Wednesday it was time to check in with our delinquent renters and push and prod to keep them on the books. Eviction was the pits, for everybody, and most of the time our people would make some attempt to catch up if they were approached with a little finesse.

I got to Linda Meadows' around three-thirty. She had been

on my mind, afflicting my thoughts with an anticipation I hoped was not primarily sexual. She was a poverty case, obviously busted out, but she was in touch with something I knew I needed to pull me back from too many bad months, recurrent intimations of worthlessness that kept coming over me after Janice bailed out.

The problem was not to be burned out merely jacking up my endorphins. Several times I'd driven out to Fort De Soto and found myself swimming out so far I could not see the cannon blocks of the fortification, then floating back exhausted on the afternoon tide. I rode the cracked, mold-streaked, faded-rose concrete bi-ways of the Pink Streets as fast as I could get my touring bike to go, an hour at a time, and dismounted afterwards streaming sweat, bug-bitten, sinuses aching from early pollens, unrelieved. I was obviously depleted in some existential way.

I'd meant to call Linda first. But she had no listed phone, so I just turned up again. Before I could knock, Penelope let loose her sharp, soulful bark, so Linda had that much warning. She opened the door immediately and conferred on me that one-sided smile, as if she had been expecting me at precisely that moment.

"It's me again," I said.

"You took a long time."

"Can't harass the tenants. It's the law."

"So many laws here," Linda said. She let her breath out. Penelope had leapt up onto the table and was regarding me appraisingly, eye to eye. I stepped back before she could lick my face.

"Penelope is so crazy about you," Linda laughed. "And see, look, you leave her in the lurch. Are you always so demanding with your females?" I thought she was on the point of touching my wrist, but I wasn't sure. We were on dangerous ground. Tenant-landlord relations are covered very specifically in the St. Pete housing code. Things could get messy, especially in the local newspapers, for any property owner suspected of taking out his rent in trade.

"It's really so good you came today," Linda said. She reached into the pocket of her shift and pulled up a roll of bills. "Three hundred dollars. Count it, go ahead. A lot of wampum. Twenties mostly. Some tens."

I took the money, somewhere beyond floored. "Look, I didn't mean for you to, you know, impoverish yourself—"

"It's my share. Part of my share. My brother, Sonny, came through in the morning from Lawton. Where the rez is, Oklahoma. He is on leave from the Army. We get the trust fund payout twice every year. It was OK this time. I was surprised."

"If you're sure this won't—"

"Alice don't come back. Doesn't. Besides, I think I have something at the Walmart. At the checkout."

"Great news. You should celebrate."

"I was thinking about that. What would you think about a little pool? I played that a lot on the road. Charlie was stone bonkers about pool. Especially if I let him slurp down a little firewater every time he scratched. There is a nice place right up MLK, nine or ten blocks north of Central. Penelope needs a walk. I'll get her collar."

It was still light by the time we got to the Flamingo Bar. An extremely old yellow dog of no definable breed lay sprawled across the entrance. Penelope barked at it in hopes of fellowship but it wouldn't move. There was a badly faded portrait of Jack Kerouac in a frame screwed onto the front façade.

A few men and a mountainous middle-aged woman sat drinking at the big horseshoe bar itself. Pool tables surrounded the bar, one in use. We both ordered Heinekens, which the voluptuous bartender skated across to us in heavy frosted glasses.

I had played quite a lot of pool, eight-ball mostly, at Amherst in the Deke House. Linda was out of my class. Her black hair fantailing across her back, she hit the long shots with the kind of power and brio that almost always made them sure things. She chalked a lot, especially when she wanted enough sideways English to tap the close ones into the middle pockets. At one point she came close to running the table while I went after another beer and passed the time of day with the owner, who had been badly damaged by Agent Orange in Viet Nam and came home and bought the bar and helped Jack Kerouac drink himself into an early grave. Penelope sat by and watched the yellow dog with great concern and lapped water repeatedly out of its dish.

Around seven o'clock or so I paid up and Linda racked her cue. I was feeling the Heinekens. "Could Charlie keep up with you at that game?" I wanted to know.

"Oh, no," Linda said, somehow a little sadly. "But Charlie was, you know, a canoe Indian. My people are horse Indians."

"That explains everything."

She hit me lightly on the shoulder. "Also, Charlie had to have – you know – the firewater...."

I looked around. "It's getting dark," I said. "Lots of people on the street. Let's get a cab." I had already spotted a dusty scarlet Crown Victoria with *P.J.'s Cabs* painted above a rear fender. We walked up the street. A very tall, portly man with a heavy white brush mustache, smelling defiantly of garlic, was seated at the wheel.

"You going to give us a ride?" I asked him.

"If I feel like it," the driver said.

We got in.

"Why don't I buy you dinner?" I said while I was paying off the cabbie.

"No, no. You spent enough already. I can fix us something."

Upstairs in Muldavey Court the dog flopped down in a corner and yawned hugely and lapped one paw over her muzzle. I took my chair and Linda crouched in front of me. "Does something hurt you?" she asked me after a moment.

"I'm –look, maybe I'm like you. My marriage broke up and I guess I've forgotten the generational moves. Also – I'm a little buzzed."

"Will you try something?"

"Whatcha got? Not too outlandish, preferably."

"Traditional." Linda rummaged in a drawer and brought out perhaps a dozen rough puckered greenish quarter-size blobs and dropped them on the table. "These are very important for the Native American Church. Sonny left them for me

64

this morning."

"Peyote buttons! I never saw any before. What the hell, they probably go great with too much beer."

Linda was regarding me through half-closed ink-black eyes. I had said something wrong.

"No," I said. "I mean, why not?" Flip obviously wasn't working. "You *are* my hostess. Fuck! How are you supposed to ingest these things?" I was at once exhilarated, still somewhat fried, and full of foreboding.

"You have to cook them a little first." Linda said. She scooped the buttons up and diced them and fed them into a tiny sauce pan in an inch of water and squeezed some lemon juice on them and put the pan on a burner. Everything boiled almost immediately. "Now we have to wait," Linda said.

The room was close, starting to get shadowy. I pulled a handkerchief out and blotted my brow. Linda crossed over to the closet and retrieved a fan from an upper shelf and plugged it in and set it up to blow in my direction. Then she walked over to the futon and divested herself of her shift and stepped rather daintily out of her panties. I stood; she crossed over and gently pressed me back down into my chair. Her tits were everything I had anticipated, and then some. Then she slipped over to the stove to mash and stir the mush in the saucepan.

"You're like my Dad," I heard myself saying. "You like to confront your inspirations sans culottes."

Linda obviously did not understand any of that. "When the spirits come," she informed me, "they want everything simple."

I suppose I half understood. After another minute or so I

stood up and pulled off my tie and peeled my shirt off and shrugged carefully out of my trousers and – half-hesitatingly – my underwear and sox and shoes. I piled everything neatly behind my chair. By then my prick spoke for me.

At some point Linda went over to what passed for a refrigerator in this woebegone efficiency we rented her and came back with some sort of wheat flatbread and buttered each of us a top-heavy piece. This greenish puree form of the peyote smelt very forbidding, bitter. I ate mine in awkward little bites, sacrificing myself to get it down. I think I sensed that I was being given what might turn out to be my last chance.

In time she presented me with another piece. "You have beautiful shoulders," she said to me, but she did not allow me to touch her. In the corner, Penelope had started whining.

The light show I'd heard about came over me little by little, juggling against a nausea I fought for what seemed a very long time before I had to stumble over to her tiny john and heave up the Heinekens and whatever remnants of lunch survived and the slimy green residue of the peyote. By then the twilight was deepening into dark. Linda was a moving silhouette, wrapped flirtatiously for a moment in a flowered shawl and executing some kind of dance step. I broke a cold sweat: At that instant an overwhelming conviction of completeness flushed over me, an awareness that I was a cluster of atoms in a universe of atoms where nothing could possibly be a boundary.

It was if I was shedding some kind of crust, a kind of poisonous all-afflicting scab that the many disappointments and frustrations of the last few years had allowed to toxify my emotions. A white, vibrating energy was coming off everything in the room, Linda especially. As I slid out of the chair and onto my back on the Navaho rug I sensed Penelope easing herself onto her feet and starting toward me, her muzzle now expanding until it was bigger than the visage of a lion, with gigantic burning eyes that reprimanded me for all my weaknesses and all the sins of my misguided ancestors.

I lay there in shame, acutely chilled and throbbing with energy while my neglected cock kept stiffening and stiffening and took on a size I would have thought was mythological. It glowed, bluish white, and out of the darkness I felt Linda approach, and stand like a priestess with her legs spread above me. The shawl floated down. I lay there watching her dark aboriginal pussy inflate like a dripping mandala as she lowered it slowly onto my suffering cock and socketed herself, taking me in entirely. Her smell was intoxicating, of succulent healing yeasts. She began to squeeze, quite gently at first, and it could well have been hours before she came finally and so allowed everything in me to burst.

I was too overstimulated by now to detumesce; I rolled Linda onto her back and made it to my knees and gripped her so that my urgent fingers met at the mouth of her sphincter and I began to probe her from the front to invite her hungriest, most unappeasable cravings. Suddenly I felt something a little chilly and very wet investigating *my* asshole: Penelope's nose.

By then it really didn't matter.

CHAPTER VII

In time we needed sleep. Linda pulled the futon open and we both crawled onto it and I spooned her beneath a summer blanket. Within seconds I had fallen into the deepest slumber I can ever remember. I dreamt of a Bucks County steeplechase in which all the mounts were naked women, a freezing lake where I was swimming frantically to avoid dozens of converging bears. I think I slowly came awake around 5:30. The single window off the landing admitted enough gray light to put a shine on Linda's dusky shoulder-blades. Penelope was asleep across our feet. Beneath the window, next to the door, a long form was wrapped in a blanket. I could make out a head of very black cropped hair and a big, boney hand holding the blanket closed. In the hand I saw the butt of a large knife.

Just then Linda came to and sat up. She saw the man on the floor and wrapped herself in the summer blanket in one motion. I scrambled for my jockey shorts and had myself halfway into my trousers when the man on the floor rolled over and spoke. "Did I miss the floor show?" the man said. Penelope had jumped off the futon and was hunched above him, eagerly licking his face.

The man rolled up. He was quite tall and extremely spare, late twenties perhaps, with the classical pointed jaw and high-bridged nose of the pure-bred Plains Indian. There was the tattoo of a snake engorging a dragon on his left shoulder. His skin looked burnished. He had been sleeping in his boxers.

"You must be—"

"Sonny," Linda said. "The brother."

We shook hands. Sonny had absent-mindedly transferred the knife to his left hand. It was a serious knife.

"Sonny stands for...." I hoped to prompt him: "You must be named after your father—"

"Just Sonny," he said, and smiled.

"His tribal name is Buffalo Hump," Linda said, with that sideways smirk. "We only use it on the reservation."

"And then it's only on feast days," Sonny said. "When we are barbequing a paleface or something really special."

A few minutes later, when everybody had clothes on and Linda was frying up some eggs, Sonny filled in a little of his background. Their father had been chief of police on the reservation, a graduate of the Indian Police Academy in New Mexico. As the children of a dignitary, Linda and Sonny got top-drawer treatment. Linda had emerged in her early teens as a kind of prodigy among the powwow dancers. The parents had separated. Linda remained with the mother and Sonny helped out around the station house off and on and picked up one of the scholarships reserved for teenage boys of Native American blood at Valley Forge Military Academy. After high school Sonny enlisted in the Army and trained as a Calvary scout.

This was a tradition: Indians had been put to use as trackers and guides in the American army since before the Revolution. At home in Lawton Sonny had apprenticed himself to one of his father's seasoned deputies and helped run down every variety of workaday violation on Indian land all the way to Fort Sill. This came very naturally: One of their grandfathers was awarded the Congressional Medal of Honor during World War

Two as a scout in the China-Burma-India Theater, a leader among the legendary Codetalkers who radioed back and forth in Indian dialects to flummox the Japanese in the jungles of Mindanao and Leyte.

Sonny had been little more than a recruit when U.S. Forces invaded Afghanistan after 9/11. There had been a perfunctory attempt to trap Osama Bin Laden without committing mainline troops to Bora Bora. Sonny's years of experience tracking Mexican horse thieves and convenience-store stickup artists persuaded his battalion commander to release him TDY from the 113 Calvalry for long enough to infiltrate the mountains of Bora Bora. Our top brass was after coordinates for a fighter strike on Al Qaeda provisional headquarters. Bin Laden had already decamped, but Sonny had found his way into the cave that sheltered Mullah Omar and managed to purloin the Taliban elder's false teeth as he lay sleeping on a cot in battle gear. Sonny still carried them around in his rucksack in a malachite case, for luck. They were his totem.

He showed them to us. They weren't pretty. The eggs were excellent; I was extremely hungry, with a gathering eagerness that morning to begin my life again. Linda started coffee brewing, and then my cell-phone broke into its idiotic chime: *None But The Lonely Heart.* I suppose I was trying to chide myself out of my slump.

It was Maximillian, the elderly black caretaker Dad relied on to watch his place whenever he was gone. "Mistah Michael?" Max opened, "You need to jump right on over here."

"What's up?"

"We had some visitors, what it is."

"Somebody came by?"

"Some fool busted in. Tore up your pa's study pretty good. You tell me what you want to do." Max, normally placid, sounded angry. "I tell you one thing, I catch that muthuh-fuckuh, I intend to go up side his head! You want the police?"

I told Max to wait until I got there and tapped off and explained the situation.

"If you could use some backup," Sonny offered, "This is the sort of petty crap I got fairly good at around the reservation."

"Sure. If you really want to help. You must have things to do—"

"Nothing you'd want to worry about. We're supposed to get a couple of years Stateside for every year in the field. I just got back after Christmas from Mogadishu. Division put me through college, on the internet, mostly. Languages come easy. They had a shortage, so now I'm an Arabic speaker. Somebody my color can get by in a pinch in a cesspool like Somalia. The DIA needed somebody on the ground so those coneheads in the Pentagon could start doping out the clans."

We hurried out to Snell Isle in my aging BMW. With months to kill, it turned out, Sonny was enrolling in September in courses leading to a PHD in environmental sciences at the University of Oklahoma. "You know the drill," he opened up, "redskins like me worry all the time about what's happening to the material world. We think it's alive, like us, and if we abuse it enough it will give up on our species and wipe us off the planet. The Great Spirit, what the Sioux call the Taku Skan-

skan—the force which moves upon the waters. Our feeling is, it's reaching the end of its patience with us – especially with the White Man. That's what we think. Probably some dumb collective neurosis."

"You ought to talk with my father. He's ready to join your tribe."

"Dances-like-Fire – Linda – she gets really upset. Especially after they took her baby. I was surprised to find you two at – you know – close quarters."

"But wasn't her husband a Native American too? Some kind of Seminole?"

"Whatever they call themselves. Basically, a spinoff. The way we see it, all these tribes down here are nothing but waterlogged Creeks who hid out in the Swamp and bred with the blacks while our ancestors were fighting Custer. Now they're getting rich like whites and we're still licking our wounds from the Trail of Tears. The Long Walk."

"So you hate us?"

"Don't judge by me. I'm Regular Army. I've been co-opted."

We were pulling in below the portcullis of Dad's palazzo. Max was waiting. He always seemed to be wearing clean gray freshly ironed coveralls. Even his bald head looked scrubbed and polished. I introduced Max to Sonny.

"This a genu-ine outrage," Max said. "I had this place locked up *real good.* I come by yesterday cause I needed to check the locks, especially in the front. Sometimes your pa get forgetful, you know what I'm drivin' at. Absent-minded professor. Yesterday everything tight as a snappin' turtle's asshole, everything in real good order.

"Then today I thought, Ima get me some of Anastasia's peach cobbler for breakfast, but before I do that I believe I will swing through and examine the property. Relieve my mind. And when I make my rounds and check that study there I see right away nothing *like* what it oughta be. Papers all over everyplace. File drawers wide open—"

Sonny had mounted the steps to the big heavy carved front door. There was a bronzed lock and a deadbolt. He ran his hand along the sills. "Nobody forced this," he said. A path ran alongside the building toward a pergola that overlooked the water; years earlier Mother had directed the construction of a low stacked-stone wall as a kind of running planter for clumps of pinks and impatiens. Halfway along, beneath one of the tall casement windows, Sonny stopped. He grabbed the stone sill of the window, which cropped out, and hoisted himself to examine the space inside. "He got in here," Sonny decided. "You can see where the pry-bar bit into the casing."

Now I saw where the plantings had been trampled and not quite recovered. Sonny crouched. "Enough of a footprint to give us a start. Man, probably on the tall side. Big. Size thirteen boot. You can see where he tried to compensate by digging in a little harder with his right foot and dragging his left toe. Won't let it take any too much weight. Look where he started to jack himself up and squeeze through."

Inside, there was a smear of dirt in the corridor. Dad's record storage area had definitely been pulled apart; he relied on a cheap battery-operated motion-sensor alarm he supposedly could hear from their bedroom, where he had concealed a Beretta in his bed-table drawer from Mother. The alarm must have been triggered at about the time the intruder went to work among Dad's legal papers.

By then whoever it was had succeeded in levering open a number of the locked drawers. No doubt the alarm had panicked the burglar; he could not have known it was not wired into the local station-house. Probably that was why papers and entire files had been pulled out and dumped helter-skelter around this alcove before the intruder had fled. It would be hard later on to tell what he had had in mind. What he was after.

"Looks like second-degree breaking and entering," Sonny said. "What do the bedrooms look like?" We trudged through, checking out the master bedroom suite and Mother's combination gallery and sitting room. "Whoever did this never got this far," Sonny said. "I do this kind of entry a lot. Line of duty."

Sonny checked the night-table drawer. "Usually burglars start in the bedrooms. Heirloom jewelry, cash stashed under the handkerchiefs. They want a quick payoff in case they get interrupted. Even without that – I would see the footprints."

"How? On polished tile?"

"You track enough, it's almost like a shadow. On anything – a grain field where a buck went through, hairs under a leaf –" Sonny steepled his long, muscular fingers. "You have to start with, what was he after? Then work back. You'd have to think the forensic guys will pick up on something. Maybe even a shred of DNA their little vacuums catch, skin. Might have scraped off while he was dragging on that pinch-bar."

"I think," I said, "I had better wait before we get the authorities involved." I had a premonition, an ugly one. "My father will definitely want to be in on this. He's getting back over the weekend."

"Don't want to let the trail cool, ever" Sonny advised.

Max had been looking on, saturnine, brow rumpled. "This gentleman is definitely correct," he said suddenly. "Why your pa want to come home to this? You ain't got to worry about no problems with *him*. He gonna be over*joyed* you get this foolishness under control."

"Still, we're going to wait." I was surprising myself. "Leave everything the way it is. Let's see whether he can figure it out."

I let Dad know about the break-in while he was still at Heathrow. I offered to pick the place up but, as I anticipated, he preferred to look around for himself. The trick was going to be to protect Mother – stretches on the airplane tended to leave her very stiff, her usual regimen of corticosteroids and diuretics wasn't really enough. But she loved Europe – their friends in Europe – and bore up cheerfully. Cheerfully, but drained. Dad wouldn't have confided in her about any prowler. It would have affronted her to think their privacy could be so violated.

We got together for lunch on the esplanade of pavers beneath a huge blue umbrella outside one of those up-market restaurants on Beach Drive across from the museum. The sailboat harborage vis-a-vis was visible between the stupendous – prehistoric – banyan trees that dominated the park, profoundly sculpted and exploding tendrils and alive just then with squirmy little children, black and white, hanging upside-down and shrugging their way along the lower boughs.

"This place is definitely looking up," Dad opened. "We're starting to have Avenues. Like Paris."

Our wine arrived; I asked for a bleu-cheese cheeseburger and Dad wanted the smoked salmon plate. Dad seemed a little fatigued still from his trip, almost pasty and noticeably popeyed. "Are you OK?" I asked him after we clinked glasses.

"Riding airplanes is death. Then there's the ordeal of following your mother all over Mayfair, from gallery to gallery, while she tries to hunt down the perfect additions to her collection. What she's after, obviously, is pornography. Except *refined* pornography, and only by geniuses. She's still secretly enchanted with sex. Which bucks me up, long-term."

"You two are hopeless."

"We're degenerates. Probably Hitler was right. In the New Order men should die young in wars and women should pull plows. No energy for hanky-panky."

"How did the research go?"

"Mostly a waste of time. The editor the publisher planted on my neck agonizes day and night over cockamamie legal issues. She wants at least three verifying documents for every reference to Keynes' homosexuality, for example. The fact is, Keynes was a perennial mama's boy and a polished charmer who liked to boast in his diaries about his conquests. He seems to have tangled assholes with just about every male cutie from Duncan Grant to Lytton Strachey. Old news, except to my editor. I tracked down source notes behind a piece in *The Econ-*

omist that authenticates every single smear on the old boy's bedsheets.

"The best thing that happened was that I ran into a don in Cambridge who agreed to critique in advance my chapter on probability theory. *That* stuff gets abstruse. For me, at least."

We drank more wine. "We'll have to deal with the break-in," Dad acknowledged after a long swallow. "Max really had the jitters. I calmed him down and went all over the place myself."

"We think your discount-house alarm system scared the guy off."

"I beg your pardon. I got that thing at Radio Shack. Top of the line." Dad smacked his lips. "Who would this 'we' be? Max told me you had somebody with you."

"That was the kid brother of that Indian woman I told you about. He's in the military. He was a lot of help. Sonny."

"That's his name, Sonny?"

"It's actually Buffalo Hump, but when he signs like that it invalidates his credit card."

"I see." Dad let his eyes roll into his head. "And you were where when all this transpired? He found the mayhem the guy left early in the morning, Max says."

"I was…with Linda. Our tenant."

"Hmmm. One night stand? You know that sort of thing is fraught with peril. Tenants tend to rat you out to the rental authorities."

"You're missing the point. The thing was largely spiritual. Closer to transcendental meditation. Out-of-body."

"Well, my diagnosis is, either you're starting to grow up

or you're losing your marbles."

"Both, I hope. I never felt better."

Our entrees arrived.

Dad's salmon had been scrolled into a cone on a leaf of lettuce. He unscrolled a couple of inches onto a crisp of toast daubed up with cream cheese and chives after brushing the capers aside. Dad didn't like capers.

"Sonny has some police experience," I said while Dad chewed. "He thought the whole thing wasn't particularly professional."

"The break-in? Probably not." Dad patted the crumbs off his lip with his napkin. "I have a feeling the bastard got what he was after."

"Which was?"

"Legal papers. Whoever broke into the files cleaned out all my copies of everything that pertained to any kind of financial arrangements. Wills. Trusts going back a couple of generations in your mother's family. Our mortgage here. That inch-thick packet of documents Prescott Wallaye came up with when we got tangled up with Ricky's mishpokhe in Miami." Dad raised his thick, grizzled eyebrows.

Wallaye, a shrewd, laid-back deal specialist, did our corporation's legal work in Florida. "You think it might have something to do with that?" I asked.

"It could have. Nobody was after finesse, maybe they were sending a message."

"And that would be?"

"Leave well enough alone." Dad took a swig of the house white. "Maybe somebody got wind of the fact that we just might renege on our participation in those collateralized bonds and turned out not to be too crazy about the idea." Dad was examining me, closely.

"OK," I said finally. "Carol had Wendy and Rick and me over last Tuesday for bratwurst and the hedge fund business came up. I think I indicated that we might have to – you know – sort of reconsider."

"Sometimes you're a lox." Dad said, and grinned. "Too much integrity. You keep this up, they're likely to drum you out of the legal profession." Dad took a little more salmon. "Maybe I'm wrong," he said.

"You're not wrong. One thing Sonny picked up on was the fact that whoever broke in was big and powerful and had a bum left leg."

Dad nodded. "Rick, is what you're thinking?"

"It makes a certain amount of sense. He knows his way around the place."

"Except that – Jesus – he's in our family now. We have to consider Wendy. They might be depending on that as cheap insurance. It's an edifying picture – Enrique in some lockup and Wendy dropping by in those *short* short shorts of hers on visitors' day."

"That could be calculated too," I said. "Incitement to riot." I'd taken maybe one bite out of my cheeseburger, but now I had no appetite. "What I don't understand is what would be the point of the exercise? Other people would have copies of all those papers. Wallaye, certainly."

"Probably it was largely a gesture," Dad said. "A shot across the bow."

CHAPTER VIII

Dad paid the bill and asked me to get over to Wallaye's office ASAP and ask for double printouts of everything his firm had prepared for us since we'd showed up in town. I had a brief due later in the week, and I needed the rest of the afternoon to work on the discovery. Tomorrow would be soon enough to drop by Wallaye's building. I went back to the office and plowed through background details until after five. I'd left it with Linda Meadows that I would pick her up for dinner at Muldavey Court around 5:30.

This was to constitute, I suppose, our second date. I was at a loss for protocol. What is the appropriate follow-up to a hallucinogenic orgy? Bare tit? What could we pick things up by? I remember standing there holding a bottle of good vermouth in a paper bag and my knees starting to tremble the moment Penelope greeted me with that low, resonant yip. I waited for the door to open.

Linda was wearing a dress, colored medallions on cotton. It was mildly décollete. A necklace strung with what turned out to be very large elk's teeth lay along her prominent collarbone.

"All dressed up," I said, and regretted that immediately. We sat down.

"I didn't think you would call or anything."

"How could I not call? The woman who saved me from terminal depression?" My untrustworthy sinuses were kicking up, and I needed to blow my nose.

"I thought, you know, that was too much for you the other

night. First too much beer, and after that the vision quest…."

"The peyote. I loved it. Also, I hated it, but wasn't I supposed to? What I keep remembering is you. Straddling me like that."

Linda's canted black eyes, examining me, seemed to be waiting for some signal. She tossed her mane. "Maybe it's me can't handle it. Why are you sniffing like that?"

"Pollens. Dust. Nothing unusual."

She crossed over to her bedside table and felt for a small bottle and opened it and came back. She shook the bottle a few times and handed it to me.

"What's this for?"

"Powdered sneezeweed. My mother is a puhakut, an eagle doctor. Medicine woman. Take a few breaths of this and you will be OK."

I sniffed. There was a mild stinging; slowly my sinuses cleared. "What can't you deal with?" I said.

"You. You're my first white. I want you, but how do I come out? Afterward?"

"What did you have in mind? A treaty?" Penelope had started to lick my ankle.

"I don't know nothing about treaties. Except – we keep signing treaties, and look how it is now."

"It could be worse. Sonny seems to be doing all right."

"Sonny is going to die pretty soon fighting the white man's wars."

"You're pretty sure of that?"

"His ghost comes and tells me that sometimes in the night."

"Heavy," I said. "I need to use the john."

Inside the john I flicked the switch and the dusty little dome light over the medicine cabinet came on and half-a-dozen cockroaches skittered to escape. I took a little while. Pissing can be quite a project through a semi-hard-on. Once I had done what I could I turned the light off and rejoined Linda.

"Pretty nasty in there, right?" Linda wanted to know immediately.

"It definitely needs renovation. Scored wallboard around the shower stall. Invites mildew. Blame the landlord."

"You saw the cucarachas?"

"Palmetto Bugs? They're Florida's state mascot."

Linda bent to kiss me, very lightly, on the lips.

"What happened to what's-her-name? The lizard. Your best friend. She seems to be falling down on the job."

"Isabella-Yearns-For-Water? She decided it was time to move on. One afternoon she sat there looking at Penelope, and Penelope looks at Isabella, and Isabella pledges her soul."

"I'm not sure—"

"Penelope ate Isabella," Linda said. "It was her nature."

I withdrew the vermouth from the paper bag and proposed a toast to Isabella's sacrifice. Linda produced a pair of tumblers and some tiny cubes of ice from a tray in her little refrigerator and we worked on the vermouth for a while. Neither of us had much to say. After a few minutes Linda stood up and pulled closed the curtain on the window that looked out on the landing. Then she sat down and smiled at me and poured herself another vermouth.

After a few moments more I said: "What do you think."

"What I think? I think what you think. Un poco loco, both

of us. You tease me like a boy. Shy, always so shy. When does the fucking start?"

Our clothes dropped off of us, although Linda retained the necklace. Her body in open daylight had an old-fashioned impact I had never quite experienced before. The weight – the gravity – of her unencumbered breasts with their big, expanding aureoles and her massive pubic triangle concentrated for me exactly what Mother's wildest picture selections were about. Woman! It had become fashionable among the girls I dated to shave the pubis, the easier for the fingers of their dates halfway into a movie to navigate toward the more responsive corners. Linda had remained untouched, her wooly black sporran initially concealing, then more and more exposing glimpses of an extraordinary fullness, swollen fold inside fold for me to explore and enrich. Stretched out alongside each other on the futon we groped and fondled, stroked, kissed deeply and licked each others' ears.

Her thighs opened and I was about to enter her when I heard her whispering something. "The best thing is," she was whispering, " to travel as wide as we can stand it first underneath the buffalo robe." I stopped. "Even Penelope can tell how you are somebody who understands a woman's needs…."

Penelope was chewing lightly on my big toe. "You want me – I'd better take the scenic route—"

I doubled back down and fell to as requested. I remembered the yeasts, but now there was a sweetness, a sharp whiff of the ammonias of birth to oil her slippery stiffening bud, her swollen labia the taste of which was starting to befuddle me.

Man and boy I had experienced my share of head. This was

an exotic dimension. Her rough dimpled tongue continually worked its way around my frenulum, she understood just when and how to modulate the suction to keep me on the ecstatic edge of climax without quite pulling me over. When she had had enough she let me know and shrugged back and I rolled up and lost myself in liquescence as she began to buck into orgasm; this stampeded us both to where she intended to finish all along. We both collapsed slowly after an agonizing last volley. Penelope was after my backside; I could barely catch my breath.

"Injun good time," Linda breathed, and kissed my nose. "You like?"

"I definitely like"

"Why do you frown?"

"I just hope neither of us got Penelope pregnant."

That night we ate the duck special at The Brasserie on Central. I stayed over. Sonny, Linda confided, was bivouacked now with a buddy from the 113 Cavalry in Clearwater.

The futon was small; around three we bumped each other awake and slipped into another groggy round. I woke up again a few minutes after seven and Linda made coffee and it was well after eight before I got a shower and dressed and descended the plank staircase to my BMW. I was pretty sure Wallaye's office was open by then. It was no more than six or eight blocks away, just north of Central.

I heard the racket before I could see the offices. Squad cars were lined up halfway around the block, several with their sirens wailing. The building itself was on a corner, a low, solid-looking structure of white painted, deeply pointed brick that might have been the overseer's residence on an anti-bellum plantation. There was a sweeping veranda on both the street sides with high double-hung windows, a number of which had been blown out. Black smoke was billowing out everywhere.

I parked as close as the cops would let me and joined the mob outside. Prescott Wallaye – a tall, youthful-seeming man in his early fifties with a big debonair crest of graying hair and a lot of the misleading Southern politesse that made you wonder much of the time whether he quite caught the gist – Wallaye stood there exchanging pleasantries with a couple of the local police and a thick-set fellow in a brimmed hat. I hailed Wallaye, who introduced me as a client of his firm to the man in the hat. He was Special Agent in Charge Vincent Hardagon from the Tampa field office of the FBI.

"What happened?" I asked Special Agent Hardagon. We were exchanging cards.

"Hahd tellin', not knowin," Hardagon said. He was obviously from the badlands of Greater Boston. "It ain't malicious mischief, you can bet your ass on that. I'm just droppin' by until the goonsquad from Alcohol, Tobacco and Firearms shows up to dust for prints," He forced an Irish grin, a rictus of exceedingly thin lips around teeth so white they looked artificial.

"Somebody set a fire?"

"Somebody blew a safe."

"We had this *enormous* antique document safe we kept our duplicates in," Prescott Wallaye said. I remembered the safe; a vast beige crackle-finished Victorian relic on iron casters with pocked-chromium rod handles hanging down beside the tumbler. It had presided over the bullpen in which Wallaye's perky assistants in their tropical frocks labored desk by desk at their outdated computers. The rest I could already feel in my gut.

"They took everything?" I asked.

"There wasn't a hellova lot left to take, Bud," Hardagon said. "A lot of the safe wound up in the can. Quite a detonation. Our own explosives guy has come and went. Some kind of limpet mine or something, he thinks. Prick knew his business. One of those shaped charges."

I'd heard of limpet mines. I couldn't remember where.

"Prick took no prisoners," Hardagon said. "Went through everything, the computers especially. Poured some kind of oily shit all over every one of 'em, then lit it. Stank more or less like kerosene. Knock out the storage disks, what we could tell."

"You are looking at a law office," Prescott Wallaye said gently, "on which a lobotomy has been performed."

"That wouldn't have helped anything," Dad said when I apologized for not having gone immediately to Wallaye's offices to pick up copies of our documents. "He'd have wanted one of his girls to copy them, and nobody is ever in a hurry over there. You know how it is in the South. The real problem is, we're a day late and a nickel short altogether. We're kind of bouncing around still, and they're going to swat us like a couple of flies."

I was cocked back in the Barcalounger. "They being Rick and his father?"

"They being all those Cuban meshuginas. At the very least. I talked with Wallaye just before you showed up and he said they had a pretty good security setup at the office – remote cameras, motion detectors, entry sensors, what have you. Wired into one of the services. When those guys finally got there there was nothing – the sensors had been blocked, nothing on the tapes, never even a peep back at their command center. That wasn't just Ricky doing his pa a favor. They're bringing in the specialists. By the way, where were you last night? I called your house."

"I was…I had a date?"

"The Indian girl?"

"She's a woman."

"I can see that. When you flounced in here your feet weren't touching the floor. I never saw anybody so cunt-struck –"

"Dad, look—"

"I'm sorry. You're right. That was off the reservation. So to speak."

We both broke out laughing.

"I'm just….," I said, "She gets to me like nobody I ever ran into. Authentic, she is absolutely authentic."

Dad fiddled with his letter opener. "We need some help," he said, finally. "We're operating on very bad intelligence. For example, can you tell me whether our real estate bonds are registered someplace? With the Securities and Exchange Commission, for example?"

"I can find out. Maybe we can get some kind of lead from that FBI team. I finally remember where I first heard about limpet explosives. That reporter in Miami kept talking about stuff like that in connection with the Cubans."

"Freddy Wilmot."

"Yes. Rick's dad, Ramon, had worked for a guy who at one stage anted up enough cash to get them started in the munitions business."

"Riiight! You mentioned that. How is it that all roads in Miami lead back to the late, great Jorge Mas Canosa?"

"I could go talk with Wilmot and maybe shake out more background. Then – I also thought it might not be too bad an idea to see if we could come up with somebody in the trade, maybe a private investigator, to go down there and infiltrate their operation. So they would, like, back off—"

"Back off or kill us all. What we're probably getting this week is the Havana version of humane treatment. No blood just yet. The family exemption."

"And you intend to just..look away? Just let them clean us out? This is fucking *war*!" I was getting carried away; I couldn't help it. "I really am astonished at how you're reacting to this!"

"What you're really doing is losing your sense of proportion. It's only money, Michael. I never saw you when your blood was up like this. Where did you get that from?"

"Look. They want war, this isn't going to stop. Why did I think your standing as a veteran—"

"You're challenging my manhood? Jesus, that woman is bringing out in you a level of hutspah I honest to God never saw before. OK, not a Comanche word, but you know what I mean."

"I appreciate the banter, but how about this? We reconnoiter a little. First I go see what the forensics guys in Tampa

88

might have turned up. Then Sonny and I take a drive across Alligator Alley and he spooks out Mr. Perez y Cruz's business files in Coral Gables. My guess is, Ramon's got a copy of everything *we* had. And at the same time I could hunt down your friend Freddy Wilmot and see if he has anything else on your Cuban partners."

"*Our* Cuban partners." Dad grimaced. " It's all in the family."

"Wendy is your daughter. I'm just the assistant zookeeper."

"Already deserting the sinking ship?" Dad knit his brow. "Sonny. That must be Buffalo Whatshisface. The girlfriend's brother. How could he help?"

"That's what he does, I thought I told you. He infiltrates, he's a professional scout. Get him to show you Mullah Omar's dentures sometime."

Dad looked sideways, reflecting. "You want to just, sort of, reach in."

"They're reaching in."

Dad looked at me and let his heavy eyelids close slowly. "We would pay Sonny, obviously," he said after a moment.

"Obviously. Just don't bring that up if you're talking to him. My sense is that he has a very highly developed sense of honor. We've got to go slow with anything that looks like buying him off."

"You're operating on very thin ice, and on a very limited acquaintance," Dad concluded after a moment's thought. "You're right about one thing, though. Whatever we do, we definitely better get our butts in gear. The stock market lost more than two hundred points this morning. The real estate market isn't going to lag things by a hellova lot."

CHAPTER IX

Early the next morning I pulled into the secure visitors' parking area under the FBI field office in Tampa. Special Agent in Charge Vincent Hardagon had left my name with the attendant, who had a four-hour clip-on badge with my name printed on it ready in his stall. The moment I left my car a tall well-groomed man stepped out from behind a concrete pillar, patted me down matter-of-factly, and accompanied me to the elevator that took us to the second floor. Special Agent Hardagon's office was all the way down the corridor.

Hardagon had his suitcoat hung over the back of his swivel chair and both his feet crossed at the ankles on the blotter of his desk. He looked very pink underneath the florescent lights. His belly obscured his belt. As I walked in he nodded.

"I appreciate your making time available on such short notice," I opened.

"Your government is on the job twenty-four hours every day of the entire goddamned year." Hardagon said, and passed me a very fat wink. Behind him, flanking the window, were official photographs of FBI Director Robert Mueller and J. Edgar Hoover as a young man. Hoover looked impressively clean-shaven and steely-eyed. On a side wall I noticed a framed diploma from Boston College Law School.

"I got my legal training in Boston too," I said. "BU. We had a lot of regard for the BC faculty," I said. "A couple of my most outstanding professors came over from there."

That certainly sounded lame as hell to me, but I could see Hardagon responding. With evident effort, he returned both feet to the floor. "We can hold our own," Hardagon said.

"You definitely got to Wallaye's offices fast enough."

"We don't like bombings. You run those douche bags down within forty-eight hours or the next thing you know those Terrorism Center lunatics start showing up and the next thing after that you have to subpoena your own evidence out of Washington."

"It's a bureaucratic world."

"You can bet your ass on that. Mister Hoover would not have cared for any of it, these days." He shuffled through the papers on his desk. "Not really a hellova lot, so far. No prints. Nothing in the carpets, nothing like that. ATF agrees that it was a limpet bomb, one of those old Navy numbers got stolen thirty years ago from a warehouse in Portsmouth, New Hampshire and most of 'em been floatin' around the Third World black market ever since. Al Qaeda probably used one of 'em on that destroyer in the Persian Gulf." Hardagon folded his tongue double in his open mouth, and bit it. "Prick that took out that safe knew his onions, though. Surgical, definitely surgical."

"I think I know who was behind that," I said. "Wallaye had worked up the boilerplate when our family transferred a number of prime real-estate properties of ours to a hedge-fund outfit in Coral Gables. We had the right to buy them back if we wanted to. You have to infer that the Cubans who ran the fund had already put them up as collateral, and when they heard that we were thinking about redeeming them it made sense to obliterate the document base."

That got Hardagon's attention. He sat up in his chair. "Holy shit, that's what this is about? You really think that?"

"Absolutely. Two nights earlier they got a man into my father's study at home and rifled his files there.'

"How come you didn't you report *that*?"

"Personal reasons. We had…connections with those people. We still thought we could work everything out."

"So what's your next step?"

"Get down to Miami. Maybe talk some sense into somebody. What are the chances you could get in touch with your counterpart down there in case I need something?"

Hardagon looked me in the eyes. "I could do that," he said slowly. He picked a card out of a translucent organizer on his desk next to a leather-framed snapshot of a worried-looking woman with a large family lolling on the sand. Hardagon wrote down two names, both Hispanic, and several e-mail addresses and telephone numbers. "These lads work out of North Miami Beach." His voice dropped. "Be careful with those Miami cowboys of ours. Off the record, you are dealing down there with spiks from the community. They have a way of playing it a little political, if you know what I'm getting' at." Hardagon paused for emphasis. "You're takin' a hellova walk on the wild side, Buddy, I hope you realize that. I hope and pray you know what the bleep you're doing."

From Tampa I went directly to the St. Petersburg courthouse, where I was well known. A steely-haired matron from one of the better old families around town, Miss Daphne Millsap, ran the archives. She had expended a lot of energy over the previous two years attempting to introduce me to her niece, whom I had already encountered, repeatedly, and preferred to duck.

I explained to Miss Daphne that we were updating our office files, and needed fresh copies of the deed for every property Dad had acquired since we showed up in town, whether we still had title to it or whether we didn't.

There was something mule-like about Miss Millsap's long face. It had years earlier fallen into dry, luxuriant gray folds. She could be stubborn. When I set forth my request Miss Millsap looked a little aggrieved. That could take time, she only had one girl and that annoying colored teenager they made her hire, Obediah she thought his name was, poor soul couldn't really read properly, one more federal regulation....

I couldn't be more sympathetic, I told her. The problem was, I needed the information before I left town in a day or so. How was her niece? Lorna, wasn't that? I had hoped to get in touch with her once I got back.

Miss Daphne studied me a moment through her milky cataracts. I was about to leave town? This was an emergency? Well, Lord knows *she* was sympathetic. Miss Millsap declared that she would pull those files *personally.* Would two o'clock be soon enough?

I said I could live with that.

Back in our office Buckley had already returned from lunch. One of his clients, a tackle with the Buccaneers until recently whose bonuses had long since departed up his nose, Andy Brunosovich, was developing fast at another high-paying sport. His athletic reflexes were intact enough still so that he could lie in wait for an eighteen-wheeler to jump a traffic light and dodge in under the tires and emerge with enough contusions to demand a hell of an insurance settlement. Buckley had already won him a couple of lucrative payouts. "This time it's Travelers gonna pay the piper," Buckley crowed as he danced by my door. "Up to their alligators in assholes, like the man says. You ought to see how that bozo has mucked up his legs this time. He's got some raw clots going to sure 'nuf knock *any* jury flat. Where have you been all morning?"

"Running down some paperwork for Dad."

"Better you than me. Hear about that explosion on Second Avenue?"

"I went by to check it out. Prescott Wallaye does most of the corporate fine-tuning for Dad."

"Could you tell what happened? Somebody said a pressure tank blew up."

I looked at Buckley. It made sense that he would be out of the loop. "Whatever it was," I said, "you ought to see the mess. Look, I'm going to be in and out for a while. Dad wants to pick up a little property on the other coast."

"Sounds like fun stuff to me," Buckley said. I never had seen him in a better mood.

Knowing Daphne Millsap, I was not surprised when she pulled all the files I requested before two. The whole pile ran to perhaps a thousand pages, way, way too much to reproduce on the antiquated machines around the courthouse. It was municipal policy that no documents were to leave the building. I pushed my status as an officer of the court – tinctured by a few dropped references to Lorna – and prevailed after a few minutes. Everything would be back in her hands inside an hour.

There was a Mister Speedy up 31st just beyond the central Post Office. The huge, cheerful, raffish beast in charge of the place did a fair amount of duplicating for us. He reproduced the entire groaning armful I brought in, collated and stapled, in triplicate, in less than forty-five minutes. I turned the originals back over to Miss Millsap ahead of time. Then I stashed one set in a safe-deposit box, wrapped one set up for Dad, and mailed the last to an Amherst classmate in Connecticut. I intended to call him before it got there.

Linda Meadows had given me Sonny's telephone number in Clearwater. He indicated that he was free, and I agreed to wait for him at one of the rib houses on upper Gulf Boulevard. They were still serving the lunch menu when he arrived.

There are critical moments in life when you have to take a chance on somebody. By then Sonny had impressed me enough so that I told him everything. He sat there cocked back in his captain's chair, watching me working down my Margarita and looking a little bemused, obviously taking everything I told him in.

"How about you," I asked him when I had finished talking. "Could you use a drink?"

"With my bloodlines? How can I take the chance? That's how you palefaces finally got us down, you know. Passing out bad whiskey and free beef and blankets from corpses who died from the smallpox. Christianity, maybe."

"Linda will take a drink."

"She'll take a drink with you. Whatever she thinks you want she'll do it your way. You've turned her into a squaw. Overnight, I can't believe it. First she watched Charlie degenerate into a total boozehound, and in the end he takes away her little boy, and all of a sudden the spirit moves her and she is in love again?"

"I know what you're trying to say," I said. "Please understand it's very much the same on my end."

Sonny seemed to smile, perhaps a little grimly. "She is unprotected," he said finally. "I went away, and she got dragged through those horseshit schools on the reservation. When she was thirteen they began to train her up as a powwow dancer. She had those quick moves, and the tribe made money every time she performed. She wound up what they call a Gallop Tribal Princess. Except that it wrecked her knees and ankles, it got so bad she was pretty much addicted for a while there to Flexeril. One day she was dancing in a pavilion on a beach off Lake Okeechobee and Savage Owl – Charlie – was playing the bass and that was that. He got a job up here, but then he dumped her."

"She told me some of that."

"If you wind up making it worse," Sonny said, "I will probably kill you."

"Big Brother is watching."

Sonny broke into an enormous smirk. "I read that book," he said. "I've got a thing for Orwell."

The waiter had returned, and both of us decided on the salad bar. Sonny got back to the table first, and I could tell from the look of resolution on his hollow face that he had made up his mind. "What you want," Sonny said, "is for me to penetrate those Cubans' office and take their documents. So you can sue."

"Something like that. Maybe both of us." I think that surprised me at least as much as it did Sonny. "Wouldn't it be safer if I were involved to at least, you know, keep watch...?"

Sonny picked at his cottage cheese. "I took too many bacon bits," he said. "They taste artificial." He ate a segment of canned peach. "Are you in any kind of shape?"

"Better than you might think. A lot of time on the bicycle."

"We're going to need a number of things, equipment-wise," Sonny said.

"There is a mall not that far from here. We could start there. I hope you understand" – I decided to risk it – "any expenses, certainly including your time, we expect to take care of—"

"My God I hope so," Sonny said.

We spent the rest of the afternoon shopping. Sonny had a rented Chevy Equinox, which we used. It would be harder to identify with either one of us once it had been turned in. I had been able to come up with the street address of Mr. Perez y Cruz' headquarters by tracking down correspondence between Dad and Ramon. Sonny had his laptop in his car; it took him the best part of an hour to hack into the Coral Gables telephone records and nail down the supplier and the regulation voltage range it took to service the building.

Then I stopped off at my bank and withdrew a couple of thousand dollars in hundreds and fifties. After that we scrounged around the Tyrone Mall, dividing up Sonny's check-list. It took just over an hour to acquire boots, coveralls, a sewing kit, small, high-intensity flashlights, some kind of graphite spray Sonny found in a hair salon and a number of caps machine-embroidered with the Verizon emblem and made-up names, Sam Pinchot for me and Bob Roundtree for

Sonny.

I remembered a big gun shop just off the 54th St. Exit of the turnpike where the outspoken proprietor would sell you anything this side of a howitzer, no questions asked. I had no permit to carry. Gun law prohibitions in Florida are probably a little less stringent than those in Northern Mexico, but they remain in force. Sonny looked skeptical, but I was able to sweet-talk the proprietor into parting company – allegedly a "private sale," in the alley behind the place – with a couple of snub-nosed nickel-plated thirty-eights along with a box of jacketed hollow-point cartridges. Technically a private sale, no registration required. I pushed about half of the cartridges immediately into the clips.

One sideline of the shop was a locksmith. Our place of business had a lot of corroded locks that tended to jam sometimes, Sonny explained to the grizzled clerk. What would he charge for a set of picks and angle bars? They settled on $23.

We paid for everything with cash. Our shopping spree ended at the familiar Home Depot off 22nd Ave. We each ended up with a black, jumbo-sized tool kit with a top handle and deep drawers, along with pliers and screwdrivers and alligator clips and a lot of latex gloves and a box of the discardable elastic booties painters wear. "The Marx Brothers man up for a life of crime," I attempted to joke to Sonny, who grunted uneasily.

Just then Sonny was living day by day, bunking with a fellow veteran in Clearwater. Around five he lugged his duffel bag into my bungalow off the Oval Crescent Annex in the Pink Streets. It needed picking up. "You must have some kind of a printer with your computer here," he suggested as he rather delicately relocated my rain gear and a plate that had recently held most of a carrot cake onto the floor and off-loaded his duffel bag onto my couch. "We're going to need some kind of telephone-company credentials." My computer was in the bedroom. He clicked onto Paintbrush immediately and pieced together two fairly convincing Verizon ID cards, each embellished with serial numbers and grainy portraits we took with my cell phone. Then he dug a two-inch roll of translucent packaging tape out of his duffel bag and covered the cards and trimmed the edges.

"The Army taught you all this?" I asked.

"Some of it. For the kind of duty I tend to wind up catching I put in a couple of semesters with the Agency's Technical Services Division. Safe-crackers, guys with breaking-and-entering PhDs, forgers, arsonists. More often than not on restricted furlough from San Quentin or Sing Sing." He had already settled down on the bed and was fastidiously clipping the embroidered names out of several of the hats we bought and sewing them onto the coveralls. "Actually, a lot of this stuff I figured out earlier. Busting guys out of dear old Valley Forge Military Academy. After a while even those grungy rich-kid classmates of mine got sick of beating their big-deal meat. Not to speak of the maggots in the oatmeal. There was a strip joint not that far down Eagle Road."

"It's all about preparation," Sonny picked it up once we were on the road around five the next morning. "Whatever you are able to anticipate won't bite you in the ass. Tribal wisdom."

"Which tribe?" I was starting to pick up on Sonny's variety of leg pull.

"The Levites, actually. You'll find it in Leviticus."

"We must be from the same tribe."

"I don't think so," Sonny said. "You haven't got enough of a nose."

We were passing over the Sunshine Skyway Bridge; early morning glare was turning the Gulf into one endless sheet of pewter all the way to the horizon. Pelicans were capering, hungry. "I think I mentioned this," I said after a while. "You'd like my father. He's also very good at putting people on."

"Maybe I would. What's his nose like?"

"Bigger than mine."

"I suppose there's hope."

We got off the turnpike just east of Naples and gassed up and ate breakfast quickly at a Dunkin' Donuts before starting east on U.S. #41. A lot of coffee helped. Merely passing through the Everglades makes it evident that most of the interior of Florida is basically a bog of grasslands punctuated by cattle ranches and orange groves. Looking out the window of the BMW made Sonny thoughtful. "I keep reading that the communities on the coasts are sucking up the water from the Swamp," Sonny said after a while. "People are afraid the entire shootin' match is going to parch out. I would bet you that long before that happens we'll all be dead of cow farts. Have you ever seen so many Black Angus?"

Then we kept still for a while. Just before the Tamiami Canal was some kind of Welcome Center, complete with a dock for airboat rides and rental canoes and a makeshift zoo you could tour for five dollars. Sonny pulled a couple of Orange Crushes from an upright freezer and handed me one and extended a ten-dollar bill to the cherubic soul behind the counter, a short woman with a barrel of a belly and amazingly thick, spatulate fingers. "I been workin' here since I was three years old," the woman volunteered immediately. "We got a messed-up family, it goes every whicha way. Dad is an alcoholic, but none of us youngsters drink. I mean – all that much. Them there is genuine native panthers."

Both panthers pushed up onto their haunches and stretched.

"Mother raised us kids to love the Lord and keep our knees together, if you know what I'm hintin' at there. Not that I been completely pure, entirely. I got a kid by one o' my – you know where I'm goin' with this – *childhood* encounters. Erskine. He out there terrifying the livin' excrement out of some o' them slaphappy tourists we get to stop off here sometimes. In one of our finest leaky airboats."

One of the panthers yawned. The air was sultry as noon approached, harder to breathe. A pair of bottle-nosed African crocodiles lay one across the other, too sluggish to mate. Next to them a flock of cockatoos squawked at us, resenting the interruption. We moved along quickly to the adjacent black bears. Their cages stank.

Back outside the cage area a scrawny old redneck was waiting with a squirming two-foot alligator clutched in front of his overalls. Its jaws were taped just behind the nostrils. "This here's my hubby," the woman said. "He used to wrestle them ugly, brainless critters. Gettin' a little bit old for shit like that these days, not that he can't still – you know – get his you-know-what to salute like a goddamned trooper when I give him his justification."

The husband smiled, revealing very few teeth.

"I suspect you give him five dollars he will permit you to hold that varmint there while he snaps a photograph."

"Maybe next time," I said. I gave the woman the five dollars anyhow. We went to use the facilities, which smelled only a little more rank than the bear cages.

CHAPTER X

U.S. 41 intersected with the turnpike south of Miami, at the northern edge of Coral Gables. Just after we turned right into the commercial downtown Sonny spotted a run-down gas station piled up with discarded mufflers and a stack of crank cases beneath a banner announcing USED CARS. We gassed up and Sonny explained in surprisingly precise Spanish to the cubanita at the cash register that we intended to move his cousin out of her apartment now that her boyfriend had flown the coop and we would like to lease one of the vans in the back until the next morning. The deal went down for $400, no exchange of information necessary, $200 back on the return of the van.

Sonny eased the van out from among the weeds in the alley that threatened to clot the almost bald tires and jacked it around a diesel truck body on blocks. I followed him down the alley in the BMW and around a corner and into another alley, where he stopped.

"Your Spanish is terrific," I said, pulling over.

"Everybody picks up a lot of it on the rez. They hit it hard in the military because our people spend so much time sniffing around the Americas. Especially the cocaine belt."

"No small asset." I watched him transfer his stuff from the trunk of the BMW into the van. "What happens now?" He was rummaging through one of the side pockets of his duffel bag and promptly slid out a stencil set and masking tape and a pint can of spray paint.

"Where'd you get that?"

"At the Home Depot. While you were in the checkout line."

"I didn't see you get that."

"Nobody did. I boosted it." I must have looked at him. "I have to keep my hand in." Sonny pursed his lips. "Now that you mention it, I thought the mama at the counter spotted something. She couldn't really have believed I was *that* heavy hung."

"Just wasn't going to make a fuss."

"Why would she?"

Sonny had already started taping stencils onto the van's less dented left forward door. It was going to read VERIZON, with Specialty Subcontractors below that. He laid a heavy coating of white paint across the stencils. "We're doing this mostly for the security types," Sonny explained. "They won't really bother to check out the identification, especially if they see a vehicle across the street. That's almost always enough. By their cars shall ye know them, like the man said. We're Americans, after all."

Within a couple of minutes the paint was dry enough to strip the tape off the stencils. In another of the pockets of his duffel bag Sonny eased out something that looked like the pelt of a dead rat but turned out to be artificial facial hair, which he daubed lightly with a stickum that smelled like gum arabic and applied to his face while squatting in front of the van's tall driver's-side mirror. The transformation was astonishing. "You look like the Grand Vizier in Ali Baba," I said.

"Works fine most everywhere, especially in the Muslim world. I was the flavor of the month in Mogadishu for quite a while. Everybody I ran into thought I might have been his nephew. Where did you put that spray-on graphite?"

I took my blazer off and Sonny told me to pull in my lips and sprayed both cheeks and around my mouth. "We're after that five-day-growth look. I'll tell people I picked you out of the welfare pool." He cleaned up the margins with a handkerchief. "Just grunt, no considered legal opinions."

"You make it fun. Humiliating, but fun."

We put the coveralls on, and the caps. I started to extract the.38s from my rucksack when Sonny stopped me. "Leave those in the car," he said.

"What if somebody catches us?"

"So—what would you do then? Blow away the janitor? Maybe the cleaning lady?"

"I guess."

"We'll be OK."

The older office building in which Sunrise Medical Ventures/Capital Partners maintained its headquarters was on a side street a block and a half off Ponce De Leon Boulevard. I stowed the BMW in the long-term parking section of a garage a couple of blocks south. Sonny looked over the office building while I circled the block in the van. "It's pretty clear both the electrical entrance and the land-line hookups come in on the left side, somewhere towards the back," Sonny decided. Around 4:30 I parked the van itself in front, conspicuous, in one of the delivery bays. The late-afternoon sky threatened to cloud up.

According to the directory inside, Ramon operated out of Suite 306. The foyer itself was mock-Venetian, polished marble floors and red velvet chairs with griffin faces carved into the arms.

Lugging our tool kits, we roamed the entry floor until Sonny located the primary storage closet. Inside, across from an inside wall of steel shelves stacked up with mop-heads and jugs of Lysol, there was no mistaking the array of junction boxes and circuit breakers that fed the offices. "Here's an antique touch," Sonny said, picking open the cover of one. "Threaded fuses." He reached up and unscrewed the hexagonal glass fuse beneath #306. Then he screwed it back. After a few minutes he unscrewed the fuse again, then tightened it up. "Just a little flicker," Sonny said. "We'll get a better welcome."

"You're not going in *now*?"

"Just a peep. Only way to find out whether there's battery backup."

"How about me, though? They've seen me. At least Ramon has."

"Never make the connection. Just – you know, slouch. My Neanderthal apprentice. Mumble whenever I speak to you. Glare a lot. Don't touch anything."

My mouth was going dry. We took the stairs up. My ears were pounding as we reached door 306. Inside, a receptionist was picking at papers on her desk and freshening up her lipstick. Another woman with big hair and a world of cleavage was filing.

"Hey, you have problem with the power, I think, hunh?" Sonny demanded of the receptionist in a heavy glottal accent. "Kaput, comes and goes."

The receptionist looked up a moment, glanced at the Verizon IDs we'd concocted, then returned to the image in her compact.

"Mucho problema," Sonny said, and leered. "Si?"

Ramon, in an open shirt, stepped out of the inner office. I turned away.

"Big storm," Sonny assured him. "*Big* storm. But not to worry."

Ramon brushed by Sonny without bothering to nod. "Caridad, no se olvide, todos los documentos para manana, O.K.?" he muttered to the woman who was doing the filing, and gave her shoulder a squeeze and left.

There was an enclosed panel mounted next to the main door into the suite. His long back blocking everybody's view, Sonny scraped at something a moment and pocketed whatever came loose. "No worries now," he announced to the women. "We protect every-things." After one gallant flicker of his hand he led me into the hall.

We waited by the stairwell until the building had pretty well emptied out. I reparked the van, blocks away. Both of Ramon's secretaries left minutes after he did. "What was that accent?" I asked Sonny.

"Albanian. Nobody gets 'em where they live like an illiterate Albanian speaking horseshit Spanish."

"They bought it, obviously."

"Now that I copped the battery," Sonny said, obviously elated, "We turn the alarm off." We repaired to the storage closet, where Sonny quickly loosened a couple of set screws and killed all telephone service to suite #306. A couple of minutes after seven we took the stairs up and pulled on the latex gloves and the booties. Sonny picked the lock and we let ourselves in.

Originally we had decided to wait until eleven or so to ransack the place. But there were louver blinds on all the windows; better yet, one of those sundown monsoons that splash down suddenly along the Florida coastline was sweeping in from Biscayne Bay, punctuated by a lot of lightning. Our little diode-encrusted penlights weren't going to attract any attention on the street.

Sonny made his way from file cabinet to file cabinet, picking open the locks drawer by drawer. I followed him going through the files. Halfway down the second cabinet I spotted what I was after. The dozen or so deeds, bills of transfer, affidavits, letters of commitment, securitization boilerplate, statements of intent: everything that constituted the blood and bones of our understanding with Ramon's hedge fund, bulging, sequestered in one place. I eased the entire hanging file into the bottom drawer of my tool kit.

"OK?" Sonny said. He flashed a light in my face. "You've stopped sweating."

"Let's keep going. I'm getting into this."

The fourth and last cabinet dealt primarily with family affairs. I found a file full of the authorizations Rick needed to pass back and forth between Florida and Cuba. Some dealings with the property-holders in La Playa del Perro, the location of most of the shoreline the Toronto intermediaries were after. I grabbed that too.

"You ought to take it easy," Sonny said. "You need to leave enough so that nobody catches on at first that anybody's been through this place. Even then they'll never be that sure. Leave 'em confused. These are heavy-duty muchachos. You really don't want this thing to escalate. We haven't got any limpet mines."

"You sound like my father."

"You're calling the shots." The storm was driving at the windows; Sonny was re-locking the file cabinets. "You know," Sonny said. "I hate to bring it up, but there's probably a safe around here someplace."

The safe was in Ramon's inner office, behind a sliding panel adjacent to a small bar. It was a Mosler, not that formidable. "Not that I'm interested in hanging around, but I *could* probably find my way into that box." Sonny speculated. "It's still early."

"You're showing off." I was again starting to feel my stomach sinking. "Maybe a few minutes."

Sonny crouched in front of the tumblers, extracted a stethoscope from his tool kit, and peeled off the latex glove on his right hand. He had some emery paper, with which he seemed to polish his fingertips. Listening, spinning left, then right, then left again, he elicited the thunk of release on the second series. The heavy door swung open, revealing several hard-wood cases, a shoe box, and what looked like a rack of specimen bottles.

The cases contained jewelry – emerald and diamond bracelets and necklaces, a number of uncut stones, five Rolex watches. The shoe box looked much more interesting. It was entirely hand-written letters and print-outs from various ministries in Cuba. Sonny eased his glove back on and looked the letters over. "What seems to be going on is that Ramon here is doubling as a contact man for a number of Castro's bureaucrats. They know the ship is sinking. It's obvious to everybody down there – you can't miss it, I've been into and out of Havana a couple of times recently on hit-and-run missions. So – these guys have been sitting on assets confiscated since 1959. Ramon is the key guy in getting them smuggled out and into depositories all over the place – Montreal, Bern, the Cayman Islands…. Enrique comes up a lot – that's your brother-in-law, right? As a courier. Ramon appears to be scarfing up a third as his commission to help haul out this stuff. Hey, even a couple of notes from Raul!"

"Can you imagine how all this would play in the Miami Cuban community? I said. "Jorge Mas Canosa would rear up bullshit out of his mausoleum. What's in the specimen bottles?"

Sonny put his light on them. They seemed to be filled with sand, with a label on each; what looked like a map was very carefully folded and propped up next to the bottles. Sonny picked a bottle up. "Yttrium," one read, with the subscript Matanzas. "Yttrium is a rare earth," Sonny said. "The kind of crap you need for superconductors or microwave filters. The Chinese have been hogging the market, so the hunt is on to find reliable sources in the West. Advanced physical chemistry is a requirement for my environmental studies curriculum. Matanzas is a province in Cuba, probably where they pulled this core sample."

"Same for the rest?"

"Looks like that. Lanthanum – that's supposedly a catalyst

they need to crack oil in refineries. Promethium is essential for nuclear batteries, if we ever get that far– This batch apparently came from Camaguey."

"And so forth." He unfolded the map. It was of Cuba, with the site and the chemical symbol of each of the sites designated in red pencil.

It was hitting me. "Leases on the right properties could be worth billions to Sunrise Capital Partners." It wasn't nine o'-clock at night, but suddenly I was afraid the next day was going to break at any moment. "Look, kemosabe, why don't you find some envelopes and label them and pour an ounce or so of whatever priceless dirt this is into each one. Meanwhile, I'll copy the letters and the map on that machine over there?"

Sonny frowned across at me, seemed on the point of saying something, then stopped. We got it done in under fifteen minutes. I stowed away a couple of the original letters, just in case. The rain had let up, and I was afraid the glimmer from our lights might alert somebody in the street. As we were sliding out the door Sonny slipped the battery back into the alarm system after cleaning it off with some disgusting form of handi-wipe, which he was taking to every surface we might have touched.

"Ten minutes after we get out of here the battery will have recharged itself. We'll turn the telephone system back on while we're leaving."

"And that will be everything."

"Almost everything. One last item. Fuck kemosabe. In our operation, *you* represent Tonto."

The hour-plus of driving rain had washed most of the

water-soluble spray paint down the door of the van; it whitened the soaked, glossy pavement. The rest came off with a can of solvent and a rag Sonny had left on the floor in the back; after that he took the rag to his cheeks where the whiskers had been and rubbed down my entire face. My eyes stung afterwards, mostly from the evaporation. We stripped off the coveralls and the hats. The latex gloves and the booties were already stuffed into pockets. Everything went into a large plastic shopping bag Sonny had brought along.

"Do you never forget *anything?*"

"Don't butter me up. I'm still pissed."

"Because I made a suggestion?"

"Those weren't suggestions. Those were marching orders. The worst thing was, you had it figured."

"I was really starting to get jittery again, I wanted to get out of there. Nothing more than that."

Sonny tousled my hair and squeezed my scalp. "You done good," he said. "It's just that I'm used to working solo. Clean slate. Some day I'll take you back to the reservation and we smoke a pipe together and we make you an honorary Comanche. You'll have to come down with impetigo first, of course."

"Do you have that?"

"Christ, no. We save that for the palefaces."

Once everything was bagged I walked over and pulled the BMW out of the garage and picked up Sonny. It wasn't that late, but neither of us was hungry. So we threw everything in the trunk of the BMW, and locked the van, and slept the whole thing off in the Holiday Inn off Route 41.

CHAPTER XI

I paid for the room in cash. We had finished the complimentary breakfast by 7:30 and headed back downtown to return the van. Somehow I had assumed that we would just abandon the van on the street somewhere, but Sonny had that all figured out too.

"Leave a cold trail," he told me. "If that thing goes back it means that's that. No police report, no missing vehicle paperwork. It's my guess she'll be disappointed to see it in her yard. She'll never get four hundred dollars for that winner the way it stands."

Sonny was right. The cubanita confronted us looking decidedly let down, and counted out my two hundred dollars very slowly, hesitating over every bill.

I still wanted to look in on Dad's contact at the Post-Dispatch. With what we'd learned from the evidence in Ramon's safe I had a feeling we were already well ahead of the story. Since Freddy Wilmot covered the Cuban community around Miami day to day, I figured maybe he could provide some context. I called ahead and Wilmot said he could give me a few minutes.

Sonny waited in the visitor's lobby while I went up to the editorial wing and located Wilmot's cubicle. Many of the cubicles were empty. The ficus plant had died. Wilmot hadn't gotten younger. His eyes looked cloudy. He was wasting away.

"How'm I doing?" he responded to my greeting. "Brilliantly. Welcome to the remnant of the Miami Post Dispatch. Where downsizing solves all problems. Six more months and

I'll be eligible for my ever more humble pension. That is, if one of those shitheads from personnel doesn't polish me off first. How's your father?"

"Still hammering away. He thinks he'll have his big book on Keynes done before the end of the year."

"Look forward to reading that. Lord Keynes is one of my absolute heroes. Took no prisoners. The guy could write a little too, know what I mean? I mean by that – for an academic. I read a lot of the Adam Smith thing."

"I remember. You reviewed it."

"Yeah. I guess I did. Also did a feature, right? On your father? Interviewed the shit out of the poor bastard, and how many phone calls? He was very nice, excellent. Listen, mind if I light up while we talk? I know, we're not supposed to smoke in here. But look around. Nobody! Why not?" Wilmot lipped a cigarette out of an open pack and lit up.

"We appreciated the help we got with Ramon Cruz," I said. "Dad was blown away by your background knowledge of the Cuban community in Dade County. We needed chapter and verse."

"Nothing that out of the ordinary." Smoke came out both his wizened nostrils. "That's what we're supposed to be doing, news, right? You really can't help but pick up a ton of shit just living in the barrio down here the way we do. Not that I intend to dump on the Cubans exactly – my partner these days is of Cuban extraction."

"What happened with—who was that, Humberto?"

"Jiminez? Picked up on that, right? Jesus. What a slimeball he turned out to be. On half the payrolls in town. Suck anybody's johnson if the price was right. You really need to pick and choose these days." Wilmot wiped his eyes. "What do you need now?"

"More of the same, basically. We thought you might be able to update us on Ricky's father, Ramon. We've developed some business connections with his little hedge fund subsidiary, Sunrise Capital Partners. Right now there seems to be a lot of static on the line. We can't quite tell what's happening."

"Static on the line. I like that. I'll use it in my column today, if you don't object. Ramon Perez y Cruz, correct?" Wilmot swiveled in his chair and called up Perez y Cruz on his terminal. "Strictly background, OK? The paper maintains its own raw files, but nobody is permitted to print any of this stuff without an OK upstairs."

"Not a problem. I'm a lawyer."

"The gist I'm getting is that the whole Sunrise Medical Ventures thing is shaky as shit. Ramon is a fairly smooth operator, compared with the rest of them – by that I mean the first generation, all those Brigade types. A lot of those nut cases scrambled around during their first years in Miami, and you know how many wound up working for the mob or the government or anybody who could provide a buck and maybe a pat on the ass during the Kennedy years. Mongoose, Watergate, all that shit. But Ramon as you know attached himself to Mas Canosa – *there* was a loose cannon – and little by little he went respectable.

"The problem with Ramon and a few of the others was that they came over to capitalism way too fast. Drank way too much Kool-Aid. Our finance guy maintains they were under-capitalized at every stage. The Bush administrations, here and in Washington, tended to baby them, and pretty soon they were dicking around with insurance and speculating in credit default swaps, which amounts to collecting premiums but laying off the claims— a high-speed con job, but involving a lot of paperwork. They ran out of assets a long time ago.

"Then at the last minute they saw that the bubble was getting ready to pop and started to scrounge for every soft touch with collateral they could dump in as ballast."

"Soft touches like us."

"Sounds that way." Wilmot inhaled deeply. The cigarette was very short. "Then we started hearing rumors about how Ramon had something going on with his childhood buddies on the island. Exactly how or when or with whom we couldn't exactly pin down. A thing like that could blow up." Wilmot eased smoke out of one side of his mouth. "The kids don't give that much of a shit, but the boat generation is still around, and if they ever caught Cruz going soft on Fidel those animals would hunt him down and introduce his head to his rectum. He must know that."

Wilmot took a last, philosophical drag and snuffed his cigarette out. " As I say: rumors. Nothing you could base a story on. Make any sense?"

"Too much sense," I said.

I had expected that we would head west directly on the so-called Everglades Parkway – "Alligator Alley" – U.S. 75. But Sonny asked whether I would mind going back the way we came, Highway 41, and stopping off for a couple of minutes at the Seminole Museum on the Big Cypress Reservation, Ah-Tah-Thi-Ki, "A Place to Remember." Savage Owl – Charlie – worked there. Sonny had promised his sister that he would look in on her three-year-old son and drop off a present.

The museum itself looked more like a storage shed or a back-lot warehouse: one floor, a long stretch of galvanized roof with a pyramidal entry portico. It was early afternoon. The exhibition area was close to empty – a middle-aged couple in cargo shorts looking over the diorama of an early Seminole village, some elderly tourists walking along a display case of arrowheads and pottery. There was a faint, herbal odor to the place, almost like an incense.

Sonny crossed at once to greet the heavy-set fellow at the cash register, who was loading change into the collapsible paper cylinders they give you at banks. He looked up, not wanting to be disturbed, his flat coppery features impassive. Above his jeans he wore a woven shirt of tribal design; he carried his elbows away from his body, like a Somo wrestler.

"This is Charlie Osceola," Sonny said. "Who was married to my sister Linda."

Charlie Osceola nodded slowly, several times: That much was true.

"Michael Landau here knows Linda," Sonny said. "He's her landlord at the moment."

Charlie didn't say anything.

"Linda wanted me to leave something off for little Carl," Sonny said. He produced the package, neatly wrapped in brown paper. As if on signal, a three-year-old with a big bowl-shaped mop of jet-black hair ran in from behind the counter and embraced his father's thigh. Charlie handed the boy the package, with which he scrambled around the counter and settled tailor-fashion onto the braided rug in front to tear the wrapping away from his present.

"From Dances-like-Fire," Charlie informed the boy. The present was a toy fire engine. When Carl ran it across the rug it trailed a rich plume of multicolored sparks.

"You've got an office job now," Sonny attempted. "How's it going?"

"Hey, man, you know I'm into anthropology." Charlie sounded hurt. "What am I supposed to be doing, hanging thatch on chickees and carving out dugouts? *Come on!*"

Once we were headed west again Sonny made an effort to explain. At the tribe's insistence, for two years Charlie had been into a program. It made him cranky, not to say sullen.

"Maybe that accounts for it. I was expecting—"

"He's a bozo, basically. He was a lot more presentable five years ago."

"What I don't understand is: How did Linda—"

"Get hooked up with him? Well, to start with, things were a lot different. Linda was still basically pretty adolescent. She was a big star as a teenager on the powwow dancing circuit. The troupe she was in put on shows from Calgary to Zurich. That means she missed a lot of her education, even in that ding-dong high school our mother put her in. Besides which she went around a lot making house calls with mother, who is a medicine woman."

"Linda told me that."

"Also, Linda is highly mystical. She thinks she communicates with ghosts, and spirits, and they will reveal to her the mysteries of the past and sometimes even what's going to happen. Like Charlie there, she's very susceptible to cultural fads."

"That's why they got married"

"It was in the air. Four or five years ago the Native America movement went through another round of Back-to-the-Wigwam craziness. Important to purify the race, that kind of thing – not that it ever lies that far beneath any of our feelings. Our mother was very strict, so Linda didn't – how to put it – go with men. Very idealistic, in those days."

"She certainly seems to have – what – is matured the word? At least with me."

"You must have something none of us expected. I told you, Linda has always been really stand-offish in those respects. Especially with whites. We think whites smell bad, you know."

"Probably we do. But how does that explain Charlie?"

"Linda was around Florida that July four or five years ago performing in the various Green Corn Dance festivals and Charlie was a fairly big deal in one of their clans – Bear, I think it was. He was a bravura type – wrestled alligators, guided parties in the Swamp. Powerful – great build, lean, if you can believe that."

"This was before the drinking?"

"During, but he was so active he could handle it. Linda's ligaments were starting to give her trouble and getting married to somebody who wasn't co-opted or too much of a breed or anything made sense to her. At about that point the tribe here sent Charlie up to Tampa Bay to consult on the Hard Rock

Casino complex they were contracting just north of Tampa."

"I've been there."

"I can't imagine what good Charlie was supposed to do in connection with that. Cultural detailing, I suppose. You know how it is – in big organizations, the stiffs make rank the fastest."

"I guess."

"After a couple of years Charlie figured out that he was useless around the casino – no alligator pits – and by then he was drinking a lot. Little Carl was on the way. Charlie quit the casino and the two of them moved into that place of yours for a while. Charlie finally gave it up altogether, and they separated, and Charlie moved back to the Swamp. Linda stayed put and wound up living with her cousin Alice and the dog."

"Then I came along."

"More or less," Sonny said. "More or less."

Once I got back to St. Petersburg I dropped out for a day before I contacted Dad. We met for lunch in one of the back booths at Howard Seltzer's Steak House on Tyrone Boulevard.

"I picked this place because it occurred to me it would be harder to bug," I explained once we had settled in. I was quietly surveying the surrounding tables. "After the Wallaye fiasco we don't have any idea how extensive their support is."

"I think you're starting to terrorize yourself," Dad said. Our mimosas arrived. "I think you may have watched *The Bourne Ultimatum* too many times."

"You could be right. Right after we sat down I thought I spotted a nun positioning a shotgun microphone out of her rosary bag."

We sat quietly, sipping on our mimosas. Dad didn't say anything. Finally, and in some detail, I told him about our evening in Coral Gables and threw in Freddy Wilmot's appraisal.

"Jesus," Dad said after I finished finally. "My boy the burglar. You're pretty sure you got everything? All the documents?"

"More than everything. Between the rare earth samples and the letters we ought to have everything we need to exert a lot of leverage on Ramon and his pals."

"Exert leverage. That means blackmail?"

"That means – get them to leave us alone. Give us back our properties."

"I still have the feeling this isn't that simple. If they're the kind of hoodlums you say they are, we're probably still alive pretty much because of Wendy. Latins rarely exterminate family. Let's not become the exception. Incidentally, I understand that Wendy is pregnant. That might help."

"It might help, but it ain't going to get you back your property."

"More with the tough-guy talk." Dad's bulging eyes were intent, amused. "How would you handle this?"

"Bring an action." I had thought about this. "Go out of Florida, where these characters obviously have a lot of political backup, and institute a motion for recovery of our real estate within, say, ninety days according to the stipulations in the secondary agreements. They recover your shares in their hedge fund and you get your own stuff back."

"And this would work?"

"Lawyers do this all the time. Guys on the corporate side at Humper, Fardel spend half their billable hours dissolving bad financial marriages."

"Then why not do it there?"

"Why not? Now that we've got certified copies of the documents."

The lobster salads we had ordered clattered down in front of us.

Dad tried a forkful, then looked up balefully. "You probably ought to make duplicates of everything you got and give me a set and keep a set in a safe deposit box. The originals would go to Philadelphia."

"I've done all that. Your set is in my briefcase."

"Oi! Mine Sohn the Vunderkind! Who would have thought?"

"You're giving me too much credit. Sonny ran the caper. I was the schlepper."

"Caper, schlepper – you're turning into a visitor from another planet." Dad speared a curl of lobster. "How should we deal with him? Sonny?"

"Deal with?"

"Reimburse. Pay."

"With money, would be the best way. A small donation to the United Native-American College Fund isn't going to cover it."

"Wiseass! I mean: How much?"

"We never worked that out. How about ten thousand dollars? He hung his butt a long way over the line for us."

"Fine. Do you think ninety-five hundred in hundreds would do it? Ten would probably move it into a category where the bank would report it to Uncle Sam. I don't think Arthur Stillman would be enthusiastic about taking it as a deduction."

CHAPTER XII

Sonny had left me with a warning that virtually any private telephone was vulnerable nowadays to electronic evesdropping. So a day after I had lunch with Dad I stopped by the St. Petersburg Municipal Courthouse, where there was a bank of old-fashioned coin-operated payphones, and reached Ethan Stokes at Humper, Fardel in Philadelphia. Ethan, at one time a nationally ranked squash player, had a forty-year reputation as a bulldog corporate litigator. I indicated that our family needed to recover several blocs of real estate we had been misguided enough to swap into a Miami-area hedge fund. Stokes released that cold, dusty laugh of his that always struck me as closer to a cough. He strongly advised me to show up yesterday with any relevant documents. I told him I would arrive in The City of Brotherly Love the following afternoon. The call took seven quarters.

Then I picked up the $9500 in cash from Dad and headed north toward Clearwater. There I stashed the Cuban letters and the rare earth samples in a safe deposit box I rented in one of the branch banks of the Wells-Fargo system and – nervous, watching my side mirrors – slid into the parking area behind the apartment complex where Linda had told me Sonny was staying. I caught Sonny headed down the back. He led me back upstairs and I handed him the bundle of currency.

I told him how much it was. "Should be enough," I remarked, tentatively.

"Covers it," he agreed, soberly. "Definitely covers it."

For just a moment I thought he might be inclined to smile.

"I have another idea," I said.

Then I went back to my office and started to pull together folder after folder, printouts of judgments from defunct cases, the upshot of several recent discovery motions, a sheaf of newspaper clippings relevant to a very nasty divorce I had unwisely taken on. Once I had enough, I started stuffing a briefcase.

At one point Buckley looked in. "Long time no see, buddy," Buckley said. "Where you been all week?"

"Miami. Guy down there thought he might want to exchange some property with Dad. I thought it might be worth a look, but it obviously isn't going to work out."

"The world, she changes. Two years ago anything in the real estate racket was a slam-dunk. You hear that Wendy is heavy with child?"

"Dad told me."

"At this point Carol is a little batshit on the subject." Buckley's high-posted preppy face looked pinched with strain; he scratched the tight sandy curls of his scalp. Dandruff was a problem. "I'll tell you one thing," he burst out, "I'm not the one shootin' blanks. My urologist checked the numbers in September. He tells me I could get a ball bearing pregnant."

"Carol is just high-strung," I said. "You know about the anorexia?"

"Teen-age shit. A stage she went through. The problem is, nobody gets enceinte without a little whoopee on a regular basis. With us now it's a couple of times a month when the moment is optimum. According to her fucking *thermometer*! I get so backed up that when I do get the call I'm—"

"Too much information," I said. "You guys ought to find another hobby."

"I guess." Buckley rolled the knuckles of one hand inside the long, bony fingers of the other. "Got something going? Pulling all that together for one of your big-deal clients?"

"Another chore for Dad. That hedge fund you think is so wonderful. Dad wants me to turn over all the deeds and abstracts and anything we can scrounge up after the bombing to some barracuda he knows in Philly at Sullivan and Cromwell and let *that* bastard unzip the whole mess. While we can still dump the pricier properties." I snapped the hatch on the briefcase. "I'm on the 10:15 tomorrow morning. Delta."

"You know," Buckley said, "the real payoff for all of us is still waiting on that island." For several months Buckley had been referring affectionately to Cuba as "that island." His was the kind of dedication only greed can engender.

Buckley made his way back to the other office. I took a moment to check my messages, and just as I was out the door I heard Buckley tapping on his cell phone.

My plane set down a little after one. As I was disembarking a tawny fellow passenger with an unkempt beard slipped me a wink from his aisle seat. I confirmed my return flight for a little after five and headed for the escalator down; that took me out by the baggage carousels en route to ground transportation. The afternoon was damp, overhung by a well-remembered mid-Atlantic chill.

There was a long queue outside waiting for taxis. Across the terminal I took the elevated walkway into a crowd already jamming the platform that served the light rail connection. Several linked cars were approaching on the track; then, just as the train was starting to slow down with a hiss of airbrakes and the mob pressed in around me, I felt a glancing blow against the back of my hand and a corpulent, exasperated senior citizen with a gray frizz defining his jowls stumbled heavily against me, and fell. I grabbed out to clutch his shoulder, and just as he wheezed and staggered for his footing it came to me my briefcase wasn't there.

"I think I dropped something," I gasped out; by then the mob was loading into the cars. But once the mob disbursed there wasn't any brief case. "I've got to go report what happened," I found myself bellowing at the fat man. He looked quite grave – sympathetic – and lumbered toward the train and squeezed in just as the doors converged. I found myself alone on the platform except for a towering matron with a pheasant feather stabbing up out of her hat and an oversized shopping bag. Shaken, I lurched back into the terminal to leave my name and a description of my briefcase.

By then the passengers from my flight had disbursed and the curbside was empty; cabs were waiting. I took the one in front. I was just about to tell the driver to run me downtown and drop me off at Logan Circle, where Ethan Stokes practiced, when it came to me that somebody had grabbed the cab behind mine. The outline of the passenger was obscure in the smoggy mid-afternoon light. But I could spot the peak of the pheasant feather in silhouette.

"I think you better take me to Broad and Market," I instructed the driver.

"City Hall, I get that right?"

"On target."

At City Hall the principal subway systems converged. I caught the escalator down and jumped into a car on the Broad Street line as it was filling up. Just before it moved on I pushed out and hot-footed it down a level and boarded a waiting car onto the Market Street Line and stood by the door until it moved out. No pheasant feather. At the 15th St. Station I took the escalator to the surface and proceeded around JFK Plaza on foot, warily, toward Logan Circle. The executive offices of Humper, Fardle took up a large part of the twentieth floor of the commercial complex that overhung Logan Square.

Ethan Stokes had always reminded me of a semiretired veteran of the British Secret Service, MI6. One of the gray men, weary and insouciant in manner but privately intense, remorseless. What very little silver hair he still had he wore straight back, a testimony to what must once have been a pompadour. He moved now with great circumspection.

"You don't mind if I include one of our younger associates, Elena Simpson, just to make very damned sure I get everything nailed down as we go along?" Ethan wanted to know – rather, was demanding, if politely. "Ms. Simpson is absolutely top notch, Yale Law '04."

"Your shop," I said, "your ground rules." I had just seated myself on the couch after excusing myself for a couple of minutes to take advantage of the private lavatory in Ethan's suite, where I had pulled off my shirt and managed to reach around and tear off the tape holding the big legal envelope stuck to my back. Shirt tucked in and jacket and tie in place, I slid the heavy packet onto the desk next to the leather-upholstered Eames chair into which Stokes was tentatively lowering himself. A steel engraving of Oliver Wendell Holmes dominated the wall behind him.

Ethan rang for Elena Simpson. "If you need coffee there is plenty in that carafe on the sideboard. If I asked Elena to pass it around she'd probably bring me up on charges before the bar association. The Women's Movement!"

"I'll be OK."

Elena came in and sat down and crossed her short legs to support a legal tablet. She looked around thirty, dressed in a dark brown pants-suit.

Both of them were waiting for me. "I like to hope the documents that I just turned over to Attorney Stokes—"

"Ethan! Michael, you're no longer darting around these halls looking up precedents and driving the partners to the airport. You are a *colleague* now. Our Florida counterpart. I was particularly regretful when you left, you had a future with the firm, you know that."

"Thanks, really." They were both waiting. I attempted to lay out the history involving our family and the Coral Gables hedge fund. How we got into that. I showed Stokes the side documents conferring on us the option of taking the properties back at such time the hedge fund originators missed the stipulated payments. I explained that several attempts had apparently been made to destroy any records we had in storage pertaining to these arrangements. Fortunately, I indicated, we were recently able to lay our hands on uncompromised backup documents. I did not say how.

"Doesn't seem that far out of the question, not in any way,"

Ethan decided. "Things aren't precisely working out, and at this point it seems desirable to your people to go ahead and unwind. We'll want to initiate an immediate action to recover unclouded title on the aforementioned properties. Hedge funds are largely unregulated, so up or down their legal status is basically what some judge decides it is that week." He lifted himself slowly to his feet. "Arthritis! Nobody mentions arthritis when they rant away about the blessings of the retirement years."

"Would you think we could get our properties back fairly quickly?" It was an effort not to sound too urgent. "My father is starting to get antsy, he thinks this market is headed for a serious correction."

"I think we can depend on some kind of speedy resolution. We work with a number of judges on the Dade County bench. We'll want to get right on the docket. I'd say we hit these jokers with a couple of injunctions next week and you should begin locking up to most of what you turned over in, say, a month? Six weeks? Soon enough? Needless to say, we *will* need a few days to wring out the empowering documents. Sounds like boilerplate to me."

"Can't happen soon enough. My father is really on edge these days."

"How is your father?" He turned to Elena Simpson. "Michael here has got an old man who is a world-class sensation," Ethan Stokes said. "A genuine polymath. You name it: economist, professor, biographer, stock market speculator. Everything. And personality? Do you remember Jackie Mason, the Yiddish comedian? Sylvan has always reminded me of that fellow, a wonderful kind of gotcha humor that blindsides everybody—"

"He does sound unique," Elena Simpson said.

"Quite a character. I remember when he came up for the Philadelphia Club. They told me *he* was a little apprehensive, but the rest of us couldn't *wait* to have him around...."

"I know he appreciated your support,"I said; that had been unexpected.

"Never a qualm!" Ethan was rising slowly to his feet, not moving: That meant the meeting was over. "My best to your mother too," he said. "What a beautiful woman she was. Honestly, a Dresden figurine moving among us. Splendid."

I got up. "The thing is," I felt I had to add in leaving, "the Cuban businessmen we're dealing with here have been known to play pretty rough. We probably ought to make sure any papers that we get served are accompanied by officers of the court—"

"Don't worry your pretty little head about that, son." Ethan said, walking me unsteadily in the direction of the door. "White-collar gangsters are my meat and potatoes. Elena here will e-mail you a workup of the estimated billable hours. Needless to say, you'll get the rate we extend to colleagues, you certainly needn't concern yourself with *that*."

"Flying back here," I had to concede to Dad, "I felt like the guy who had just lit the fuse." I remembered that Dad held early evening office hours on Thursday. Fortunately, the one graduate student who showed up had just left.

"Have you eaten today?"

"Just what they give you on the planes."

"Nothing. Worse than nothing. Should we go out?"

"Maybe later on. I just realized I'd better get back and leave word at Humper, Fardel not to run any correspondence through our office. Buckley. I just wanted you to hear right away how everything went with Stokes."

"Ethan Stokes! He is definitely the hound you want to turn loose in a situation like this. But on the personal level? Ecked mir a liberal!"

"He's high on you. He thinks you're Jackie Mason all over again."

"Exactly. What's that old saw, a kike is a Jewish gentleman who has just left the room?"

"I think he meant that with a certain affection," I said.

"That's part of the problem. Just stay away from his sister. Besides which, I always thought he had his eye on your mother."

"You can stop worrying. Right now his arthritis is so bad he probably couldn't climb into bed."

As a precaution, Sonny and I had agreed to avoid communicating with each other for a day or so but to meet the following evening in a folk and jazz bar over by the Gulf, The Sloppy Pelican. The handful of Native Americans around town had a way of congregating here; it was a blue-jeans and tank-top crowd, lots of hair and tattoos. Blouses tended to be extremely low-cut. By nine or ten, if one of the chubby young salesgirls or recent college dropouts drinking nearby noticed you noticing her too much, she was liable to pull one breast out and aim the nipple at you. This was not entirely a friendly gesture.

Our table was on a sort of deck that adjoined the bandstand. When the little group performing that night got going the amplifiers made our table vibrate.

"I think I've been here once before," I commented to Sonny just as my Heinekens and his Diet Coke appeared. "Noisy!"

"Better that way. Keeps us from being bugged."

"Always one step ahead. Flights went off OK?"

"Easy enough. You see me on the flight going up?"

"Couldn't miss you. The wink was gratuitous."

"Whatever that means."

"That beard! It's becoming a health hazard. How about you get it dry cleaned and put that on the tab?" But I had gone too far; Sonny tipped his head and narrowed his eyes. "OK," I said, "I retract that, just yanking your chain a little."

"Don't yank," Sonny said. "We got too much to do."

Just as we arranged, Sonny had been on my flight to Philadelphia and tracked me into the terminal. "Not that you made it easy," Sonny reprimanded me. "I saw you bolting for the taxis after we landed."

"Force of habit. It hit me just in time to turn around and try for the light rail. I spotted that mob, and naturally I remembered that that was what you wanted."

"It wasn't about what I wanted. There you are, dangling that briefcase like a freaking wedge of cheese. We needed mice."

"Well, they did hit it."

"I know. I could have reached out and touched you the whole time. It was the fat man who knocked it loose – very professional moves, perfect bump and run. Before you could turn around he handed it off to the skyscraper with the mink choker, who shoved it into her shopping bag and slid back out of there."

"The babe with the hat? With the feather?"

"Yeah, I think so. I was pretty busy keeping track of the fat man. I made it into the rail car behind his and followed him back to his hotel. The woman showed up about an hour later."

"She was on my tail for quite a while. I shook her in the subway system under City Hall."

"Hey, troop!" Sonny exclaimed. We banged open palms. "It could be you're not entirely dead white meat."

"What an ugly thing to say. Is it my turn now to sulk?"

Sonny gave me a long, glowering look. "OK, you got me," he said finally. "No more prima donna."

It turned out the fat man and the tall lady were sharing a suite at the Sofitel. Sonny had slipped unnoticed into their packed elevator and spotted their room number. The problem developed when the pair had regrouped and turned up downstairs for drinks in the Liberte Urban Chic Lounge. The door to their suite, fitted out with the latest in magnetic card-key locks, was not to be picked.

"So then what?" I asked Sonny. "Punt?"

"Improvise. I don't have that much French, but I guess I had enough to convince the Concierge that I was dropping in and out on loan from Paris to spot-check serving staff in New Jersey and Pennsylvania. Once he was out of sight I tied on the official Sofitel apron and delivered a decanter of ice water to the fat man and the tall lady where they were having cocktails near the fireplace. Somehow my ice bucket slipped and water splashed up on the fat man's shoes and the tall lady's snakeskin purse. Not too much, but I insisted on wiping the shoes down and drying off the flap of the purse. Women generally tuck their cards just inside the flap. She did."

"So you did get in."

"I hope for long enough. Besides your briefcase I located a passport case for the fat guy. In it were three or four business cards printed with a name, Cedric Bougalas, and a P.O. Box and what he says he does: Strategic Opportunities. He bills himself as a retired G.S. 16 out of the DEA, Drug Enforcement Authority. There was another passport he had in another name. Both with Sarasota addresses, which I got.

"The lady seemed to be travelling light, nothing but a sort of vanity case/carry-on bag. Everything was luxus, old-fashioned, like that fur muff. *That's* where I noticed the hat with the feather. On a chair in their suite, I remember it now. Her passport said Olivia de Broulee. French maybe, except that she had more of a German accent. Hard to place. She was travelling light – a change of underwear, extra makeup besides her toilet kit. Not even a second dress."

"They obviously weren't expecting to stay in Philly long."

"Overnight. They were overnighting. She did bring along one thing I hadn't seen before. Some kind of mean-looking curved battery-powered apparatus with three protruding vibrating heads. Definitely had me puzzled for a minute or two. Why wouldn't it – backwoods brave, fingering the white lady's underwear?"

"Not a vote of confidence in Cedric Bougalas."

"Not a vote of confidence."

Just then a hefty female singer with a mezzanine that made me catch my breath began to belt out a half-forgotten Janis Joplin number against the harsh thunder of electric guitars. I had almost been about to ask Sonny whether he could recall the brand name on Olivia's apparatus so I could get one for Wendy for Christmas. Then I thought better of that. By that time, more than likely, Wendy would be a mother.

I sat there finishing my second beer, my nerves jangling. Everything was eating into me – the raw, evocative throb of the music, the smell of working-class people enjoying themselves, the unabashed sexuality the women in particular kept projecting. I was profoundly thrilled, confused.

"I don't know what's happening," I said to Sonny. "Something really has changed."

"Peyote can do that. Open things up. Besides, you've had a hard week. Probably just unwinding."

"Maybe. I admit I'm scared half out of my mind. But I think it's more your sister."

"I went by Linda's place earlier today. She's loco too. At least she's got the dog."

"I'll try and see her tomorrow."

"Try and fit it in," Sonny said. His eyes were narrowing, not a good sign. We both stayed quiet for a couple of minutes. The big singer started a new set, torch songs from the thirties.

"What do you make of that Bougalas operation?" Sonny asked once the singer took a break.

"I have no idea. You're the spook."

"Just guesswork. Those two didn't look like that much,

some kind of retirement gig, it could be. What that really means to me is that you're not dealing with IBM here. Bougalas is probably an old hand in the business, and word has gotten around that he can put things together under the table and customers come to him and he subcontracts a lot of it. He's a clearinghouse. When your boy Buckley called somebody—"

"Rick. It stands to reason he called Rick."

"OK, Rick called Bougalas. Probably Senor Cruz' go-to guy on this coast. Bougalas couldn't have handled that big safe the other day, so they brought in demolition talent. Picking off your briefcase must have looked doable to Bougalas, especially with the tall broad as backup."

"So what happens next?"

"By now they all probably know they've been had. You've got to hope your lawyer in Philadelphia lands on all those Cubans before they can regroup."

I could merely nod. The singer had launched into a jazzed-up version of *Begin the Beguine* that was all but immobilizing me. I could feel tears starting in my eyes. I was hopeless.

CHAPTER XIII

Late the following afternoon I picked Linda up and took her out to supper at The Spartan, a Greek restaurant in a neighborhood shopping mall off 62nd South. They baked a decent pizza, and the baklava was outstanding. The restaurant was blocks from my house in the Pink Streets on the Oval Crescent Annex.

Linda had packed her big flowered pouch-like carryall with what she expected she would need for a night or two. The good-natured hunchback who rented the unit on the first floor of Muldavey Court was going to look after Penelope.

"You think we can do this thing without Penelope?" I wondered once we were back in my bungalow and I had poured two glasses of Cabernet Sauvignon and we had started to settle in. "She added that unpredictable je ne sais quoi."

"I guess." Linda looked confused. "Mostly she supplies slobber. She is an old soul, but on the earth level she slobbers like a leaky hydrant."

Laughter was warming us up. Without a word of understanding we each finished our wine and stood up to strip down. I proceeded her to the bedroom. Every piece of furniture in the bedroom was part of a California fruitwood suite Janice and I had picked up cheap at The Gas Plant on lower Central. Linda took the silver clasp out of her hair and we sat in the edge of the bed and held hands.

"Your brother is a piece of work," I tried to open. " Maybe a little bit touchy at times, but gifted. Amazingly. No point in getting into it now, but without that tradecraft of his we'd already be cooked. Our family, I mean by that."

"Sonny is the one they always favor back home. When he was very young he stabbed to death a rattlesnake that was waiting underneath the blanket of the chief. After that they even let him use the sweat lodge when he was around. On the rez. Most of the time he was away at those schools."

"That's what he says about you. That you were gone mostly."

"Later, dancing. In the ceremonials. I was twelve when they put me into the group that travelled so much to perform the dances. Away and back, away and back. Never really a teenager."

"That's what Sonny indicated. He said you were very— extremely serious about your powwow dancing. No time to waste with the usual screwing around—"

Linda gave him a sidelong look, her dark eyes glittering a moment. "Did I go with men, you're trying to ask? Before Savage Owl? One. In a way."

"Look, it really isn't any business of mine—"

"No, I ought to tell you. Maybe you should know." Linda recrossed her legs and hunched her shoulders. "We were a troupe who travelled together. Six people. Eight people. Three were still very young. On one tour I was eighteen, and we had a stripling who was very ahead of himself, very dynamic, leaps very high. He was sixteen."

"Not really the age of consent."

"That wasn't a part of it. We had our own world. Because I was closest to Little Shield in years I was supposed to look after him. Help wash the paint off after the performances, make sure he stored the headdress right so the feather bustle don't get tangled. So much regalia for all the males, and after we got that all off he had such very soft buckskin leggings that he wore and sometimes I helped him get them off afterwards. So easy to snap the porcupine quills, which our head drum worried about. All the time."

"You were supposed to tend him."

"Tend to him, not let him get too homesick. Mother him. Little Shield was high strung."

"I gather that you discovered new ways of helping."

"Nobody wanted this. But one afternoon when the others were away in some town and I was cleaning Little Shield up we had some trouble getting his leggings off that day, and his breach clout came loose, and he was – his—"

"His pecker?"

"I like cock better. His cock was – you know – it stood up there so stiff and swollen and sore! *So* smooth, with all those veins! I didn't know what to do, I had to take it in my hand, and then I give Little Shield a tug. But then he had to have another tug, and I can see you know what happened after that."

"I know what happened." My cheeks were burning.

"It makes a truly wonderful face cream," Linda mused, with that half-smile. "I tried to save a little every time from then on...."

"And Little Shield – you taught him how to keep *you* from being – what's that phrase – too high strung? Those woman's needs?"

"We learned. Both of us learned. That tour lasted months. The important thing was, I couldn't get pregnant. Among us

Comanches, that would have been a disgrace. So in a way, we were just practicing."

"Saving yourself for Savage Owl?"

"Saving myself for you. I see you liked my story."

My prick was outdoing itself. I planted my fingers deep into Linda's fur and she reciprocated. After a few minutes I got up with difficulty and stripped back the coverlet. This time Linda took off her necklace of elk's teeth. "I wear this even to bed so the spirit of the elk can protect me. But you will protect me now. I think you will."

"I will," I said.

We were so excited by then that our lovemaking lasted hours. I remember waking up around three or four with my face between Linda's powerful thighs and my nose halfway up her vagina. As I came to slowly she stirred. "What are you doing down there?" she said softly.

"Just checking things out. I think I caught a taste of the baklava."

Easter came in 2008 just before the end of March. After a touchy winter the stock market began to show indications of coming back, but Dad was increasingly alarmed. "It's going to be entirely about the big banks," he assured me on Easter morning, when I stopped by the house on Snell Isle to make sure it was OK to bring Linda to the three o'clock banquet. "They're trying to lay everything off on Lehman, and more now AIG. But at this stage it should be obvious how every shagitz up and down Wall Street has been selling phony insurance policies with no more capital than I've got tits enough to

142

suckle King Kong. Derivatives, feh! Insurance is a great business until something floods or burns up."

"Isn't that what Ramon was doing? Those medical insurance startups?"

"With those you can predict, at least. Statistics mean something. But you tell me which of those Wall Street sharpshooters can gauge the foreclosure rate of a ten-billion-dollar issue of subprime mortgage bonds based on the ability of Margo the cocktail waitress and Elmo the bellhop to pay off their minimansion. Preposterous! Or Iceland to float paper based on a budget its parliament will never pass."

"But Ramon's hedge fund is different?"

"I told you. He started out underwriting health coverage for a lot of mom-and-pop start-ups and widows and orphans in the Cuban community down there. Then he got into partnerships concentrating mostly on land development. Insurance is a sideline."

"Then why did he need us?"

"Because we looked solid. Quality properties, professional mortgage-holders. With us in his fund he gets to keep on borrowing. He needed to impress the machers around Miami he thinks he wants to run with, Gomez and Geoffrey Ball and the rest of those potzes whose big interest was scams like draining the Swamp into their offshore bank accounts. Now Ramon would get to be a player. Maybe they cut him in. He obviously left those bloodsucking mob counterparties of his with the impression his hedge fund was in a position to liquidate our properties any time push came to shove. Butcher anything we turned over to him whenever his balance sheet looked a little thin and they decided he'd better recapitalize. "

"So now Ramon has got a problem?"

"If we can get out."

"I thought we were as good as out. I thought those injunctions of Ethan Stokes' froze the assets until they pass back to us."

"Their lawyers have already started to contest the injunctions. Stokes says we're likely to recover the properties but it may take a while. Time is precisely what we haven't got, with the economy falling off a cliff."

"And you think a few months—"

"We need them back in time to unload them."

By one in the afternoon, when we met in the drawing room before dinner, you'd never have been able to tell Dad had anything on his mind. Everybody else was there, working on Daiquiris, when I showed up with Linda. She had just gotten her initial paycheck from Walmart, and bought herself a very flattering dark linen dress.

Everybody had pulled up the Hepplewhite side chairs around the big parquet coffee table that fronted on the balustrade that overlooked the Bay. Linda eased into the chair next to Carol and I sat next to her beside Rick. Rick looked preoccupied, wiping off his bulging temples again and again with his giant palm once he felt his cocktail.

"Mikey here speaks so highly of you," Carol said to Linda. "He says you're extremely talented."

"Quite a performer," Wendy chimed in. I could have cut her throat.

"Michael says that you were well known while you were

still very young as part of some sort of travelling dance company," Mother said, straining to rescue that. "I know *I* have at times been reduced to all but tears by ethnic dance ensembles. When I was a girl we *never* missed the Bolshoi."

"I never saw that," Linda said.

"Outstanding!" Mother said. "Every spin made you catch your breath."

"Linda was a powwow dancer," I said. "She and her group danced here and in Europe."

"That *had* to be exhilarating," Carol said.

Linda surveyed them all and barely smiled. "Sometimes it was a blast," she said. "Sometimes it got old. The food was good, though." Dad brought her a Daiquiri, which she held but did not drink. "I liked the French."

"Who was that was telling me the other day that Native American cuisine is utterly *superb* under certain circumstances?" Buckley volunteered. "Much neglected."

"What are your favorite dishes?" Carol asked. "At home. On the reservation."

"At home?" Linda tossed her black mane and appeared to think back. I could tell by the sudden light in her eye that we were in trouble. "We like plain food. A lot of boiled dog. Sometimes we season that up a little with – what do you call them in English? – grubs. Larvae. Very excellent fried. When you eat them fast they go pop, pop, pop—"

There was a startled moment or two before the rest of them realized that Linda was putting them on. Then Wendy exploded with laughter. "This girl is a *trip*!" she got out. "You're gonna fit right in here, babe."

Dad poured another round of Daiquiris and the back-and-forth got lively fast as politics became the subject. The national party primaries were starting to heat up. As always, Buckley Glickman was our outspoken Republican. He still favored John McCain, with his years in a North Vietnamese prison camp, although he himself had to admit that George Romney came closer to looking the part. Barack Obama was showing a lot of appeal nobody had expected. That week he made a speech proclaiming that there was still a lot of black anger out there, a statement the Fox spokesman resented especially. James Carville gave an interview in which he savagely accused Governor Bill Richardson of taking on the role of Judas by espousing Obama so early and selling out the Clintons, who did so much for him.

"Whatever happened to the war in Iraq?" Dad – clearly feeling his Daiquiris – demanded of the group at large. "Kids are dying." Mother looked apprehensive – Dad sometimes went overboard railing about the senselessness of the invasion. I think Mother had started to worry about Dad's blood pressure. She looked quite attractive if extraordinarily pale and patchy-cheeked in a white silk cocktail dress, her knuckles all but submerged from the edema in her hands. Dad had told me earlier that day that Mother was on and off prednisone at this stage.

I could see that Linda was making an effort to be attentive. Ricky had just started to defend the Iraq incursion, maintaining to the best of his ability that unless we took over there Saddam Hussein would have invaded Israel with his atomic weapons, as he had attempted to do with rockets during Desert Storm.

Dad was countering that with unaccustomed gentleness when I caught Linda's eye and she planted her untouched Daiquiri on the coffee table and followed me to the door. "I thought I'd show Linda around a little," I told the others.

"It's got so many rooms!" she breathed as we explored the upper stories. "Like a museum." A central hall led into Mother's office and private library. Linda took in Mother's pictures one by one and stopped – everybody stopped – at the Klimt drawing of the full-bodied woman fellating the adolescent boy. "That's definitely right out there, isn't it?" I said.

"I didn't know it was all right to hang up pictures like that one."

"Bring back memories?"

Linda conferred on me a long look, between amusement and recrimination. She accomplished a lot with her eyes.

"The afternoon I first met you, you reminded me of the woman in that picture," I said.

"Because we both have fabulous big butts?"

"I think it was the long hair. Long dark hair."

"Ah. You appreciated the hair." She murmured that softly but full of feeling, accompanied by another look. If we had not been trapped in my father's house, I think I would have fucked her on the carpet.

By the time we got back downstairs Anastasia had come out to get us in to dinner. "Anybody 'round here hungry, I gots a little something," she announced in those lilting, musical tones: a small girl's voice, always surprising in a black woman whose waistline had gone out of control decades ago. She was

Max' wife, or whatever.

We started with lobster in cocktail sauce in Margarita glasses and moved on to rack of lamb and/or individual Cornish game hens – several of the women refused red meat. Sweet potatoes decorated with marshmallow sauce. For dessert Anastasia's amazing carrot cake, ice cream voluntary. By the time the Cointreau went around we were all breathing hard.

After that we all went back to the sitting room. Wendy was already starting to show, and Carol and then Mother couldn't resist palpating her abdomen. They invited Linda who – shyly – acceded. "You will have a boy," she said, and smiled.

"How do you know that?" Ricky immediately demanded. There was a catch in his voice. "Nobody did sonograms or nothing like that. Nada." I had never mentioned to any of them that Linda had been married before, and had a child.

"I feel the rhythm of him breathing," Linda said. "And you are carrying so low."

Mother and Wendy looked at each other.

"Male chauvinism not intended," Dad said. "But don't you think it's time the gentlemen hid out at safer altitudes? Brandy and cigars?"

We repaired to the pergola. When Enrique and Wendy got married Ramon had sent Dad a box of Cuban panatelas, the real thing, impossible to find. He broke them out on holidays or special occasions. That Easter Dad had one, and I had one, but Buckley had brought a pack of his evil-smelling cigarillos and Rick took one of them – a gesture of solidarity with Buckley, I suppose. We all smoked silently for a couple of minutes. An afternoon squall was coming in across the Bay, padded out with thunder and the very distant wrinkle of lightening. The air was extremely close.

"So you're about to have a boy?" Dad said, finally, to Rick.

"Maybe. However it comes out, I got a fifty-percent shot, 's verdad?" He raised his hand to extract the cigarillo; his enormous bicep almost grazed his wrist. It was hard for me to see Rick without envisioning him hoisting himself through the casement window and pillaging Dad's file cabinets.

"Linda has got gifts in that department," I said. "She is a little bit …telekinetic, if you know what I'm getting at. She has *insights*."

"As well as a hellova rack," Buckley put in.

"Always the one comment that raises the tone," I said.

"I would think your father would get pretty excited at the prospect of a grandson," Dad said. "Another generation to break in down the road? Ease into the business? Have you picked any names?"

"Not yet," Rick said. He looked uncomfortable.

"We've got a couple that have come down on my side of the family. How about Yonkel? Still carries a lot of prestige around the stetl." He popped his cigar back in.

Rick looked both concerned and bewildered.

"Dad's just screwing around," I said. "Sometimes he can't control his Jackie Mason side."

"What I want to explain you is, the way things look there ain' gonna be no business," Rick broke out. He was still feeling his cocktails. "You pull your real estate, I know you got your worries too, but we been dependin' on heem. We know you got your rights and your abogados in Philadelphia but you know we got some pandillaros backing *us*, bad hombres, investment gunslingers out of Miami, sabe? Who we got to have as counterparties. Who are into us, man, they get a killer risk premium—"

Dad got serious. "We don't have much of a choice. We would definitely like to participate financially in Cuba down the road. But real estate in this country in for trouble, there is a shitstorm brewing. *Whoever* has those properties in a year is going to take a tremendous beating, it's already sliding off the peaks. If I could liquidate them soon enough maybe Ramon and I could work something out–" At that moment, on cue, a heavy, driving curtain of rain broke against the pilings and threatened to swamp the pergola. "See, Nature speaks. It's time for everybody to pull in his horns."

"Economics is too complicated for a simple little ding-dang lawyer like myself," Buckley said. "And worse than that, my cigar is soaked."

We all ran together for the ocean-side door just as the sky unloaded. It let up for long enough for the girls and their husbands to scurry out into their cars on the tarmac off Brightwaters Boulevard. Linda and Mother were talking about something.

"I thought it went all right," Dad said. "Little flare-up from Ricky in the pergola. He's obviously worried about Ramon. Those 'counterparties' probably have Ramon's nuts in a vice, as the lady reminded the bishop."

"I'm not sure how that affects us."

"Maybe we ought to lay off for a couple of months. Take the pressure off. Let the legal system work its magic. But you don't agree," Dad decided. "I can see it in your face."

"What you are liable to get out of the legal system is an ever more extortionate fee schedule. That's one meter you never want to leave running. Those are our properties. Your properties. Mother's properties."

"Look, boychik, hok mir nisht a chinik about properties. We have other assets. It's only money. They are part of our family now. A grandson is on the way, remember?"

I didn't say anything. Dad was wrong, and I would have to deal with it.

"She is a *very* interesting young woman," Dad said, with a nod toward Linda. "A lot of substance. I haven't seen your mother so absorbed in conversation with anybody for a long time."

"There is a lot there," I said.

CHAPTER XIV

I spent the day after that on client work. The following morning, while Buckley was chasing down a personal injury lead, I donned a pair of latex gloves, and rescued a long-ignored Olivetti typewriter from obscurity in a dusty closet, and rolled in a piece of blank paper and typed a short note to Ramon Perez y Cruz.

"Senor," it said, "I am an admiror of yours who have been follow your activities for many years. I know that your fund is fighting the return of a number of valuble mortgages held once by the Landau famly, who I also know these years. Give them back!!!!! I have in my possession many letters from persons we both knew the old days in Cuba. You are helping this people, I think. I send you copies of a few – I have more!!!!! You no return the mortgages by Apr. 7, copies of all letters go to reporters we know in Miami Post-Dispatch, Miami New Times, New York Times, Wall St. Jernel. Others. How do your once friends from our Batista time think when that comes out?

"Es un placer trater de negocios con Ud."

The final phrase, which I found in a Berlitz paperback in the office, was no doubt the only grammatical sentence in the note. I copied and included several of the letters I had found in Ramon's safe from officials whose looted valuables he spirited off the island, including the one from Raul Castro. Mapquest supplied me with the address of the Sarasota post office closest to Cedric Bougalas' mailing address. I remember driving over the Skyway Bridge with my head buzzing. I posted my letter to the Coral Gables office priority, no return receipt requested.

I had no doubt that it would be obvious to Ramon and his people where my note originated. It also seemed to me that the spectacular clumsiness of my approach might lead Ramon to suspect that other people might also be involved, qualified extortionists and blackmailers, more insidious and without a doubt more competent in covering their tracks. Bougalas, possibly, a conniver with DEA credentials, the mention of which alone was likely to panic that generation of cocaine-smuggling Cubans. The question was: Were Ramon and his backers geared up to take that risk?

I had my answer ten days later. Ethan Stokes telephoned Dad to crow that Humper, Fardel had brought it off. Attorneys for Sunrise Capital Partners had been in contact late the previous week and decided to drop their challenge and return to us uncontested title to our real estate. Documents to follow.

I was well aware all along that extracting our commitment to Ramon's hedge fund the way we had was not going to sweeten up intra-family relations. But from the outset we hadn't attempted to terrorize anybody, certainly nothing remotely comparable to blowing the safe in Wallaye's offices. Whatever the upshot, we were at most responding. We'd gotten our properties returned, and so it seemed to me that we were back where we started.

I began to discover how naïve I was a little more than a week after we recovered our deeds. I came in late in the morning on Friday; Andrea, our part-time intern, met me with news that the FBI field office in Tampa had been trying to locate me since the previous afternoon. She had two numbers for Special

Agent Hardagon.

An hour later I was in his office. For a phlegmatic man, Vince Hardagon had a gift for cranking up threat. "There's been a development," he informed me before I could sit down. "There was a nasty incident in our Miami district." He checked his report. "That Cuban investment hotshot or whatever he is who is some kind of shirt-tail relative of yours, Ramon Whosis – some S.O.B. blew his Lexus all over bleeping LeJeune Road in Coral Gables. The wife was driving, but she had left the two little daughters in the vehicle and was gone into a boutique or someplace to pick up a watch. Some kind of magnetic device, somebody slipped it under the frame and set it off by radio. Engine went twenty feet in the air."

"Jesus," I said. "What about the girls?"

"They got lucky. Burns, shock – they won't forget that morning in a hurry. I take it you had nothing to do with anything of that nature?"

"How could I—"

"Well, you said you were headed to Miami."

"Not to blow anybody up. I've been around here the last couple of weeks, I can establish *that.*"

"Worth a shot. The thing is, we think the two cases are related. I know I haven't been in touch, and civilians like you think federal employees just sit around drinking coffee and pulling our puds all afternoon…."

"I don't think that."

"Well, it's only partly true. What I'm trying to tell you is this, it took a while but our people got around to comparing some scrapings. We're actually starting to utilize the computer these days, not like the Louis Freeh era when the lab guys were told to depend on Ouija boards or whatever the hell they used. It develops the nitro somebody used to take that safe out the other day and the nitro in Coral Gables came from the same batch. Those munitions in Portsmouth. Spectrometer readings, same chemical signature. So there's a connection."

"And you want me to—"

"Make the connection for us." He gave me that wide, insincere Irish smirk of his. "Somebody was after those documents of yours, and now the guy who supposedly wound up with the documents gets blasted—"

"It makes no sense," I said. "Ramon and his backers appear to have rethought the whole thing, and now they've decided to give us back our properties. We got the paperwork earlier this week. I doubt there's any connection."

Hardagon exhaled hard, the snort of a bloodhound giving up on a scent. "What you want to do is stay in touch with us, counselor," he conceded after another moment or two. "We'll skip the polygraph. 'jever do any good with our field office down on North Miami Beach? Hector Diaz? Cute, an exceptionally cute piece of work. Talk about dubious collaborators in high places...."

"Never got that far."

"You got lucky. As I say, stay in touch. You got my numbers."

I had to regard that summons as fair warning, a testimony to suspicions around the Bureau that there was a potentially noisy game afoot and that I – we – were implicated. A few days later, Sunday evening, I found myself mulling over the bombing in Coral Gables and the extent of my personal culpability throughout the opening-night Passover seder Mother insisted on hosting every Easter season. I never thought Dad was that enraptured with formal Judaism – he claimed he had barely survived several years of Saturdays and Sundays as a small boy in the basement of the synagogue in Minneapolis squirming through unending sessions of rote Hebrew in preparation for his bar mitzvah. But Mother was very firm in her conviction that this was part of our family tradition. We ought to recognize that too.

It developed that I was the only sibling in town that April to observe. Carol and Buckley flew up to White Plains to celebrate with Seymour Glickman, Buckley's father, and his screechy third wife, who was borderline Orthodox. Without mentioning why to our parents, Wendy and Rick drove down in Coral Gables to visit the bandaged-up little step-sisters in the hospital and support Annilita and Ramon. Earlier in the day Wendy had telephoned me to describe Ramon as withdrawn and obviously unnerved, by no means the light-footed promoter the rest of us would recognize.

To round the table out Dad had invited Rabbi Sheila Ginsburg from Seminole and her partner Angela McCarthy, a big aggressive feeder and a loud talker. I invited Linda and her brother Sonny, who was just back from a quick visit to the reservation in Oklahoma. I wanted Dad to meet Sonny.

Jews throughout the world have supposedly been celebrating the feast of the Passover for 2300 years, since Moses conducted his rabble of ex-slaves across the Red Sea and Jehovah parted the waters. As a woman of the cloth, hung with tallises,

Rabbi Ginsburg sat at the head of the table and led us through the Haggadah, back to front. Once we had gotten to the recitation dealing with the building of the pyramids, and the travail of the Israelites beneath the whips of Ramses' overseers sweating to produce bricks without straw, Sonny was resolutely studying the text.

When the time came to deposit a drop of red wine on our plates for every plague that Jehovah visited upon the Egyptians, culminating with the angel of death wiping out all their first-born males, Sonny looked up. "Big Chief Jehovah mean serious business," he commented.

"The Biblical God?" Rabbi Ginsburg responded. "Definitely a hard-ass. You don't want to yank the chain of the Lord of the Hebrews. Tit for tat. Or tat for tit, reading from left to right. But now I think I need to readjust my brassiere. "

Everybody laughed. Angela shoveled a heavy load of horosis onto a segment of matzo and scarfed it down. "That is *good stuff*," she decided, and suppressed a belch.

"Then when they finally got away?" Sonny wondered.

"Moses made them wander in the desert for forty years. Allow the slave generation time to die off."

"It's like the Trail of Tears, except with unleavened bread," Sonny said.

Several of us chuckled at that, if a little uneasily.

"Cultural overlays in tribes tend to be very much alike," Dad broke in. The red wine was getting to Dad, which invariably risked bringing out the pedagogue in him. "You want to remember that the Christians started out for several hundred years as a Jewish cult skulking around bazaars outside Athens and hiding in Roman catacombs. Humble, taking Christ's teachings seriously. Then Constantine decided to unify the Roman Empire by imposing Christianity on the infidels, and ever since then it's been the cross or the sword."

"That's very informative, Sylvan, dear," Mother said, "but what has that to do with Moses?"

"Moses was one more empire builder. He put those slaves through hell so he could turn them into an army. Exactly the same thing happened with the perception of Jesus. I remember the chorale we used to sing in chapel when I was a kid in my Episcopalian Country Day School outside Minneapolis. Supply the pipe organ accompaniment yourselves." Dad began to sing, something all of us dreaded:

" 'The Son of God goes forth to war

A kingly crown to gain,

His blood-red banner streams aloft,

Who follows in his train?'

"Whose Jesus is that, for Christ's sake?" Dad challenged us all. "I suspect that that's the Jesus who rounded up Sonny's ancestors, and Linda's ancestors, and herded them out of all that valuable prairie real estate and into the detention camps we like to refer to as reservations." Dad took another swallow of wine. "Does that sound about right to you, Sonny?"

Sonny was examining Dad, piercingly. "White man speak truth," Sonny said. "A few of the details need a little work, but who could have a problem with the bottom line?"

"And a lot of the same reasoning applies to our adventures these days in the Middle East," Dad concluded. "Which doesn't detract in any way from the sacrifice by our troops."

158

"Don't back off now, darling," Mother said. "I think you've managed to make just about everybody at this table uncomfortable, one way or another."

"Well," Rabbi Ginsburg piped up, "sometimes that's a good thing."

"I have to protect my reputation as an equal opportunity blasphemer," Dad said. We all laughed.

"I got a nephew in Afghanistan," Angela McCarthy said, snapping in half the last matzo on the common plate and starting in on that. "He is a beast. You ought to see the triceps on that mother."

Linda was the youngest at the seder, and I wanted her to participate. A few minutes later, once everybody had started to relax again, I convinced her to ask the four questions. That got her into the ceremony a little, but a few minutes later she demurred when it came to searching out the afikomen. Linda was obviously shy about roaming Dad's house unattended. When the time came to open the door for Elijah Linda perked up. I tried to explain who or what Elijah was: an ancient prophet, who returned over the millennia – dropped off no doubt from a chariot of fire – to help reconstitute the remnant of Israel. "Didn't make it to the Happy Hunting Grounds yet?" Linda mused. "With us, after four days, the ghosts of warriors aren't supposed to come back."

Mother served a light meal, chicken pot pie and salad. Anastasia was coming in later on to clear things away. Afterwards there was a cherry cheesecake, which Angela seemed to relish, several slices.

Just as Rabbi Ginsburg was leaving she drew Mother and Dad aside. "We had a very enjoyable time," the Rabbi said. "Angela I could see especially enjoyed herself. The cherry cheesecake in particular was a tremendous hit."

"Why don't you take the rest with you?" Mother offered. "We'll never eat it here."

"Don't tempt me. As it is I need a map and a compass to get around Angela when she stops all of a sudden." Rabbi Ginsburg hesitated. "Maybe it's not my place," she said, "but my mother in Boca sent me a clipping from *The Miami Herald* Tuesday. Your Cuban in-law, Ramon? The bombing? I wanted to say I was very glad to read that the children are going to be all right. I remember them from the wedding. Adorable, and so intelligent-looking." She deliberated a moment, and peered into Dad's eyes. "These Cuban business people—it's no joke, geferlekh." Rabbi Ginsburg looked away and pinched off her yamulkah and slid it into her handbag.

Dad started to say something, then stopped himself. He walked the Rabbi and Angela to their car. Mother and Linda were rounding off one of their fervent exchanges, fellow spirits; Sonny waited for Linda to detach herself so he could run her back to Muldavey Court. I touched her waist and she laid her palm on my cheek.

"Tomorrow," I said. She nodded. I started to say good-by to Dad but he gripped my forearm.

"Stick around," he said. "We have got to talk."

Mother went to bed once Anastasia showed up. Dad and I repaired to his study. When I was young and I had screwed up, Dad tended to wait until some of the dust settled. Then he would invite me into his study, and close the door, and chew my ass. We'd gone beyond that – at least I hoped we had – but something in Dad's tone as the rest of them were leaving hinted that perhaps we hadn't.

I took my place in the Barcalounger and Dad planted himself behind his desk. Then he clicked his desktop computer on, accessed the internet for a minute or so, clicked the computer off. His face darkening, Dad reached beside himself to lift the top of his humidor, decided against a cigar, and closed his humidor. He put his reading glasses on, knitted his brows, and took the glasses off. His eyes looked swollen, tired and a little bloodshot.

"I drank too much of that wine," Dad said. "Manishewicz. I guess it's sacramental, but it ain't Mouton Rothschild. I have been reading galleys for the Keynes thing all afternoon, and that isn't helping. I feel a headache coming on."

"You covered up nicely. It certainly didn't affect your singing voice."

"Thank God for that." Dad moistened his lips. "Michael," Dad wanted to know, "don't I always play it straight with you?"

"I'm not sure—"

"Yes you are. I suppose I look stupid, but at this point I like to think I have average intelligence. Wouldn't you say?"

"You want a yes or no answer?"

"Don't fuck with me!" Dad was sitting upright in his chair. He settled back. "What would *you* think?" he demanded. "Let's review the steps that got us here. First, we decide we want our properties back but Ramon and his partners attempt to stall.

Then they – probably they were the ones, we aren't that sure yet – clean out my records and dynamite Wallaye's safe. Then you and that Indian kid – who is very astute, a lot sharper even than I had any reason to believe – pull off that prodigy of breaking-and-entering and actually recover copies of the legal papers. Then we hire Stokes to land on Ramon without any warning so we can reacquire our properties. But Ramon's guys dig their heels in – which was predictable.

"By then I assumed that that would be that for a while – that we had probably exhausted normal legal remedies. Is that a fair summation so far?"

"I'd say so."

"Then all of a sudden everything starts to fall in our lap. The Coral Gables braintrust decides that it has lost interest in our properties, on which their financial survival supposedly depended a few weeks previously, and give everything back. Wonderful! Except that just about the time we get to reprocessing our documents somebody blows up Ramon's car, with two of his youngsters in the back seat. Which was absolutely news to me until the good rabbi brought it up. I see that it is all over the Miami papers. Were you aware of that?"

"Sure. The FBI in Tampa hauled me up there last Friday. The same explosives were used on the car as on Wallaye's safe."

"But you didn't tell me," Dad said.

"I'm trying to keep this business from wearing you out."

"Ah. Protect Dad, the senior citizen. Now, let's be specific. Have you any reason to think that something you did, or said, brought about this dramatic reversal of tactics by those hedge fund people?"

He had me. "I really didn't want to embroil you in this," I said. "I know how important you think timing is going to be now that the big banks are tottering. We needed to recover our assets, now. So I wrote a kind of anonymous note to Ramon in which I let him know that we – somebody – was in possession of all those letters from the Comandantes he'd been pipelining loot out of Cuba for. For whom—"

"Skip the grammar. "

"And that's it. I imagine that what I sent was enough to persuade Ramon to give us our stuff back."

"Then why blow up the car?"

"I have no idea," I said.

"Let's explore various suppositions," Dad proposed. "Let's play around with the possibility that your letter got away from Ramon and into the hands of other interested individuals. It could be those shadowy frigging 'counterparties' Rick seems so out of joint about. We can't rule out the usual flaming Batistiana soreheads around Miami. Or – this is the crowd I'd worry about – veterans of the apparatus inside Cuba, socking it away in Basel and Lichtenstein and the Cayman Islands. They've got to keep Ramon cooperating. Keep anybody else from finding out. At least until they're finished with him. They just made their statement. A bomb carries with it a lot more sincerity than an Easter card, wouldn't you say?"

"I suppose that makes sense."

"But if they really suspect he's leaking," Dad went on,"they've got to cover their tracks. Take him out."

"Do you really think"– my palms were sweating – "they'd

go that far?

"Take Ramon out? Why not? And then anybody else with knowledge – Enrique, and Wendy, and the baby, and very likely you and me."

Then neither of us said anything, for perhaps a minute.

"I thought I headed something like this off when we discussed it last time," Dad said. "Remember: 'It's only money?'"

"I remember," I said.

Dad sighed, heavily. "Well, we're into it now. We'll have to figure out who's behind all this and head for the exits early."

"I have an idea," I said. I hoped I didn't sound as bleak as I felt just then.

CHAPTER XV

I had assumed all along that Ramon's people hired Cedric Bougalas. After that exchange with Dad I wasn't all that positive. One gravy-spotted adjunct professor I studied with at B.U., who made his bones in real life hammering out custody settlements, confided to me that in the end most lawyers got to be a lot like the private detectives they depended on to scrape up the dreck when marital estrangements became inflamed. "They'd all eat just about anybody's shit if there was a fee in the offing," my burnt-out tutor concluded. There was no loyalty. I hoped I'd be able to say the same about Cedric Bougalas.

My situation was compromised to some extent in that I had caught a glimpse of Bougalas himself and given the slip to Olivia de Broulee in Philadelphia. The trick would be to bring off a plausible non-recognition scene, present myself as the preoccupied dupe not likely to have paid much attention that smoggy winter morning at the airport. And then to get them involved as much as possible in our behalf.

With enough exposure, if I were at all shrewd, I might find ways to get them to play back hints as to who their other clients were. What other forces were homing in on us. How they could be of help. If the money was right.

I started things out by running a search for private investigators in the Tampa Bay area on Google. When Bougalas' firm came up I picked his e-mail address out of a short ad and e-mailed him requesting a list of references in Tampa-St. Petersburg. Somebody in his office replied with several; I actually recognized one of the names as a tennis pal of Wendy's and called her. She told me that she had hired Bougalas a couple of years before, when a thief had broken into her condo and escaped with most of her family's heirloom jewelry. Bougalas got it back, somehow – afterwards she heard rumors he had a working arrangement with a fence in Naples. The whole thing in the end cost her at least what the jewelry was worth, but there was always the sentimental value. Besides, the insurance covered much of it.

Next I slipped out of the office and reached Ethan Stokes by cell phone. After buttering him up over the amazingly quick resolution of our action against Sunrise Capital Partners, I wondered whether his lines into Washington were still in good enough shape for him to access the raw 201 file on a Cedric Bougalas, ex-DEA. One of Stokes' Republican partners at Humper, Fardel remained the deputy attorney general in the expiring Bush administration.

Then I called Bougalas' office in Sarasota directly and told the twit who answered that I would like to have a word with the detective personally. I named Wendy's pal as my immediate reference. I got the call-back around ten the following morning.

It was Olivia. What did I have in mind?

Her inflection, while obviously flattened out a little by her years in America, sounded Germanic to me too. But the name was French.

I told her I was a lawyer whose family had business relations with a banking organization in the Miami area. Certain arrangements had recently gone sour. Once we had a more complete sense of what exactly we were dealing with, everybody on our side of the negotiations would probably be a lot more relaxed. My Google search had indicated that Mr. Bougalas had worked for the government around Miami for many years.

"That is true," Olivia de Broulee said. There was a huskiness to her response.

Perhaps Mr. Bougalas and I could meet somewhere, I proposed. My office in St. Petersburg?

"It goes better if you come to us," Olivia decided. "Here we have the records."

"Works OK for me. Sometime tomorrow afternoon?"

We settled on three o'clock.

Cedric Bougalas' *Strategic Opportunities* headquarters seemed to have been put together to guarantee that the potential client remained a little bit unnerved about to what he/she was getting into. It existed behind a blank door twenty-three floors up in a new commercial building a couple of blocks behind the extravaganza of St. Armands Circle, a radiating welter of promenades and boutique arcades and shedding royal palms and bad pseudo-antique statuary and popular-priced hotels that dead-ended the John Ringling Causeway off downtown Sarasota. Potential clients were required to press a large illuminated button; during office hours that elicited some response from inside while simultaneously triggering several cameras, above and below, which shot footage from every angle. A glass rectangle beside the entrance could accept a thumb-print.

I got there early enough to leave my BMW in a garage and walk across to Bougalas' building, which had a fountain in the atrium and escalators to the lower floors. His was the last office suite at the end of a long corridor. I pressed the large illuminated button and waited. After thirty or forty seconds the voice of the twit demanded my name and I gave it to her. She released the lock.

The waiting room inside was very sterile, carriage-trade Danish modern of the sort Janice liked so much. The twit, who had a fluffed-out gamin haircut, watched me very carefully until Olivia de Broulee came through to usher me into the back. The twit and Olivia paused for an exchange of elevated eyebrows. Nothing I could decipher.

Bougalas had the primary office. A floor-to-ceiling tinted window took up the corner and looked out into the Gulf of Mexico. What walls there were carried bright signed posters of late work by Andy Warhol and a copy of the New World canvas by Salvador Dali. Three leather-covered Barcelona chairs faced Bougalas' formidable desk. Beside the door was mounted a huge, intricately carved and gilded Baroque crucifix, obviously looted from some medieval chapel, with an expiring savior several feet high hanging out into the room. Its stigmata dripped faded vermillion tears.

Bougalas nodded; I sat down, and then Olivia sat down next to me. Impressively smooth-limbed, she wore an expensive-looking frock and a ruby choker and shoulder-length hair, beautifully cut and streaked. Her rich, European features were large, expressive; except for the suggestion of spider veins in her cheeks she could have been forty. Well cared for, I thought. Then suddenly I found myself fighting the image of Olivia on her back attempting to insert the ferociously buzzing contraption Sonny had discovered in her things, struggling with the final vibrator–

I wasn't here for that, I reminded myself. Bougalas was obviously waiting. Even without a word he carried authority. While seventy-five or a hundred pounds overweight, he was still on his feet, aggressively bald in the way kings and rock stars go bald these days. That old-Bolshevik fringe of clipped beard, totally silver. He was Perry Mason or Sidney Green-street in *The Maltese Falcon – "By Gad, I'll tell you right out that I'm a man who likes talking to a man who likes to talk... ."* – a totally engaging scoundrel. He knew – and he had to assume that I was likely to be aware – that weeks earlier he was the one that light-fingered my briefcase on that platform in Philadelphia. Neither of us had any intention of getting into that.

"We've got a depressingly heavy agenda these days," Bougalas began, "but I have to admit I went ahead and did a little unremunerated snooping. It is just possible we are in a position to help you."

"Not me so much. Our family. As I think I indicated to – to Olivia here, a few of our investments with some hedge fund managers in the Miami area backfired. We took legal steps to recover important assets. That seemed to be paying off, but just the other day we discovered that a car belonging to the father of my brother-in-law got bombed. My father in particular is extremely concerned. Those people are family."

"I saw that item," Bougalas noted. "I go through the Post-Dispatch every morning. Partly, I like to believe, for nostalgic reasons. But also – who isn't human? – out of Schadenfreude, perhaps?" Olivia snickered; Bougalas opened his palms out:

Nothing hidden there.

"You know the world, don't we all relish a little bad news, especially about the people we thought we trusted? Would you believe that certain of my ex-colleagues in the DEA have fallen into evil practices? Not hesitated to cross the line? In fact, quite a number are doing time. Literally, as we speak. Reflects abominably on our society as a whole. But then, let's not forget that even Our Lord sometimes spoke ill of those he thought were close to him. Judas?"

I nodded. Sealed records Ethan Stokes had faxed to me spelled out how, once he began to recover from being gut-shot in Salt Lake City in 1996, Bougalas had plea-bargained his way out of at least a dozen years in Atlanta for collaborating with a prominent drug-lord while smuggling Renaissance art works in and out of the country by way of Mexico. Obviously, he had known too much, had too much on too many Iran-Contra-era bureaucrats. The papers never picked it up. He had agreed to forsake his pension, all charges were expunged from the unclassified documents, and nobody thought to go after his off-shore accounts.

"I guess it's basically blowing up that car that's got us upset," I said.

"Nobody really likes violence," Bougalas said. "For forty years I lived with a woman whose nerves were so delicately constructed a popcorn fart could land her in a sanitarium. It's just as well she's in a better world."

"I'm sorry for your loss."

"Selena? Selena isn't dead. Not totally. She's in Oregon. I got hurt badly in the line of duty during the middle nineties, and when I finally made it out of rehab we both decided to consecrate our lives to Jesus. Selena took it all the way. She's with the Celestine Sisters. They have an encampment."

"A life of prayer?

"A life of peeling potatoes, judging from her Christmas cards."

"Heaven is what you make of it."

Bougalas was regarding me, sizing me up with those warm mocha eyes.

"What we would like," I began again, "is some sense of who's behind all this. Who's all over us. Why."

"We understand your predicament," Bougalas said, "but I'm not at all sure—"

I decided to play my ace. "We ought to start with the bombings," I said. "The top guys in the FBI field office in Tampa have called me in a couple of times this winter. They've already established that the nitroglycerine in the charge that blew up that attorney's place in St. Pete and in the bomb under our relative's car came from the same batch. They think they know who's subcontracting this whores' picnic."

Bougalas kept very still for perhaps half a minute. This was a shift of tone he hadn't expected.

"You're not the whole explanation," I pushed, "but you and Mata Hari here are definitely in the middle of a lot of it. Whoever blew that safe came directly out of your Rolodex. You got delegated to waylay me in Philadelphia and grab my briefcase, except that there wasn't anything in there. Because we set you up – we have a cassette of videotape of you jostling the briefcase loose, and of your girlfriend here scampering around the subway in Philly attempting to pick up my trail–"

"I find that—to laugh at," Olivia broke out. "I do not scamper!"

"We even managed to make a home movie of your night in the Sofitel," I added. "Not entirely fit for family consumption."

Bougalas closed his eyes. "What do you want?" he finally said.

A lot of what I claimed to have was bogus, but he didn't know that. At least not which part.

"We want to find out who's doing what. Ramon and his hangers-on? The Mas Canosa irreconcilables? Somebody in Havana, possibly?"

I had to be very cautious here. The letters were dynamite, and Bougalas wasn't likely to know about them.

"What if we don't really know that much?"

"Find out. If we don't get this thing doped out pretty soon the Bureau will decide to fatten up its arrest record and move in on all of us. They tend to be pretty comprehensive, and before you know it that shootout of yours in Salt Lake City and everything leading up to it could wind up in court. Not to mention the newspapers. I gather the statute of limitations hasn't run out."

"When do you want answers by?"

"Soon. Now. Let's start with who hired the car bombing."

"That definitely wasn't us." Bougalas paused, then took a chance. "There is a contractor in Houston who specializes in break-ins and the demolition of evidence and—the sort of thing that happened in your attorney's shop. All we did there was pass the money orders through. The car bombing was laid on by somebody else, I assure you we would not do that, I assume that whoever it was hired the Houston team directly. A coincidence. Not that there are that many people anybody can choose from. Explosive technicians willing to go that far aren't listed in the yellow pages."

"Why *would* somebody go that far? You're in the business."

"Maybe somebody got scared. Ramon Cruz might have known something, or maybe he had been dealing with some people who didn't want their involvement to get out. They must have decided that something was starting to leak."

"Leak where?"

"Start with the office. That Medical Ventures fiasco. Olivia here knows incomparably more about that than I do. She flew over to Miami personally a couple of times to nail down our piece of the— pertaining to practical arrangements. Her Spanish is A number one."

A number one. I really was dealing with a gaffer. "So what was your take?" I asked Olivia.

Olivia recrossed her endless legs. Suddenly I could smell her perfume. "Nothing so special," she said after a moment. "Everything goes very Latin over there. Ramon is the big boss. El Jefe, gets everything he wants."

"That isn't so surprising."

"One of the things he wants, natuerlich, is one of those secretarias in the office."

"I bet I know which one," I said. "The one with the boobs."

"You been there!"

173

"I stopped by, at one point."

"Except that gets problematic. One afternoon when Ramon was late the one with the boobs saw how I knew Spanish. She is called Caridad. One time I got there early, and we were there alone, and she started to cry, and then she explained to me how Ramon was not being attentive like he was the first two years. He has decided now he is going to remain with his wife. But then the one with the boobs gets excited, and I started to hear all about how she worked before she came to Ramon at the Venezuelan consulate. The people over there love her. Maybe she will go back...."

"Isn't that where most of our business with the Cuban regime gets processed?" I asked Bougalas.

"Pretty much." Bougalas pushed out his lips and bulged down his brow. "You think the secretary might have stumbled across something in the office and ratted Ramon out to interested individuals on the island? Who arranged to bomb his car? Stupefying! What in God's name could she have picked up on?"

"Lord knows," I said, standing up. But I knew.

"You'll need to establish that," Bougalas announced. "This might be a context in which we could be of service. As you might expect, I know the Miami expatriate community intimately. For years a lot of what got those cabelleros into business in the first place was – should I be delicate? – drug-related. I was DEA. To operate effectively they required – I'm sure you can fill in the blanks. Protection. That's how I first got to know Olivia."

"She was a DEA agent?"

"She was a perpetrator. For several years the most interesting thing inside those padded, push-up brassieres everybody admired so much was not Olivia. It was cocaine. Heroin."

"She was a smuggler?"

"She was a courier. She is Alsatian. As a French national she was free to move in and out of Cuba every month. Drugs paid a lot of the bills for the Castro regime, Olivia's Spanish was serviceable and she understood how to make herself very useful at a profit to movers and shakers in Havana all up and down the line. She still knows a lot of the power players down there."

"She brought in drugs mostly?"

"She brought in everything. Diamonds. Rare manuscripts. Whatever."

"In her bra?"

"There are other places."

Olivia turned to me. "Where the sun don't shine," she said, and arched her well-plucked eyebrows and minced her lips a little.

"Olivia is very versatile," Bougalas said. "She doesn't go cheap, but she gets it done."

"I'll remember that."

Exhaling heavily, Bougalas levered himself out of his office chair with both hands and rounded his desk to escort me out the door. "I take it everything between us remains privileged, isn't that right, counselor? I would also assume you're aware that everything that goes on in this office we videotape. You know how that goes."

"Likewise, I'm sure," I said, and tapped my belly just

below my necktie where I had taped on my microrecorder. "Let's work this together from now on."

I walked out toward the elevators with as much aplomb as I could muster. Going down my mouth was dry, I was awash in perspiration. I was totally out of adrenalin. The more I began to figure this whole thing out, the more the hairs on the back of my neck were standing up.

CHAPTER XVI

By May, as ever, the tourists and Snowbirds had pretty largely given up on Florida and round-the-clock mugginess was setting in. The prospect of the summer's hurricanes put an edge of drama on our workaday lives. By that point Linda and Penelope were spending more time on the Pink Streets than at Mulcahey Court. Linda's job at Walmart seemed to be panning out; Penelope was excited by our fenced-in yard in the back and kept the squirrels jumping and rolled back and forth among the fallen calamandons. Waiting for Linda to get off shift I occasionally took Penelope to the pet compound at Lake Vista Park, where she could fetch sticks with the other dogs. I was getting domesticated.

Once Dad's properties got returned to us the events of the winter began to feel like episodes in somebody else's life. Conceivably my visit to Bougalas had resulted in word processing down the line that we would not make trouble if we were left alone. Nobody wanted the Bureau involved.

We had fought our battles; perhaps we had won. My law practice was picking up, with a lot of foreclosure renegotiation starting to come in as adjustable-rate mortgages reset. Halfway into April a Palm Beach brokerage that plugged overseas buyers into Florida investments approached Dad about disposing of a number of our up-market properties through their international clearinghouse. Newly rich Danes and Greeks and Irishmen had started to panic about the sovereign debt overhang to the Common Market and yearned to have their capital locked up in something substantial in the First World, something they could touch, like real estate in Tampa Bay.

Lawyers for the Palm Beach brokerage with power of attorney had prospects waiting. Most of the big luxury condominiums we had taken back from Ramon were still fully priced. The quickest way to transact business was for Dad personally to show up at the Bank of America complex in Miami and sign over the properties. We picked the first Monday in May; he insisted that I come along, to review the transfer documents. We could expect to receive a bank check in the neighborhood of twenty-two million dollars unless there was something none of us expected tainting any of the deeds.

At that moment averages on the Big Board were slipping into free fall, a precursor to the spring and summer of demolition that lay ahead. "It's 1987 all over again, only bigger!" Dad huffed as we started south that Sunday. "Hunting season!" People were getting hurt, he understood that, but his blood was up.

I think Dad needed somebody to talk to. I had been really bearing down in my office the previous few weeks. Everybody seemed to be someplace else. Sonny was spending time at the reservation in Oklahoma, after which he intended to drive their mother back to Florida in his Equinox to look in on Linda. It took some heavy-duty arm-twisting, but Linda, who had been tossing in her sleep lately dreaming of her abandoned son, wheedled Savage Owl into letting us pick up three-year-old Carl at the Ah-Tah-Thi-Ki museum at the Reservation on our way back through on Monday. His chance to meet his grandmother. Meanwhile, Mother was in Philadelphia for a workup by her trusted rheumatologists.

It had occurred to Dad that five hours was a long time in

my BMW for little Carl to sit placidly in the back and look out the window. I remembered the Welcome Center just off the Tamiami Canal. Carl might enjoy that cockamamie zoo, and possibly an airboat ride? Dad wasn't that captivated by the idea. We needed a second opinion. Hadn't Enrique grown up in Coral Gables, a few miles up the road? He probably knew the place, which sounded like a dump to Dad. As things were working out, Rick wasn't that far away, Rick had been in and out of Ramon's offices ever since the bombing in mid-April, keeping an eye on security there, showing the flag. Maybe he would join us.

Frankly, in view of the winter's events, I was leery of involving Rick. Dad was absolutely convinced that we were beyond that, everything was straightened out and including Rick that morning would amount to a vote of confidence. I certainly wasn't convinced but – as always with Dad – I didn't get much of a vote.

To celebrate the recovery of so much capital we splurged and stayed at The Four Seasons on South Ocean Beach. I had gone downstairs to take care of the extra room charges on our bill while Dad closed up his rollaboard and packed his pajamas and toilet kit in the scruffy little canvas top-loader duffel he always hauled along on camping trips or weekends in British country houses – wherever, a place to stow last-minute items and bottles of water and energy bars.

I got back into the room just as Dad was finishing up an exchange on his cell phone with somebody in Ramon's office. If she would just get the word to Enrique? We expected to pick Carl up close to ten at the reservation, just off Alligator Alley, then head south to Route #41 and show up at the Welcome Center at – what? – eleven o'clock in the morning or thereabouts. We'd have the little fellow with us. If Rick could make it, we'd love to have him along.

"I hope she got at least part of that," Dad mused as he clicked off. "The English wasn't wonderful. Bilingual, Caina hora! At least, we tried."

We did pick little Carl up around ten at the Big Cypress Reservation museum. I introduced Savage Owl to Dad as Charlie. Charlie was sullen, suspicious. He had not packed any kind of a bag for the child; as Carl was clambering into the back Charlie hung over the BMW as if he were tempted to grapple with the car and heave it into the Swamp. Possibly he was waiting for some kind of tip to justify parting with Carl, which he didn't get.

We did in fact get to the Welcome Center no more than a few minutes after eleven. By then a lot of the sky across the west was darkening. The roll of very distant thunder, no doubt opening up just then over Venice and Naples, boomed faintly across the sultry late morning. Dad took Carl by the hand and showed him the gorilla — which was defecating with an expression of pensive concern stressing his leather features, a major primate solving a great riddle – in a high cage behind the lavatories. The African crocodiles were as logy as on our last visit. I left Dad and Carl on their way to the aviary and went back toward the office to buy tickets for the next scheduled departure of one of the air boats. The atmosphere was very heavy.

The parking lot was filling up. I noticed a Jeep Cherokee

that reminded me a lot of Ricky's. A couple of compact-looking Latinos with thinning hair were sitting in their car with the doors open, smoking filtered cigarettes. The plump little woman we'd joked around with last time waited behind the counter, selling the tickets.

"Finally gonna get it right?" she demanded as I handed over a fifty-dollar bill. "Go get your rocks off playin' with them 'gators? You wait and see. It'll be rewardin' for you, guy! We had one woman here last week, didn't want to go near the marsh, she come back and she told me it was *the* greatest single experience of her en-tire life. Soaked her britches, though. She had on one of them old-fashioned mini-shirts, and you could easily see what she done from the back. How many in your party?"

"Three. An adult, a senior, and a three-year-old child."

"Which are you?"

"The three-year-old. "

"I like you," the woman said. "You got a sense of humor. I b'lieve I might jist run your irreverent ass 'round the Swamp myself. Ever' onct in a while I experience a personal cravin' to cut loose and whale the motherhumpin' piss out of the surrounding countryside. You'll forgive my language, I know you will."

"It's that time of day," I said.

"You got that right. You all hafta meet me over on that landing you can see over there on the left in maybe five minutes. Boat on the right. Take any place you wanna sit. We don't go no-place lessn every swingin' dick got on his life preserver. That's the law."

As we were pulling out and headed around the first wide break in the surrounding sawgrass I saw the two Latinos climbing into the other airboat. They were carrying what looked like big bags of camera equipment. "Erskine can run them fellas around," the plump woman said. She adjusted the tiller. "He's my son by an earlier relationship. Not that my hubby these days shootin' blanks. I can allus tell."

Now that we were moving faster and into the Swamp it was getting hard to follow her patter. The huge caged propeller above and behind us that drove the boat set up an intense droning whirr. Dad was holding Carl, who was very excited. His tiny hand kept jerking out to point at a flight of roseate spoonbills lifting off the water as we powered around the first bend and into the depths of the course. A gigantic carp exploded into an arc in front of us and rebroke the surface; a stippling of very fine raindrops little more than a thickened fog swept through a grove of cypress to our left and roughened the greenish water. The woman gunned the engine and executed a hairpin turn, which raised a sheet of spray.

"Moptop here is starting to get soaked," Dad said. He clawed into the little duffel between his knees and worked out a light scrolled windbreaker, which he pulled open and wrapped around Carl's shoulders. "You want some water, Buddy?"

Carl nodded, solemnly. Dad unscrewed the top of a water bottle and turned it over to him.

The squall showed signs of turning into a downpour. Thunder cracked; a bolt of lightning hit somewhere, miles to the west.

"You think I should take it in?" the woman said.

"How about you, soldier," Dad queried Carl. "Had enough?"

The child shook his head, with vigor.

"Let's go find us some alligators," the woman said. She throttled the boat up again and another heavy spray rose as we powered ahead into the depths of the preserve. The thunder was abating now; I thought I could make out the controlled sputter of the other airboat, on some parallel course. We plowed through a deserted pond of lily pads and spooked a whitetail doe and a couple of fawns, which pranced in great lunging leaps through the enveloping muck and were lost at once in the high grass. Suddenly we were hedged in on three sides by mangrove. "This little corner of our universe here is *gator heaven*," the woman said. "See them openings in the briars? Them's gator holes, they live and breed and look after their young down there in such places. Whichever babies they refrain from eatin' themselves."

Where the mangroves ended there was what looked through the incoming rain like a stand of willow. I thought I heard the engine of the other airboat just beyond there for a few seconds; then it stopped. Just where the waterline met the willows I thought I glimpsed the silhouette of a canoe. Another squall was starting to sweep in. At that moment it occurred to me that it might actually have been Rick's Cherokee I saw in the parking lot.

"Dad," I found myself shouting, "when you called Ramon's office this morning. Who did you speak with?"

"Who? I don't know. Some secretary. Unusual name."

"Caridad?"

"Yeah. That's right. I remember noticing that. Charity, doesn't it mean?"

"Let's hope so." But I could feel my stomach tightening.

The squall hit, unloading a real soaker, and the thunder opened up, and the sputter of the other airboat among the willows stopped and I could see the outline of one of the Latinos standing stiffly in the bow. There was the regular throb of something exploding in sequence; feet from our boat, muck was kicking up all along the gunnel.

"That's automatic weapon fire," I heard Dad mutter; he was milling a little frantically in his open duffel. "Sounds like an old-fashioned AK 47. He's establishing the range. Any second he'll raise his sights and finish us all." Moments later I watched Dad shove a clip of cartridges into the handle of his Beretta, steady his right wrist with his left hand, and get off the first couple of shots. The Latino seemed to be reeling momentarily in place; his weapon continued to fire on its own but wildly, high and into the overhanging foliage.

"I think I took his shoulder out," Dad said. He seemed ice-cold, academic. "You always want to hit just a little bit below and to the left of the muzzle flash."

The chunky woman running our boat was coming out of her paralysis. "Erskine!," she bellowed across the water as the main torrent of the storm struck. "Baby, it's time you get your shit together now. You bail out, hear? You get your randy little can out that boat, you hear me? I mean that, honey – forget about the boat–"

But by then the sky had opened up, the air was a waterfall,

the shooting had stopped, and there was nothing any of us could do except to wait for the monsoon to clear. Dad crouched in front of little Carl in an attempt to reassure him. "It'll be all right, pal." Dad said

The child looked up, round-eyed and excited. "Bang Bang," Carl said with tremendous enthusiasm. "Bang, bang, bang."

The storm passed over with as little warning as when it struck. A hatch of deerflies poured up out of the thicket of mangrove and descended to pepper us, something to slap away as we trolled warily closer and closer to the high boat stranded in the willows. As we came alongside it became clear that we were confronted by two bodies, the Latinos, both unconscious from multiple lacerations and heavy bleeding. Dad's bullets had in fact torn away much of the right shoulder of one of them. The AK 47, if that was what it was, had already disappeared into the muck.

Erskine, who had been alert enough to splash out into the willows when the machine guns started sliding out of one of the camera bags, had scrambled and swum to where the crud was solid enough for footing behind a stand of bulrushes. Once the rainstorm passed over, and he could see us pulling alongside, he was starting back.

One of the Latinos had toppled into the swamp water. Blood was spreading and scintillating around him, like oil. The Swamp smelt rancid.

"You leave him that way," the woman said, calming down, "them 'gators movin' in over yonder gonna drag his foul little carcass into their nest until he swells up. They'll feast on every morsel." A pair of what looked like long, knobby gray logs had started to slide out of the mangrove thicket in our direction. Something in the woman's tone suggested that abandoning the shooter might be a practical alternative.

"Let's get him back into the boat, and for God's sake both of you dimwits get in yourselves, chop-chop," Dad urged. I was already in the water grabbing the Latino around the ribs while Erskine helped. Both alligators now pulled up as close as twenty feet, then opened their jaws at us as if to yawn, then stopped. We were clambering aboard. "There must be some kind of shore patrol or rescue squad service or *somebody* we could call," Dad proposed once he was satisfied that everybody was out of the water.

"Just Elvis McKechnie. Works with the sheriff. Got his own boat."

"Let's get him out here ASAP," Dad said. He dug his cell phone out. "Will 911 make it happen?"

While we were waiting around the Welcome Center an hour later it occurred to me that now might be our chance to end this once and for all. "Let me get in touch with that FBI agent in Tampa," I proposed to Dad. "Get those people involved. Find out who put these stiffs up to something like this."

Dad thought it over, then nodded, not entirely persuaded. I made the call. Elvis McKechnie had proposed that the whole incident go on the books as an alligator attack, that the two Latinos be advised once they came to in the local infirmary that unauthorized possession of or the unprovoked discharge of an automatic weapon in Dade County amounted to a felony. A second AK 47 had turned up in the bilge at the bottom of

Erskine's boat. The County would extract a very heavy fine before either perpetrator went free. Swamp justice.

I think Dad liked the idea of putting the whole incident behind us without a lot of follow-up. That way we wouldn't have to wait around, sign depositions, no doubt come back on some inconvenient date to appear in court. Dad was already impatient because we were being held up throughout that midday waiting for the FBI. Except for two Ford Explorers with their launch trailers from the sheriff's department and a couple of rescue ambulances, the Welcome Center tarmac was deserted once we all straggled back onto shore. The downpour had probably scared away tourists for the rest of the afternoon. The car of the Latinos was still in the lot, but the Jeep Cherokee had disappeared. One of the Center's rental canoes seemed to have drifted to shore; apparently somebody had slipped it out of the racks much earlier without leaving money down.

I understood perfectly well why Dad detested the idea of tangling both of us up in some hillbilly court case. Apart from his teaching load, he was already looking at an autumn and winter of flogging his big book about Keynes, which was being published in September. This was a situation where he had his priorities, and I had mine. I liked the idea of establishing precisely who kept setting us up, and why. That way we might stay alive.

Tampa's Special Agent in Charge Vincent Hardagon, his deputy, and one technician landed in a Bureau chopper on the parking area of the Welcome Center barely an hour after he got my call. Paramedics from the infirmary were still flowing in plasma and smearing antibiotic ointments on the many wounds preliminary to binding the two Latinos up. The shoulder was effectively shattered. The FBI technician worked adroitly around the paramedics to collect fingerprints. Hardagon relieved himself of his jacket and his tie and handed them to an assistant to put back in the helicopter.

"I would imagine even you realize that we are a long way out of our jurisdiction," Hardagon breathed at me while his technician was running the prints electronically. "Only for you." His breath smelled of blended whiskey.

"You were the one who warned me off the Miami field office. Everybody in the tank?"

"In the tank. That's beautiful. You get that off some George Raft movie?"

"I'm not cool, is that what you're trying to say? Dude!"

"I don't know why I bothered with this motherhumper today," Hardagon said. "You are a pippin."

"You know you trust my judgment. This could be a really big collar, reputation-making."

"When I need you to pump up my career—" Hardagon stopped. The technician had just handed him a printout from the FBI Biometric Center. "Holy *shit!*" Hardagon said. He pulled a flat chromed flask from inside his jacket. "I think we got us a couple of live ones here."

The Latinos were Colombians, brothers, Cesar and Victor Percado. "Not your plain-brown-wrapper hit men, these two," Hardagon had to admit. "Big league, in demand, top of the Interpol wish list. Have a drink."

I took a short pull from Hardagon's flask. Awful!

"These shitheads been around a while," Hardagon said.

"Our intel people picked up on the pair of them fifteen years ago, when they were first started pulling Liberal politicians out of their apartments in Cartagena at three in the morning for the Marulanda wing of FARC. Kidnappings, a source of income for the FARC guerillas second only to cocaine. The last few years they been on notice to deal with some of the skuzzier chores certain of the international corporations and even, I'm told, certain questionable governments around the hemisphere need them to take care of. They supposedly pull down a very serious dollar."

"But why us?"

"That is the question, Bud. Why you? You probably know, but until you start to level with us you can expect to deal with clowns like these two from time to time. On this occasion I guess it worked out, but—"

"Un hunh," I said. I had a decision to make, and I made it. "I think this might have something to do with that Cuban family I told you about that my sister Wendy married into. Ramon Perez y Cruz. He came over early, when Castro let the Battalion survivors out, and he has been very active socially and in a business way in émigré affairs."

"What a surprise," Vincent Hardagon said. "You know, it started with those bums. Then came the freakin' Marilitos, the boat people. The day a couple of hundred thousand of those jailbirds arrived courtesy of Ronald Reagan Miami was absolutely dead-ass *gone*. Not that those Bay of Pigs jerkoffs were a walk in the park. I guess the Agency loved them, but they were the heart and soul of Watergate, and you can't tell me they weren't right in the middle of offing JFK. No matter what Mister Hoover wanted middle-level pogues like us to think." Hardagon took a minute to check something on his laptop.

"There's something else," I said. I took a breath. "I have reason to believe, and a certain amount of evidence for this has come my way, that Ramon has been in touch with elements on the island and has been making certain....specific arrangements for them. Getting their assets out. Against the day when Castro isn't around any more."

"That I can believe," Hardagon said. "When Gorbachev pulled the economic plug down there those campesinos were left with a choice between chopping sugar cane and peddling their overripe pussies to whatever half-ass tourists made it through the blockade. They poured in here, and – what a surprise – their whole freaking barrio turned into a political tinderbox." Hardagon arched his back and absent-mindedly started to knead his breasts. "Fucking hot!" he said. "What evidence?"

"I'll have to let that slide. For the moment. We have just managed to extract ourselves from a potentially very damaging business relationship with Ramon and his people. We need whatever leverage we can hang onto."

"What evidence?"

"That's all I can let you have. You'll probably have to get a subpoena."

Hardagon let his breath out. "You're very cute," he said. "You know that? Not that it makes me no nevermind, but I think I'm going to throw you at least part of a fish. We have our lines into Havana too. Fidel is a dead man walking, and he has been for ten years. When he goes down the termites will own the place. People in power – top people, all the way up – are cannibalizing what little is left and exporting whatever they can. They'll join their bank accounts when the opportunity arises. If the last of the bardados don't put them against the wall on the way out."

"What else is new?"

"What else is new, wiseass, is the fact that no prisoners are being taken. The pipeline is in operation, and people are dying on both ends of it. That's why you merit the Percado brothers – you know too much, and here was a chance to catch you off your home turf. You obviously did some things right – you will notice I haven't even mentioned that shoulder wound."

"That's a blessing," I said.

"I just ran your in-law, Ramon Cruz. He's no boy scout. Along with the usual fascists he was a regular asshole buddy with Miguel Recarey, another bleeding heart in the medical field who managed to scam HUD out of millions before he fled the country. All tied in closely with Governor Bush, and the late Trafficante, Jr., and a couple of fast-talking Batista knuck-ledusters from the rubber-hose era who managed to squeeze their way onto FBI payrolls. As I say, it's no boy scout troop down here."

"So what should we do?"

"Do? Come clean with us, for one thing. Then arrange to look away. Pull in your horns. These types will take one an-other out, if you leave them alone long enough."

"I wish we could," I told Hardagon.

CHAPTER XVII

By 3:30 we had managed to explain away whatever the sheriff thought he was going to need. We signed a packet of releases. The fact that I was an attorney did a lot for us. If the locals were going to make a mistake, it had better not be in front of me. It was easiest to release us on our own recognizance. Meanwhile, the FBI delegation had long since lifted off.

Dad was certainly grateful. "I had dark visions of two weeks in the no-tell motel in adorable downtown Sweetwater," he confided once we were back on Highway 41 headed west.

"What good could we do? I have a feeling from what Hardagon was implying that this is going to be the event that never was. Our hostess will have another drink and tell whoever will listen about the time two nutcases who didn't wear their life preservers turned into an alligator's dinner. The Bureau will grab both those hairpins the day they can walk again and pop them black into some off-the-books dungeon in Transylvania, where they will live on in transcripts from their interrogations. Only Carl here will get it right. 'Bang bang. Bang, bang, bang.'"

"I'm getting very depressed at having raised such a cynic," Dad said. "What did you make of Rick?"

"Of Rick?"

"Absolutely. Who else do you imagine got in behind those thugs in that canoe and disabled the living shit out of both of them?"

"You think it was Rick."

"Either him, or a saber-toothed tiger. Either he got my message, or he caught enough of my back-and-forth with Caridad and maybe heard her dial up her support group at the Venezuelan consulate and doped the rest out. So Ricky got there first. You must have seen his Cherokee."

"I thought you had things pretty well in hand. The Beretta was a surprise."

"On a visit to the Miami area? Wouldn't leave home without it." Dad put his hand on my knee. "Are you under the impression that I am totally out to lunch? I get the message that you're trying to protect me, but how could I miss what we're up against. Don't confuse yourself – I got a lucky round or two off, but against a couple of pros with machine guns? Never happen. Rick made all the difference."

"You could be right. I realize you always expected he would come around."

"Ricky is in our family. He is the father of my grandson. Look, I don't want to get all epistimological on you, but sometimes things go the way you want them to because you want them to go that way badly enough. Meanwhile – pull over at that rest stop up there. Doff gehn pischen. In Middle-High German that means: My back teeth are floating. I'm sure Carl here will join me."

We showed up in St. Petersburg not long before eight. The sunset over the Gulf of Mexico once we started north was stunning, indescribable. On Snell Isle I took Carl in to introduce him to Mother, who had gotten back from Philadelphia hours earlier. Dad poured a round of vermouths and we sat around briefly to compare notes.

Dad had cashed out in Palm Beach, which was wonderful.

We had stopped off briefly for a look at a unique zoo and an air-boat ride. Mother fussed over little Carl for several minutes, then hurried off into the kitchen to get him a small dish of ice cream and strawberries. But something wasn't right. Mother seemed distracted.

"So," Dad wanted to know, "how was Philadelphia? Overflowing brotherly love?"

"The same as always," Mother said. "Stuffy. Well organized." She started to say something, then couldn't, then started again. "The doctors weren't particularly encouraging."

"Anything too radical?" I could see the blood draining out of Dad's face.

"Not radical, exactly. It's just that things aren't progressing in what we all hoped would be a desirable direction. They've upped the prednisone. Quite a lot."

"Well," Dad said. "You knew that could happen."

"But this is obviously quite serious." Mother examined us all, her look of peaked grandeur. "They're telling me I will have to be very, very deliberate from now on. Step off the curb wrong and I could snap my femur. They raised the possibility of some motorized thingamajig. That I would ride around in. I mean – talk about *awful!*" Mother was fighting it, but I could spot tears forming. "I have to *live* in this body, Sylvan!"

"Hey, Weeze," Dad said. "We could get used to it." He forced the legendary grin. "I suppose that means sex with the trapeze is out for a while."

As I was taking the last turn off Serpentine Drive onto the Oval Crescent Annex I spotted Linda's ramshackle Volkswagen in my drive. Sonny had dropped off Linda's mother and left a few minutes before. I grabbed my carry-on and un-snapped Carl's safety belt in the back and let us both in. Linda and her mother were waiting in the living room, quietly. Penelope was sprawled out next to the door.

Linda's mother was a short but muscular woman still in her forties dressed in a shawl and a woven skirt along one seam of which raven feathers and silver studs had been stitched for ornamentation. Her hair, still dark, was braided into one plait and pinned in a tight bun above her neck. What was most striking was her eyes, like Linda's a little bit canted but even blacker, pools, as alert as a deer's, constantly searching.

"Sonny says to tell you give him a call," Linda said. "He wants to know about Palm Beach."

"I'll call him tomorrow."

Carl was standing his ground, examining his grandmother. The enormous knitted satchel with which she had just arrived sat in the floor next to his grandmother, who had settled into the sofa. Obviously, Carl liked the looks of the satchel.

"He don't know me," Linda's mother said. "I saw him two times. He know I brought. Somethings."

"Mother uses the dialect mostly back on the rez," Linda said, and smiled up at me in an extraordinarily bewitching way: our secret. "She is very, very excited to see Carl."

"And you're not?"

Linda was hunkering down to confront the child face to face. He took a step to her and she engulfed him in her hug, tears flowing down her cheeks. I'd had no idea she'd needed this so badly.

Penelope shrugged and hauled herself to her feet and began

to sniff at the mother's satchel, which smelt of peat fires in the teepees.

I arranged to meet Sonny for lunch the next day at Harvey's, a dimly lit restaurant in a small shopping center up Fourth Street North. Its management was cultivating a reputation as hip but civilized – no adult customer could expect to be blared at throughout the meal by the overhanging plasma television monitors demanded by the city's sports fanatics, or chivied cheek-to-jowl over a quick one at the bar by the singles crowd. They served the best Margaritas in town.

We passed on drinks but ordered Harvey's world-class chili. Sonny wanted to know how our trip had gone.

"Dade County is always exciting," I had to acknowledge. I detailed our adventure in the airboat, and the aftermath. "So – what's your take?" I asked when I had finished.

"I think you have made it onto the screen of some heavy, heavy hitters. Cesar and Victor Percado – congratulations, nobody sends them after just anybody. Even a back-country pissant like me runs across their debris every once in a while. I've got to think you browned off somebody with a dollar to spend. Wha'd you do?"

I hadn't had it in me before to tell Sonny about my ransom note to Ramon. Now I did. He gave me a very long look and shook his head.

"That's what got us our properties back," I said.

"I hope you'll be around long enough to enjoy 'em. I gather you don't think Ramon is your problem at this point."

"They're after him too, they blew up his car a couple of

weeks ago. They've got him thoroughly wired, from what I can tell. I think I know how."

Sonny remembered the secretary with the jugs; he too had noticed the tell-tale pinch on the shoulder. I filled him in on Olivia's comments.

"Everything certainly fits," Sonny acknowledged.

"So what do we do?"

"Arrange something. Give the letters back."

" Sure. Where? During the Friday afternoon cocktail reception at the Vinoy?" The Vinoy was the landmark hotel in town across from the yacht basin.

"I'd go to Havana," Sonny said. "Those old Sierra Maestra hands around Castro will understand the gesture. Valentia, valor, that's what they like to think it's all been about even at this late date, while they're hobbling toward the lifeboats. They stood up to Batista, and they stood up to John F. Kennedy and el gigante del norde, and then they hung on when the Soviets deserted them. They built their hard-core socialism in one country, no matter how grubby it turned out."

"Will you come along and translate?"

"That wouldn't work. I know I look like a human being, but I'm still Regular Army. I can't take meetings, especially with the functionaries of blacklisted regimes."

"Can you help at all? We're pretty generous."

"We'll have to play it as it lays. Lies."

"I guess," I said. "The first thing we'll have to do is convince Ramon he's got to give up the originals. That he should write that entire project off. That won't appeal to him."

"It just might," Sonny said. "More than another bomb."

Once the chili showed up we worked on that for a couple of minutes. We both ordered tea. "I met your mother," I remarked to Sonny. "How was the ride?"

"With my mother? Across six states? Long."

"It gave you a chance to catch up, though."

"On what? You've got to understand. She's a solid citizen, she's got a lot of amazing qualities. But she's a throwback. A refugee from the stone age. She knows a few words of English, but most of her life has been spent grinding stuff up and memorizing chants. I grew up with my father, who at least made it most of the way into the nineteenth century, and as the token aborigine in military boarding schools where the off-duty staff supervised the showers and you got demerits if you refused to grab your ankles."

"Look, I didn't mean to—"

"In my world you had to look after yourself. Whatever protection you got came basically from the tribe. At that Passover thing the other night I got a feeling for what your family is all about. Rough once in a while, but basically love."

"I guess so," I said. I didn't know what to say. "We have our ups and downs. My mother is getting pretty sick. She's in an advanced stage of lupus, which is—"

"I know what lupus is."

"I think it's worse than she lets on."

Sonny nodded, sipping at his tea. Beneath his thatch of straight ebony-black hair his face over the rim of his teacup seemed preternaturally narrow, the jaw so hollow the cheekbones cast shadows almost to his jutting chin.

"I didn't mean to put our mother down," Sonny commented after a moment. "She did what she could do." He continued to examine me. "I imagine Linda already told you this, but our mother is a healer. An eagle doctor. I suspect Linda tipped her off when she called to let mother know when I would pick her up, because I couldn't get her out of that hutch she lives in until she had packed all her roots and dried herbs and powders so she could stuff everything in that carryall of hers. She spent an hour trying to find her charcoal burner."

"You think Linda—"

"Linda loves your mother. She thinks they're kindred spirits or some such. It may be that she feels that our mother and those supposedly supernatural powers of hers could help."

"That's going to be a hard sell," I said.

"You think your mother would object?"

"Dad, possibly. Carol, certainly. We'll change Linda's name from Dances Like Fire to Plays With Fire. "

"But how do you feel?"

"Me?" I finished my tea. "What's to lose?"

I started by broaching the idea of letting Linda's mother loose on Mother to Dad. He was basically noncommittal, which was uncharacteristic and probably an index to the level of his desperation, now that Mother was losing ground so fast. Ultimately, the decision was up to Mother. I stopped by late one afternoon, while Dad was teaching his post-modern-capitalism seminar.

"But can you tell me in specific terms what this sort of procedure actually *amounts* to, Mikey?" Mother inquired. She looked as pale as her ivory dressing gown. The butterfly on her left cheek seemed to have grown darker, appeared to throb, palpably. "So often this sort of thing doesn't seem worth the discomfort. I'm not that infatuated with colonoscopies, for example."

"I'll ask, if you want me to. But I don't think what Linda's mother has got in mind involves a lot of – you know – orifice-invasion-type activity. Anything like that."

"But what–?"

"My sense is that it is closer to massage. Laying on of hands. Prayers – that sort of thing."

"Not that I would care that much whatever she did to me. If it worked. I've never been particularly...persnickety about my person, as you well know. I just want something that works. I've gotten to feel so listless these last months I suspect I've died already and everybody around here is too polite to tell me about it." She conferred on me the suggestion of a smile, her indication of agreement. "I gather that Linda thinks this is a good idea, " Mother concluded, fatalistically. "Why don't you set the whole thing up, Mike, and tell me when and where?"

I arranged for the treatment itself to take place the following Monday morning, when I knew Dad would be teaching his course on top-down economic management in authoritarian societies. The place Mother and I selected was her second-floor office-sitting-room suite, where there was a sofa and privacy and a kitchenette where Mother could brew herself tea when she was going through her art books or reading during the afternoons. I asked Anastasia to make sure the area got a good vacuuming and that the drapes off the balcony were drawn and that the overhead ventilation system in the adjacent bathroom worked. I remembered the charcoal burner. I explained that Linda's mother was a Native American healer, an expert in ancient tribal ritual we thought might help Mother.

Anastasia dropped her heavy shoulders and looked at me, her you-white-people-all-crazy look, between amused and horrified. "You don' wanna mess with nothin' like that, Mike!" she broke out. "That voodoo, the devil like to play around with spells and all that foolish damn exorcisms like you hear about. I had a friend of mines stroked *out* after she went into one of them spells like you're talkin'." Anastasia and Max were Christians, hard-shell Baptists.

"I think she'll be all right. Conventional medicine certainly isn't making it."

At ten sharp Linda appeared in her Volkswagen with her mother and her mother's satchel. By agreement both mothers had fasted for twenty-four hours to clean out and purify their bodies. Linda had told me that it was important that Mother not be encumbered with tight clothes – or many clothes – so mother came in from her bedroom in her dressing gown and underwear. Linda's mother introduced herself. She was Sakwa. She held Mother for a moment by both shoulders and indicated that she must now lie down on the Pakistani area rug on the tile floor. There was a linen closet across the hall in Mother's bathroom, and I hurried over and grabbed a couple of clean sheets and spread them out on the rug for Mother.

Mother eased out of her dressing gown and lay down on her back. I showed Sakwa where she could ignite the charcoal burner under the window in the bathroom. It was as if a single very high note, almost higher than any of us could hear, had been struck by a tuning fork. For perhaps a minute I could not speak.

"Look, Mother, would you be more comfortable—"

"Stay," Mother said. "It wouldn't be the first time you'd gazed upon thy aging mother's nakedness, would it Mike? This is your party, after all."

Sakwa pulled the charcoal burner from her satchel and went into the bathroom to prop it up on the window sill and light it with a wooden match. Then she came back and removed a shapeless object bigger than a softball covered by some unidentifiable animal's hair out of the satchel and pulled it open.

"That is my mother's medicine bundle," Linda said. "She believes that everything inside there is magic."

Sakwa tugged several clumps of dried sage grass and three semi-translucent stones and a big tuft of weeds that were still green and something black from the medicine bundle and went into the bathroom and heaped everything onto the small grate of the charcoal burner and watched it a while until it started to smoulder. The smell was heavy, a little bit dizzying.

"The black thing is something she has kept for a long, long time," Linda whispered to me. "She will now sacrifice it for you. It is the belly button of an antelope. The antelope is a holy animal for us."

Sakwa knelt beside Mother. Impassively and with great diligence Sakwa unhooked and lifted off Mother's brassiere and slid her panties down off her legs. Mother gazed back, registering little. She looked so wasted to me, like the last survivor from a concentration camp.

Sakwa felt the top of Mother's scalp. Then she looked up and muttered something in her dialect to Linda. "She says the top of your mother's head is very wet.," Linda said. "Somebody put a curse on her a long time ago. That is why she is sick. Mother will try and take out the curse."

Sakwa pulled slowly from her satchel a golden eagle's feather, the tip of which she let play all along the shrunken muscles of the front of Mother's body. Then, gingerly, she rolled Mother over and traced the lines of Mothers legs and back and shoulders. Then she placed Mother on her back again and rooted in the satchel before withdrawing a jar of what looked like glass slivers from broken beer bottles. Carefully selecting each sliver Sakwa began to make a series of crisscrossing incisions in Mother's stomach, under each lapsed breast just below the areole, in the bony hump of her mons Venus, and at the top of each thigh. Then Sakwa found another jar of what looked like a heavy paste and smeared it onto each of the incision areas. Sakwa waited several minutes before pressing her thin lips against the treated areas one by one, expectorating delicately into a rag after sucking out the paste.

"Mother is trying to be extremely careful not to swallow the paste," Linda whispered to me. "Sometimes she uses a sucking horn, but now she wants to be sure. She needs to think every second, have I got all of it out? Not swallowing even a little bit."

"What if she swallowed some?"

"That would kill her. It comes from grinding up a chunk of pork we let a water moccasin strike over and over. Then that is very powerful from the venom, so mother mixes it a little with lard."

"But how about my mother?"

"Sakwa will lick everything out in time. The tiny little bit that is left in your mother will get rid of the curse. Scare away all that water that makes everything swell up so bad so it will go away."

"I hope you're right," I said. I was genuinely terrified, my stomach was in a knot. Smoke off the charcoal burner was making my eyes water. I was supremely glad Dad wasn't around.

"My mother has done this her whole life," Linda said. "For a medicine woman it is all about fingers and lips."

"I've noticed that," I whispered thickly to Linda. "Part of your training." That was very clumsy, but I was depleted. "I suppose it makes some sense," I said. "I know they use bee-stings to help M.S. victims."

Sakwa rolled mother over and cross-hatched her buttocks at four points and then the backs of her thighs and the wings of her shoulder blades and the nape of Mother's neck. She applied the lard. Sakwa waited briefly before bending down to recover this last round. Then she traced Mother's body back and front one last time with the tip of the eagle feather.

"The important thing now is to recover the eagle feather which we cannot see but which was in your mother to make the curse get worse and worse. Sakwa thinks she has pulled it out, but the ghost of the curse will stay in this house for four days, so she must talk to the spirits now and convince them to make the ghost go away."

Squatting on her hams, Sakwa raised her palms and lost

herself for over a minute in a crooning, soaring atonal chant. Then she retrieved something from her medicine bundle and blew through it, five shrill blasts.

"What was that all about?" I asked Linda.

"That is a special protection. The sound from the eagle-bone whistle can be heard even by the Great Spirit."

Then Sakwa eased herself back down to her knees and began to dab something on each of the abrasions.

"What do you suppose that was?" I whispered to Linda.

Sakwa looked up. "Bacitracin," she said. "Don't want infection."

CHAPTER XVIII

I stopped by Brightwaters Boulevard around noon the next morning to find out how Mother was doing. Max, who was devoting the day to his regular pruning chores, put down his clippers and intercepted me before I got to the door. The day was already very hot, at least 100 degrees, and getting hotter.

"She asleep," Max said. Max pulled a bandana out of the side pocket of his immaculate coveralls and mopped off his shiny bald skull. "If she ain't been out she been close to out fo' twenty-fo' hours. That not natural, you know it, Mike, and I know it. Anastasia and I been debatin', hadn't we ought to maybe call 911 or somebody, relieve our minds. That woman done something to your mother, just sleepin' and sleepin' like she doin' ain't natural."

"Let me go up. Is Anastasia around?"

"She keepin' an eye out, nobody going to leave her alone in this condition."

Full of foreboding, I pulled open the heavy carved front door and crossed into the cool of the foyer. The long winding staircase to the central corridor of the second floor felt like the ascent to the gallows. I knew I'd have to answer for this one.

I knocked on the door to my parents' bedroom. Dad was inside, and told me to come in. Mother was up, stretched out in a bathrobe on a chaise lounge.

"I ran into Max," I said. "He thinks the Antichrist has carried you off."

"I wouldn't rule that out," Mother said. "I'm feeling a little bit flirtatious. Maybe I'll have a fling."

"Your mother has always been hard to control," Dad said, and grinned. "Now that she's feeling better we may have to post a guard."

"Somebody ought go and relieve Max' mind. He and Anastasia are obviously close to hysteria."

"They're just traditional," Dad said. "When I'm on my deathbed I intend to inform them both about the Emancipation Proclamation."

"But not before," I said

"Absolutely not. We could never replace those two."

"So you're feeling better?" I asked Mother.

"Better? Reborn. Except that my scrofulous old hide is so chopped up I look like a victim of Rocky Mountain Spotted Fever, and everything itches, I'm another girl entirely. Look, Mickey, look. Look! My hand?" She made a fist. "See, knuckles! They're back! I'm returning to duty, back on the job to meet all reasonable needs. What's next?"

I let a long breath out, very slowly. "Well," I said, stupidly, "Let's hope it's permanent." I could still make out the butterfly on her left cheek, but it was very faint.

When I got back to the office I found that the window air conditioners we depended on couldn't handle the heat. Buckley was a little beside himself. "They're diabolical, the summers here, they really are," he honked as I slid by his office. "It's like a career on Devil's Island, except that it pours every day at five o'clock and lays waste utterly to the cocktail hour. You never brought any of that up."

"I'm an unreliable recruiter," I said. "They pay me by the truckload."

"Guess who's back in town. The big guy."

"Enrique? Things must be settling down in Coral Gables."

"It could be that. My guess is, your sister laid the law down. She's getting pretty far along."

"Wendy can certainly do that," I said. Buckley obviously was undecided about where to go with this. The day we recovered our units from Sunrise Capital Partners the backstage collaboration between Buckley and Rick had ended, abruptly. No more strategizing lunches in Tampa. The dream of a career-inflating sideline in Cuban beachfront properties went up like a runaway balloon, and Buckley was back to ambulance chasing.

Andrea was in. Nothing urgent that morning – a couple of calls I would return later. I realized I ought to get in touch with Wendy and tell her what was going on with Mother. Carol could wait – the idea that Mother had put herself in the hands of a Comanche medicine woman was likely to send Carol into conniption.

Wendy picked up on the second ring. "Hey, bro," she boomed. "Keepin' Dad under control? I know I haven't been in touch, but we've been down in Coral Gables a lot and that little fucker in the oven is starting to kick. It is a boy, they've done the sonogram. Miniwawa or whatever her name is was right."

"Linda. Here's the bulletin of the day. Linda's Mother is a practitioner of tribal medicine, and she stopped by yesterday and did what she does and Mother is much improved."

"Really? Send her up to Tampa. I am not enjoying morning sickness. Listen, Ricky and I are leaving for your neck of the woods in an hour or so. Remember Gretchen Loomis, my doubles partner? That head case has managed to get herself into the finals of the women's singles runoff at Bartlett Park this week, can you believe that? *Singles*, and without my trusty backhand to carry the bitch. Ricky and I are headed down to dumpy old St. Pete to take in the match. Three P.M. Interested in joining us?"

I was about to beg off, but then it occurred to me that this might be the chance to pull Rick aside and sound him out.

"Why not," I said. "I'm not doing anything."

The tennis-center clubhouse at Bartlett Park – a kind of public-private collaboration intended to generate an oasis of upbeat activity in what was one of the slackest patches of dug-in ghetto in South St. Petersburg – was on the way out. A sagging green structure redolent of generation after generation of mildew and compounding rot, rumor had it the clubhouse went up during the Flagler era and has been programmatically neglected ever since. The building was scheduled to be razed and replaced. The regulars who played on its twelve clay courts absolutely loved the place.

Everybody in our family had taken lessons there, despite the fact that Dad insisted on joining the much more upmarket St. Petersburg Country Club. We preferred Bartlett Park for the same reason Roman senators hung out around the public bathhouses. The atmosphere was real. An elderly Cuban with outspread ears of great distinction ran the tournaments at Bartlett, backed up by the imperturbable Jackie, who supervised every breath he drew. By the time I got there Wendy and Rick had settled into Adirondack chairs on the cluttered veranda and

Gretchen Loomis was down 2-4 in the opening set.

I dragged a third Adirondack chair in next to Rick and attempted to follow the match. Gretchen won her serve but was losing the receiving game; Wendy rocked onto her feet and hooted "Go-go-go, woman! Don't let her drop-shot you like that." Wendy spotted me and gave me the finger, a traditional gesture of purest affection.

"When did you get in?" I asked Rick

"Twelve, twelve-thirty. I flew. They were supposed to take off at seven, and three times I wen' to the gate an' three times there is a problem. They didn't take off. What happen, something with the gas line. So they keep saying, no importanta, but still nobody boards."

"But you got off."

"Absoluto. Three hours late."

"Still, you got here." Rick shrugged. His cheeks and forehead and the backs of his hands looked badly scratched up.

A few minutes later Gretchen lost the first set and Wendy hoisted herself to her feet and turned to me. "You're sure Mother is all right, Mikey?"

"I think so. Maybe better than she's been for quite a while. Lupus is tricky."

"Everything is tricky. Try pregnancy. I've been here forty-five minutes and I have to hit the head again."

That seemed like a good idea; I trailed Rick into the men's toilet. Nobody else was there. There was one urinal, which was perennially backed up. It gave off a stench somewhere between congealed uric acid and a decomposing animal. A poster of Jim Courier was tacked up on the curling sheetrock above the urinal. Rick unslung his mighty pecker and directed a stream that might have come from a fire-hose into the beak of the urinal. As he was zipping up I thought I might as well say something.

"Listen, pal," I started. "We owe you. We know we owe you. How did you figure out what was coming down?"

Rick hesitated. His eyes grew calculating and he started to clench his heavy jaw. "That just happen," he said after a moment. "I pick up the extension and Caridad was telling some dude in Miami she knows how you was going to that Welcome Center, which I know where it is, and whoever that was says, well, we have backup here. We take care of this.

"I don't think Caridad understood what that means. But I understood. So I got there first."

"Needless to say—"

"You let us down with the stakeholders importante. Nobody forgets that. But you are in our family," Rick said. "It's like the SEALS: Nobody gets left behind."

"That's how Dad feels. You are the father of his first grandson. In any case, the same torpedoes who are after you are after us, apparently. "

"I get the picture," Rick said.

"I think I've figured out where the problem is, and what they're after, and how we can get them off our backs. But first I need to sit down and talk with your father. Can you make that happen? Don't tell Caridad."

"With Ramon? He can be a mule, but I will make him talk to you." Rick smiled, broadly, a rare event. He put his giant hand on my shoulder. "Don't push too hard. Since that bomb went off he is un hombre cambiando. No mismo, not the same."

"Get him to call me on my cell phone, but not from his office. We'll pick some neutral spot and work the details through. Tell your father I promise I will be mucho agreeable."

"Your Spanish is like my English," Rick said. "A horrors show."

I got the call from Ramon around three the next afternoon. I had left our office around noon to run Sakwa over to Snell Isle to check Mother out. Like any medical practitioner of integrity she insisted on a follow-up visit, and Linda had to put in her stint at Wal-Mart. Sonny expected to head back to the reservation with his mother the next morning, after swinging through Big Cypress to drop off Carl with his father.

I think Sakwa was deeply pleased to find Mother so reinvigorated. But given her heritage she was at great pains to remain impassive, prodding Mother somberly here and there to ascertain the blood flow and interpret Mother's vital signs. Mother's scalp was dry now and tingled, Sakwa indicated – excellent omens, that meant the ghosts had probably given up and fled. When Mother suggested that she would like to reimburse Sakwa for everything she had done Sakwa shook her weatherbeaten face, very gravely. This was for Linda, she told Mother. Mother had been kind to Linda. Once she got back to the reservation Sakwa would have to find herself another antelope belly-button.

Carl had come visiting with us. He intrigued Mother. Between the Prince Valiant haircut and his dusky, self-contained Swamp-Indian personality the three-year-old was an utter novelty. A doll from everybody's primeval origins, like a tiny onlooker in a George Catlin tableau of a traditional prairie rain dance. Carl *was* willing to accept another bowl of ice cream and strawberries.

I had just run Sakwa and Carl back to the Oval Crescent Annex and let Penelope out to chase Carl around in the yard when Ramon telephoned. At first his manner was wary, if not hostile, but he was listening. He was out of his office. Yes, he understood that we certainly had nothing to do with the dynamiting of his Lexus. Yes, Enrique had divulged to him that there had been an attack on us, on Dad, sometime the week before. Ramon hoped we would understand that as a matter of honor he would not have known in advance about anything like that, he personally would have prevented such an indescribable brutalidad. He was very proud that Enrique had taken it upon himself to help….

The difficulty appeared to be, I attempted to suggest to Ramon, that information about Ramon's more—more confidential sidelines, if that was the right word, had leaked. Caridad in his office was in touch with her ex-officemates in the Venezuelan consulate. Ramon's most substantial clients – people of importance on the island – these people were alarmed. They had written letters, and Ramon was holding these letters. And so much exposure was extremely dangerous for people of such importance, Fidel was still potent enough to exact a terrible revenge on even the closest of his life-long comrades once he had determined that they intended to abandon the revolution—

There was a long, long pause on Ramon's end. So, he said finally, what did I propose that he should do?

I said I felt that there was only one way. Meet me. Give me the originals of all the letters. I had a way to return them to their senders. Along with that I would need all the contact information he could come up with about his clients – addresses, telephone, bank account numbers and locations. Enough so that when they realized how much damage we could do them they would feel compelled to back off.

Once I got all the ammunition I would need I would turn up in Havana personally and turn over the originals myself to Ramon's list of disillusioned functionaries. Along with that I had a few ideas about how to keep them worried enough to leave us alone from now on.

Ramon was silent for some time. But what if the comrades refused to do a thing like this? he asked when he had decided to speak.

Then they would probably kill all of us, one by one. But that's what they've obviously decided to do in any case. Let's try and make it too expensive for them to think about.

Perhaps a minute passed. Ramon's inflection when he did decide to respond was heavy, resigned. Where did I want to meet? he asked.

There is a Hilton Garden Inn on the main road to the raceway where Interstate 4 deadends at Interstate 95 just west of Daytona Beach. I had stayed over there during Bike Week a couple of times during a passing flirtation with a Harley toward the end of my teens. The motel was two-plus hours from Coral Gables and perhaps four from St. Pete, enough of a haul to discourage in-town surveillance. Anybody tracking our cars on the highway should be easy to spot.

I got there perhaps forty minutes before Ramon and settled into a chair in the lobby with a clear view of the entrance. That week the first real stint of insufferable heat was settling in, day after day, and everybody was scurrying from one air-conditioned refuge to the next. Ramon appeared in the kind of cord suit and hand-painted necktie I had not seen in Florida for years.

He walked in and looked around, but I wasn't at all sure he recognized me. He looked a lot older than he had at Ricky's wedding a few years earlier. His hair was thinning fast and he was permitting it to go to gray and beneath his eyes had developed the tell-tale pouches of a man for whom sleep didn't come easily.

As I stood slowly and approached Ramon he did summon up that hard professional smile. "It has been too long a time," he greeted me with. "Enrique tells me every time what is happening with your part of the family, and Annilita and I myself speak very often how we should just hop in the buggy and come see our Tampa relatives."

"We'd like that," I said. Ramon's stilted, transliterated English struck me now as moving. Endearing.

We sat down; Ramon put his attaché case down so that it leaned against his chair. "All during the drive on the Interstate I think about what you say," he opened. "The letters." Ramon extruded his lower lip. "Maybe that works, I don't know. But how do you bring the letters to Havana? I don't think through the customs. The inspectors will just grab them, don't you think?"

"I certainly wouldn't carry them in with me," I said. "I'll

have them there when the time is right."

"Ah. The certitude of the young. When the time is right, si. Claro." Ramon looked down, an expression between irony and resignation lighting up his pinched face. "But I can tell you do things sometimes by which I have been surprise. You or the father. You get what you are after."

"What I am after here, Ramon, is putting together some kind of an arrangement following which your unhappy ex-clients in Havana don't blow all our miserable asses to smithereens." The vehemence of my own response startled me. I knew that I was bluffing to a certain extent; probably I was overcompensating. "This a dangerous fucking game, Ramon, and nobody in our group wants another round of tribal warfare, or whatever the hell this is."

Ramon looked at me.

"You're going to have a grandson pretty soon," I pressed on. "We don't want him looking over his shoulder until he's ninety years old. We're all going to have to take some chances. Your cover is blown, and our cover is blown, so let's bring this thing to a head one way or another. I'm really not here to negotiate."

Ramon continued to examine me, his brow drawn down, on the edge of surly. At that moment I thought I had overplayed it.

He stood up. I stood up. Ramon opened his attaché case and extracted a large, thick mailer. Still rigid with bruised machismo he handed it to me and headed toward the revolving door. A gusher of heat enveloped the lobby.

CHAPTER XIX

Making arrangements for Havana turned out to be – on the logistical level – a lot easier than I expected. In the post-Soviet austerity tourism was stressed; entry procedures for foreigners were comparatively lax – none of the groping and orifice-searching that plagues us in the States. No incoming ninety-one-year-old incontinent would have to worry about the authorities wringing out her dignity breeches before she got her shoes back on to make sure her overflow wasn't combustible.

Little by little, as the Mas Canosa generation continued to age, the U.S. government began to relax its ruinous embargo. Interest groups, professional associations, could bloc-book and fly in directly and take advantage of the dollar as against the discredited peso. Like an antiquated leper colony, post-Cold-War Cuba was absorbing to scientists, economists in particular. Academic groups from the frozen north liked to collect in conference rooms and auditoriums around Havana; such groups rarely scheduled meetings into the late spring.

One did that year. The Global Round Table on Preemptive Debt Reduction had arranged to meet in Havana the first week of June, 2008. Its chairperson, Doctor Mary-Ellen Fondling, was somebody Dad once liked to kid around with during his apprenticeship in New Haven. One call and Dad had been penciled in to read a paper on Keynes. I would accompany him as his research assistant. There was even grant money.

The hard part now was to alert that killer's row on Ramon's list and strike the deal. A B.U. classmate of mine who had migrated to Miami and built a law practice that specialized in the thin flow of business litigation authorized between the States and Havana had access to computer screens designed to spell out who was who among the Maximum Leader's favorites along with the last known contact information. It stood to reason that a number of the names and a lot of the locations Ramon had turned over to me were out of date. I'd have to find somebody savvy and connected enough around Havana to jump onto the island well ahead of both of us and make the bureaucratic rounds personally, track Ramon's clients down and set up a group meeting.

When I had hinted to Cedric Bougalas that we would be working together to deal with the Cuban problem I had been spouting bravado, misdirection. But now I realized I really did not know anybody else with savoir faire enough to work both sides of the street in that ramshackle but still very dangerous dictatorship.

As things developed, I was able to bypass the twit at the front desk and get through to Bougalas in mid-May and arrange to meet at a seafood restaurant in Palmetto, The Crab Trap, just beyond the Skyway Bridge on the highway to Brandenton. We got together over dinner one stormy Thursday evening.

Bougalas' henchwoman, Olivia Broulee, was very much along. The Trap was popular, it didn't take reservations, but we got there early enough to pick up an out-of-the-way booth for three. The place was clamorous with the initial seating of the evening, pouring down rum-based cocktails and feeding, heavily. Cedric Bougalas was obviously pleased that I had turned to him: he oozed complacency, a compound of the kittenish and the sinister.

Olivia was all attention. She wore a loose, low-cut, off-the-shoulder dress that did not leave a lot of questions about her mature poitrin. Whenever she leaned forward – which she arranged to do, several times, always in my direction – every question was answered.

To start things off we sipped a round of mimosas. "I realize you have a lot on your plate," Bougalas opened, "but before we tackle anything substantive I want to emphasize how—how incomplete we both felt when you turned on your heel and bolted our office last month. Chewed us out, made very clear what dummies you had played us for, and vamoosed. We just sat there looking at each other. And Olivia here is not the sort of female whose animal spirits you want to depress."

"Probably I was rude," I admitted. "We were under attack. I needed to sort things out."

"But now you're under the impression you have the upper hand."

"I think there might be a way to relieve ourselves of this nightmare."

An aproned waiter laid out a complementary serving of cheese-stuffed portabello mushrooms and waited for our entrée orders. I selected the rock lobster tails, Bougalas took the crab au gratin, and Olivia decided on the alligator bites.

"You *are* an adventurous eater," I said. "Alligator?"

"They are extremely tasty," Olivia assured me in her saucy Alsatian inflection. "Gamey, and a bischen oily sometimes, but always very flavor full."

'Still – alligator?"

"It's worse than you think," Bougalas said, about to rock with laughter. "These people are attempting to remain genteel, but all over Creole country this dish is advertised as alligator balls. And why not? People eat hanger steaks and nobody thinks anything about that. Aren't we primarily carnivores?"

"I'm just waiting around to find out what Olivia is having for dessert," I said. That definitely broke the ice.

Once the waiter finished laying out the main course I got down to business. As I had indicated in Sarasota, our family had been attacked. There had been a follow-up attack earlier in the month. There was a lot of evidence that all this was instigated by highly placed individuals in the Cuban government who were worried as hell because we were aware of the extent of their trafficking, through Ramon Perez y Cruz – Bougalas' other recent employer, I couldn't resist adding – in valuables stolen from the bourgeoisie at the time of the revolution. These valuables were now supposedly awaiting the functionaries who had pilfered them in banks all around Europe and the Caribbean.

We knew who was corrupt. We knew where the loot was stored. We had acquired the originals of every piece of correspondence with our mutual acquaintance, Ramon Perez y Cruz, as well as receipted vouchers and deposit numbers from quite an array of foreign banks. The governments on every side of this betrayal of trust in the Revolution were guaranteed to clamp down swiftly if they got evidence of any of this. It had the makings of an international media circus. Nobody involved would survive the scandal.

"That's not too far from what we surmised," Bougalas acknowledged, suppressing a belch. "Those hypocritical greasers down there are without a doubt already moistening their knickers at the prospect of any of this getting out. Where do you see Strategic Opportunities in all this?"

"It's not that complicated. We want a truce. You might send somebody like Olivia, who you say knows her way around Havana and speaks the language. Let her hand-deliver our assurances to any of Ramon's old clients that we have their letters and all that paperwork from the depositories. That we would like to trade. After that we make an appearance in Cuba and give them their correspondence back, and they forget about us."

"That sounds like a lot of assumptions," Bougalas said. "But what the hey, nothing is totally out of the question. How many on the list?"

"I researched that. Fourteen over the years, but three have died. Two in front of firing squads. Three women, eight men left. A couple of the men have made it all the way to the top – deputies, elected to the Council of State, just under Raul. One is still a delegate to the People's Assembly, three work in the agricultural bureaucracy, and two in the office that watches over the media on the island. Such as they are. The rest appear to be retired. I managed to track down recent addresses."

"But even if you bring off a thing like that," Bougalas asked, "How will you enforce it? You know, these garlic mashed potatoes are tremendously good. Do you think they'd bring me another serving?"

"I assume it would be self-enforcing. The ones that agreed to the standoff wouldn't want to compromise themselves further by going after us. They'd have to keep an eye on the others. If there was trouble – and I would stress this in Havana – any of us that survived and/or friends they would never identify in time would get the facts into the public domain in a hellova hurry."

"Again," Bougalas said; he was signaling the waiter. "Olivia slips into Cuba and rounds all these people up. Then?"

"My father and I will be at the hoary old Hotel Nacional at a sort of convention on the island the weekend of June 8. We'll book some sort of room where we can talk directly to everybody involved. If Olivia would bring them in, and translate wherever that is necessary, we'll take care of the rest. I hope we will. We'll reserve a room for her."

The waiter made it to the table. "I don't suppose there would be one last serving of these delectable potatoes left in the kitchen for a wounded old combat veteran like myself," Bougalas wanted to know. The waiter nodded, and disappeared.

"Care for more potatoes?" Bougalas asked Olivia.

"I believe, no."

"How are the alligator balls?" I asked.

"Quite rich," Olivia said, and bestowed on me the mildest of smiles. "In places, stringy. I think they need to marinate them perhaps a little bit longer. Still, the idea is entzuckend." She examined Bougalas for a moment. "What about the money?"

"Women!" Bougalas erupted. "Forever preoccupied with

animal needs! Narcissists every blooming one of them." He turned in his chair to confront me, full-face. "Let us say fifty thousand dollars."

"That could happen," I said. "Half shortly, half afterwards?"

Bougalas managed to look stricken. "Do I detect an element of mistrust?"

"At least an element."

"You're not an easy man to do business with," Bougalas said. "I had an afterthought. Something to sweeten the deal. What if you were to turn over to my associate here and myself the overseas banking locations and account numbers of the Comrades who are already dead? Perhaps the firing-squad victims."

"So you could con your way into those safe deposit boxes, and pretty soon their survivors are hunting us down? Get serious. What did my law-school pals from Chelsea say: 'Don't make me laugh, my lips are chapped.'"

"I think you spent a little too long in law school, lad," Bougalas said. "It has warped your relationships with your fellow man."

"It's worse than you think," I said. Outside, the rainstorm was pounding against the low metal roof above our heads. "It's starting to pour," I said. "And here we are with three months at least to go before the hurricane season."

"Let's not invite catastrophe," Bougalas said He was finishing the potatoes.

Perhaps a half hour later, when we finally left, it was really coming down. We had to splash all the way through the parking lot to make it to our cars.

CHAPTER XX

When we arrived to board our flight to Havana on June 6, Dad and I discovered that our fellow members of The Global Round Table on Preemptive Debt Reduction took up most of the American Airlines charter. Which was just as well, because the dozen or so Cubans on American Eagle Flight 17 needed every leftover inch of space – I spotted several microwave ovens still in their discount-house cartons, many unidentifiable items in shrink-wrapped packaging, a half-a-dozen Queen Size blankets stuffed into one garbage bag, a duffel so packed with canned goods it took two Cuban heavies to chivvy it into an overhead rack, a cage with parrots, canaries and something that looked like a Plymouth Rock hen which one extremely swarthy and rotund traveler cradled on her lap. I have no idea what made it in the baggage compartment.

I had assumed it would be foolhardy to carry that precious trove of letters from Ramon's safe into Cuba myself. Both Dad and I would have to get by with vestigial high-school Spanish at best to explain away anything the inspectors turned up while we were processing through customs. Still, when our little charter banged onto the crumbling runway of the Jose Marti International Airport outside Havana I began to wonder whether I had been too apprehensive. Emerging from that airless cabin – which, after an hour and a half, stank overpoweringly of chicken shit – our delegation was barely questioned. Nobody ransacked the bags. The languid airport security clerks showed very little interest in our passports. We all trudged directly onto the big air-conditioned bus in front of a nostalgic

billboard of Che Guevara and another of George W. Bush sub-
titled Terrorista! We were on our way to the hotel in fifteen
minutes.

The Hotel Nacional de Cuba, where all The Global Round
Table members would be staying and where our colloquia were
booked in conference rooms, is itself a kind of massive cultural
artifact, a showplace for the furtive nostalgia even many Cas-
tro-era Cubans nurture for the disappearing past. Crowned by
its Iberian bell towers, after more than eighty years the Nacional conveys a kind of soiled dignity all its own, a sprawling
high-rise layer-cake in its own park that overhangs the swarm-
ing pedestrian life along the Malecon and affords guests lucky
enough to book rooms on the water side unbroken exposure to
the Straits of Florida.

The Nacional opened up for business in 1930 and immediately attracted an American clientele that knew what it liked.
Hollywood hard cases consorted with Joe Kennedy and his
feckless son Jack here, the Mob held Commission meetings to
welcome Lucky Luciano back from exile in Italy – Frank Sinatra sang – and agree on Bugsy Siegel's execution. Meyer Lansky oversaw the Casino. Until Castro took over, the susceptible
flocked to Havana to partake of what Graham Greene later
characterized as the "louche atmosphere" of the capital, "the
brothel life, the roulette in every hotel...I liked the idea that
one could obtain anything at will, whether drugs, women or
goats...."

By June of 2008 goats were hard to find around the Nacional, but there were plenty of suggestions that even the
sternest revolutionaries were not above a secret hankering for

the old indulgent days. Incapacitated by diverticulitus, Fidel had handed off the presidency to Raul a few months earlier, but as long as el Caballo was conscious there was no doubt on the street about where the power lay. The Nacional was a relic, a museum of capitalist temptations with which to tempt the tourists. Huge posters of George Raft and Frank Sinatra and Rita Hayworth were plastered up around the walls of the Cafeteria el Rincon del Cine in the basement of the Nacional. Movies of the era ran non-stop on the giant TV screen.

Dad and I identified the Cafeteria immediately as a potential hideout between – in my case, usually, during – the jargon-choked presentations the academics in our party were so eager to share with their fellow Round Table conscripts. Several times even Dad sat one or another of the papers out. Once Mary-Ellen Fondling herself sneaked out after she had made the introduction and found us in the Cafeteria.

"I heard Maxine give an earlier version of that paper in Albuquerque," Mary-Ellen offered by way of apology as she seated herself at our table. "They'll have to forgive me." She gave Dad what I suspect she thought as a very wicked look. "I've gotten a lot better at forgiving myself since my divorce from Stanley," she wanted Dad to know.

Mary-Ellen was a pleasant looking woman in her fifties, perhaps a little bit fully packed but assertively in the game. When she scurried off to introduce the next speaker I asked how long Dad had known Mary-Ellen.

"I was her tutor at Yale."

"At least that. How was she?"

"How was she?" Dad gave me a mischievous look. "Pretty

good shtupping, actually. Except that afterwards there were always the tears. She came from serious Irish-Catholic stock, the O'Shaughnessys. The day your mother came along that was all over. Things got a lot more cheerful."

"I'm sorry I asked," I said. It was eleven AM. Just before I met Dad downstairs I had found Olivia Broulee in the lobby as prearranged and pinned down our timetable. Olivia had on a perfectly tailored black pants-suit and a velvet cloche trimmed with what might have been woodcock feathers. I was beginning to catch on that for Olivia, as with Sakwa, feathers were very important.

Olivia had been able to locate and alert nine of the eleven survivors on Ramon's list and all but one agreed to meet Olivia at the hotel entrance at three, when she would conduct the party directly to one of the smaller conference rooms. I had booked Seminario Casa C. "The ones I talked with have told me they can deal with the others." Olivia said. "I think you have them entirely frightened."

"That's fine with me. I just don't want any State Seguridad types busting in when we make the trade."

"Have you got the letters?"

"They're on the way," I assured Olivia. They had better be, I couldn't help thinking.

"I got the room across from you," Olivia put in, brightly. "From you and der Vati."

"How did you work that out?"

"How? Liebling, I make a lot of business in this hotel."

By 2:30 I was back in the lobby, flopped into one of the overstuffed chairs within sight of the main entrance. The lobby was enormous, one grouping after another of badly faded art deco furniture. Stupendous overhanging chandeliers. I watched the door for a couple of minutes and then headed – mostly for something to do, I was very nervous – toward the Gentlemen's Lavatory somewhere behind the lines forming at the check-in desk. I made my way by a couple arguing and a nun in a wheelchair and a puffy-faced gaffer in a baseball cap with grizzled hair flowing down his back and Koolray sunglasses and a prosthetic limb of some kind clamped on to replace his left calf, which stuck out sideways while he dozed. Just as I was passing I heard the old man attempting to clatter to his feet and begin stumping along behind me. I pushed through into the Men's Room and, just as I had begun to organize myself, the gaffer staggered into the urinal stall next to the one I was using and grabbed the intervening marble barrier for balance.

"Are you OK?" I said. "Can I help? Ayudar?"

"What did you have in mind?" the gaffer wanted to know, popping something that looked like a pair of small foam-rubber water wings out of his mouth. "I catch you anywhere near my parts and you are in for heap big trouble, white boy. Is this the sort of behavior you indulge in on foreign soil? I've heard about people like you. Caucasians, mostly."

"Jesus," I said. "Sonny! I was just about to run down to the Malecon and jump into the sea. You've got the letters and the rest of that stuff?"

"I said you'd have everything by 2:45, and here we are. Do you always transact business with your pecker out?"

"Lately I seem to. It just works better that way."

"I'm having second thoughts about you. You may not be

brother-in-law material after all."

I took the plump dark postal mailer Sonny had extended to me and sighed, heavily. I was at the same time relieved to have the letters and banking confirmations as promised and petrified that this entire transaction could go sour in a New York minute and there I would be, implicated by enough evidence for a dozen lifetimes in one of Castro's blackest lockups.

"I'm still very high on *you*," I assured Sonny. "What are you going to do now?"

"Stick around. Catch up on my sleep in the lobby. If you aren't back down here by four I'll figure out what else I have to do to make sure you get out of this piss-hole in one piece."

"That wasn't part of the arrangement," I said. "You don't have to do that."

"I'm not doing this for you. I'm doing it for the father of my newest nephew. Or niece. Even Linda isn't sure yet."

"What?"

"Obviously the last to know. And you're surprised? Didn't they teach sex education at B. U. Law School? If you will please zip up I will be on my way. The caballero that just walked in is eyeing you. He may be cruising for a date, and how could I explain your motives?" Sonny slipped the water wings back into place, adjusted his cap, and hobbled towards the door.

My head buzzing, I made my way across the lobby and headed up to our room on the fourteenth floor for ten minutes to catch my breath. I tucked Sonny's envelope into a document case and stretched out on one of the beds. I was too tense. I got up and went back out and summoned the elevator.

Back in the lobby I identified the correct side corridor and spotted Seminario Casa C. For most of the previous hour Dad had been holding forth in front of the Roundtable group about Keynes and countercyclical public spending during the Great Depression. But he had shut the questions off early and joined me at three precisely.

For five minutes nobody else showed up, which was unnerving in and of itself. Seminario Casa C was truly a dump – the walls were stained with mold streaks the color of black tea and much of the plaster ceiling had come away in big shags that revealed the underlying wooden lath. The air was dusty, a dry putrescence from inside the walls.

Havana itself was like that, I had been reading. Twenty-three percent of the housing, including the atrocious high-rises the Soviets had contributed, was in constant danger of collapse. Houses were falling in on themselves every day, brought down as often as not by an afternoon rainstorm, crushing inhabitants and piling up as rubble for months or years before the authorities got around to clearing the sites.

They didn't need that many parking lots for the cranky Ladas and vintage 1958 Pontiacs that survived on the streets. Bicycle rickshaws were a commonplace. Everything was controlled, forbidden for the most part. Citizens, hungry all the time on their reduced quotas of rice and beans, were living in a kind of time-lapse demolition site. Meat was so precious that rumors were going around that used condoms got mixed with the sauce to thicken pizzas as they were sliding into the oven.

Around ten minutes after three we heard the delegation approaching in the hall. Olivia conducted them in. Seven had actually showed up. Two of the men – I had to assume that they were the deputies to the State Council – were way up in their seventies or early eighties, both dressed in the olive-drab fatigues of the revolutionary militia, both with the emblems of rank and full if scraggy beards and glittery eyes and capped teeth that marked Fidel himself. That should have tipped me off that this was not going to be that simple, but I was elated that we had gotten this far. The other five looked like ordinary Cubans – the three men in slacks and open shirts and the women in middle-class skirts and unadorned rayon blouses, very buttoned-up.

Olivia introduced them all; it was confusing at first to keep their names straight. One of the women, a short, wiry editor from the staff of the official daily *Granma* with a stupefying wen underneath one eye, stepped forward and announced immediately that she commanded enough English to interpret for the group. She came over as inherently disapproving, her lacquered hair pulled back in a tight bun. One of the younger arrivals, a moon-faced civilian named Lopez whom Olivia identified as the delegate to the People's Assembly, positioned himself above the short woman's shoulder. Her commissar, I suspected, proctoring every word.

In simplified but coherent Spanish Olivia laid out what case we had. We were, above all, innocent parties. It happened that a daughter of el Senor Landau here had married into a family of Cuban immigrants in Florida. An influential member of that family, Ramon Perez y Cruz, seems to have developed a professional sideline by means of which he was able to help transfer certain—certain assets that individuals associated with the regime had collected to depositories abroad for safekeeping. There was correspondence involved, bank vouchers. Paperwork which could prove confusing to the authorities in Havana.

By accident Senor Landau came into possession of this information. Purely by accident. We have now been made aware that individuals implicated in these transfers – people in this room, let us remain honest – people here discovered the situation and were so alarmed that incidents of violence have now occurred in the United States. Against the families of Senor Landau and Senor Ramon. We wish these incidents to stop.

We have come here to give to you the evidence we have. We wish the matter to end with this meeting. We ask nothing – no payback, no remuneration. You take the evidence, the letters, the deposit slips…. Whatever you do after that we do not wish to discover. You are people of honor. We require only the word of all here who made use of Senor Ramon's services that when you take these papers back we will disappear from any future transactions. That you will ignore us after this.

Olivia stopped talking. I had the documents from Sonny in the zip-up briefcase under my arm. I expected the editor to respond for the group, but instead a kind of low-grade tumult broke out. There was obviously disagreement, fierce at moments, too frantic for me to begin to comprehend.

"Perhaps we step out in the hall," Olivia said, letting her voice rise. But the exchange was much too intense for any of them to respond. "We go into the hall," Olivia said, very loud. Dad and I followed her out.

Outside in the corridor stood two burly specimens in

checked shirts I had not been aware of earlier, probably plain-clothes policemen. "This wasn't part of the deal, as I under-stood the deal," I complained immediately to Olivia.

"I did not understand this either," Olivia said. Dad and I walked down the hall a few steps, and Olivia followed. She slipped into place to where we could shield her from the stares of the policemen and opened her copious handbag.

"A Walther with a silencer!" Dad burst out, then covered his mouth.

"By me I have also a concussion grenade," Olivia said. "Wenn this goes too bad stay by me near the door, and I will roll it in there under the window and we go blitzschnell through to the back. We have a van waiting. To a private aircraft."

"You guys are full service providers," Dad mumbled. The cops in the hall had started to watch us.

"Exit strategy. Remember: Strategic Investments? Also, we like to collect the other $25,000."

"You better let me blow the whistle on that pistol. I really don't want anybody to get killed."

Olivia nodded agreement, not happy. The door to Semi-nario Casa C was coming open, slowly. The editor stepped out. We followed her back in.

"What's with the meatloaf in the hall?" I wanted to know. "This was supposed to be an off-the-record-type meeting."

The editor shrugged. "In socialist society no secrets all the time, like with you," she informed me. "Our leadership says, sunlight makes purificacion for everything." She looked to Olivia.

"Makes clean," Olivia said.

"Yes. Cleans. Here we discuss all matters in a democratic fashion, and then comes the decision."

"What are the choices here, would you say?" Dad asked.

"Comrades in this group have commit crimes against the state. Against Cuba. And now you want to cov—"

Suddenly one of the veterans in the green uniform of a Co-mandante was starting to rant. Olivia attempted to interpret for us. He was, Olivia translated, an old man now. He had been side by side with The Maximum Leader when they stormed the Moncada barracks. He sat in prison with Fidel. They fought together again in the Sierra Maestra. During the evil time of the Special Period after the Russians sold them out he had become disheartened, la lucha seemed too hard. He had been contacted by one of those maggots in Miami, and he had agreed with this gusano to place some heirloom jewelry from his family in safekeeping outside the country.

Tears streamed from the old man's eyes. That was a terrible mistake. Now he must die in Cuba. If the leadership decided that he would die in prison, he was prepared to accept that.

The emotion rising from all the others was palpable, like steam. The editor confronted Dad and me.

"We have made our plebiscite," she informed us. "Keep the documents. We are every one of us in agreement with the honored companero here. Cuba must remain foremost. Several of us have already seen the inside of the Combinada del Este."

"That is the main prison in Cuba," Olivia said.

CHAPTER XXI

There was a kind of restrained collective grunt emerging from the delegation; at just that moment a face looked in from the slightly ajar door: Mary-Ellen Fondling. Horrified, Dad took a step to push her out again but she had edged into the seminar room while one of the guards outside slammed the door shut.

I heard Dad take a very deep breath. "Please tell the madam editor that I would really appreciate the opportunity to say something to the group myself," Dad said.

The editor translated; there was general ascent. "This is a democratic society," the editor said. "Please, not at too great length, because the guards outside are waiting to take you directly to the State Security Offices in Villa Marista."

"I can't wait," Dad said. He put his arm around Olivia's shoulders. "Jetzt muss du uebersetzen," Dad breathed at her.

"Du sprichts Deutsch?"

"Genugend," Dad said.

"En Espanol o English, por favor," the editor said.

A cold sweat was appearing across Dad's temples. "But first," he said, "the lady who just turned up came in by accident. She's one of those precious tourists the government keeps trying to attract. She just wanted a word with me. You should let her leave."

"Too late," the editor said. "The authorities must decide those things."

"Why am I not surprised?" Dad said. "OK, this is where I'm coming from. First, my son here and I are at most the messengers. We had nothing to do with any of this. No matter how things work out we will not profit one penny. All we ever wanted was for the whole thing to end quietly. I think that right now Senor Ramon feels the same way. He is prepared to turn the whole schlamazel over to anybody available around here and just walk away."

"I don't know schlamazel," Olivia said when she got that far.

"Mess is fine," Dad said. "The point is, we're turning over to your people every bit of the evidence that involves the entire matter. You work it out, decide who gets what or maybe the regime gets whatever there is, and that ends it. You dick us over and pretty soon people in the States, in the government, are going to look into this thing. That's not going to help with your embargo problem."

"Dick man over?" Olivia questioned.

"Schwierigkeit machen," Dad said. "You guys will catch the blame."

I could sense the uneasiness beginning to sweep the group.

"What has any of this to do with socialist principles?" the editor demanded.

"What good are your socialist principles going to do you if the regime isn't around in five years. I hadn't expected to have to bring this up, but something else surfaced you ought to think about."

Lopez, the delegate to the People's Assembly who had been attending rather languidly until now, suddenly spoke up. "At times socialist principles require flexibility," he put in. His English was almost without identifiable accent. "What else is there?"

All right," Dad said. He took a deep breath. "Over the course of this kerfuffle we picked up a geodetic survey map of this island on which are pinpointed the important deposits of rare earth, where, the specific types, and estimated tonnages. Plus core samples from each location. We—"

"We waste time," the editor said, sharply. "I told the guards before four o'clock—"

"Calmese!" Lopez commanded. "We must hear this."

"I've talked with a number of my colleagues in the scientific community," Dad continued, "and every one of them says that if word of these mineral finds ever gets around, the isolation the regime keeps complaining about will collapse in a heartbeat. The question is, will Molycorp or BHP Billiton take the place over first? Remember, U.S. Marines never did leave Guatanamo."

"How will that be?" Lopez said. Olivia continued to translate, but sketchily.

"What has kept Cuba socialist all these years is the fact that the place is fundamentally worthless." Dad was warming to his subject. "Cane brakes and soggy putas. Historians I've spoken with suspect that the only reason the Kennedys were so apeshit to take the island back was because old Joe still controlled the Coca Cola franchise and Meyer Lansky had his ass in a crack about losing his gambling rights."

"What is ass-in-a-crack?" Olivia wanted to know.

"Pissed off. Now – after water, rare earth is probably the most sought-after commodity on the planet. The age of computers would flame out overnight without these specialized minerals. China holds the important deposits, and they've already started to dole the stuff out very sparingly."

Lopez looked extremely earnest.

"You let us alone and this will be our secret. If any of us have to get anywhere near socialist justice my colleagues are under instruction to plaster up word of this bonanza on every media outlet you can imagine. The same holds if anybody in our family, or Ramon's family, even stubs his or her toe back in the States."

The editor from *Granma* had gone from shock to anger. "Please do not think that you can—" she began; the wen beneath her eye seemed to darken, to throb.

Lopez shut her down. "These are new facts," he announced. "We will have to hold another plebiscite. You must wait in the hall," he instructed us.

"Fine," Dad said. "But I expect you to let this colleague of mine go." He nodded toward Mary-Ellen Fondling. "She is a mere economist, she really doesn't understand anything about how the world works. This has nothing to do with her."

"Thanks a bunch!" Mary-Ellen gasped at Dad. But she had picked up enough on the drift of events not to waste any time before scuttering through the door.

The plebiscite did not take long. Lopez himself came out to deliver the news. We were free to go. Or stay.

I unzipped my document case and solemnly turned the sealed mailer inside over to delegate Lopez. He accepted it without emotion. This exchange of views had never happened, he suggested. He hoped we would enjoy the remaining days of our convention in Cuba and that we would recommend the island to our friends. He had found my father very eloquent.

CHAPTER XXII

There was a patio under the eaves on the Gulf side of the hotel set out in handsome native furniture, the ideal place to order the drinks we all needed badly by then. Dad led Olivia and me out of Seminario Casa C and up the corridor and into the lobby. It was perhaps a minute before four: Behind one of the pillars I spotted the geezer version of Sonny, already beginning to pull his wooden leg in under him, preparing to rescue us all.

"Dad nailed it," I informed Sonny under my breath as we went by. "Find us on the patio."

We settled into the big woven-raffia armchairs around a glass-topped coffee table and requested a round of mojitos while Olivia went up to change out of her working clothes.

"Things really got squared away, from what I could tell," I said to Dad. "You done good."

"None of the other options had a lot of appeal. My retirement years in some vermin-infested hoosgow, or getting caught in the crossfire when Olivia and those two gonnifs in the hall opened up. I've made my peace with enough gunshot wounds. After that exchange of pleasantries in the Swamp I had reverbs for a couple of nights."

"That doesn't make you less of a stand-up guy."

"Stand-up comedian would be closer to it. A Jackie Mason lookalike, isn't that what Ethan Stokes said?"

"You get it done." I toasted Dad with my mojito glass. "And – you've still got it. Our tour leader is obviously trying to hunt you down."

"Never happen," Dad said. "We're too far out of touch. Lovemaking is a very open conversation carried on by two people's genitals. As time goes by not many can keep that going. Sick as she's been, your mother and I have never quite given up on amour, and that's probably what saved us."

"Still, a lot of casual sex is available these days."

"Casual is the word. Condoms. Lap dances. Peekaboo on the internet. Techniques to avoid involvement."

"You are a throwback," I said.

"Eighteenth century. My emotional development ended with the eighteenth century."

Olivia was making her way across the lobby in our direction. The short, loose, medallion-imprinted silk dress she was wearing pointed up the power in her thighs. The neckline was uninhibited, dramatically scoop-necked.

Dad signaled the waiter and pointed to his glass. Olivia took the loveseat adjacent to our chairs and set down her sizeable hanging purse.

"No grenades in there, I assume," Dad said.

"Chust a little mustard gas," Olivia said. "Air freshener-upper."

"What did you think?" Dad wanted to know. "Could it have gone either way?"

"Sure, jah. Cuba is like that. *Impulsif*."

"For quite a while there it looked like a contest between senile idealism and common sense. I thought we could easily be goners. Were you really prepared to shoot it out?"

"In this consulting business we make a lot of verrueckte bullshit. Fun und games."

"You certainly do," Dad said. "That editor from *Granma* was after our immaculate Yankee tails, nothing was good enough until she had us tucked away in that slammer she booked. Wasn't that your impression? Could she have made that stick?"

"*Granma* is a big deal in Cuba," Olivia assured us. "Where else they gonna get their toilet paper?"

"So that was definitely in the works?" Dad looked concerned. His nerves were coming off the crisis. "Could somebody at home have ransomed us out of a cesspool like that?"

Olivia began to frame her answer; I felt the presence of people converging. First came the waiter, bringing Olivia her mojito along with a plate around which slices of papayas and mangoes had been fanned out artistically. Behind him came Sonny, out of his disguise. He took the unoccupied chair across from Olivia. I introduced them.

"How do I think we met before," Olivia wondered, with a crooked smile. "Do you remember where?"

Sonny shrugged, very much the barefoot buck just off the reservation. Dad indicated his mojito, but Sonny turned it down.

"Sonny brought the documents in," I told Dad.

"It just gets weirder and weirder with you, Michael," Dad said. "Are you really the Operations Director at the CIA?"

"Only until I get a real job." I knocked back the last of my mojito. "Sonny here was backup. In case we needed to get our butts off the island."

Dad looked amused and a little startled. "What does that mean? In case Olivia couldn't blast our way out?" He turned to Sonny. "Would this be possible?"

"I think so," Sonny said mildly. "We've worked things out with personnel in most of the penitenciaras. This regime cannibalizes everything from the black market to the dollar economy. Everybody except the Comandantes is scraping along, and nobody is going to feed himself without a payoff. Convicts with rich relatives disappear from the head count every day. Exfiltration isn't that hard."

"And who is *we?*" Olivia cooed, leaning deeply forward to pick out a slice of dripping papaya with her fingertips.

"We?" Sonny said. "My employers. The YMCA."

Olivia laid the papaya out onto her tongue.

"How does papaya taste" I asked. "Never tried any."

Olivia shot me a sidelong glance. "Papaya is something for which everybody should cultivate an appetite." She presented Sonny with a very amused wink. Without warning Sonny blushed, a backwoods lad in faster company than he could handle. Red on red.

"Time for this girlfriend to visit the Ladies," Olivia decided. She found her feet and started into the lobby.

"What was that all about?" I asked Sonny.

"Around here papaya is peasant slang for vagina."

"*That's* what it was. And here I thought you were reacting to those tremendous nipple erections she kept flashing in your face."

Not long after that Olivia decided to retreat to her hotel room to have a nap. Sonny left soon afterwards. While we were flying home late Sunday I asked Dad whether he thought those two had gotten together.

"I'd imagine they did," Dad said. "Didn't you notice? After Olivia got back from the can the pheromones off those two fogged out the coffee table."

"I hope she didn't waste Sonny too bad."

"She'd probably leave enough so he can start things up again. In time." The cabin attendant brought Dad a Sprite. "There is a variety of European woman that likes to move from one man – or woman – to the next and arranges to gratify herself by chewing the marrow out of everybody's goddamned bones. The granddaughters of Alma Mahler Gropius Werfel. They run to a type – polygamous, ambisexual and voracious. Dybbuks. These ladies flout traditional boundaries whenever it comes to meeting their needs, they never mind gorging on *anybody's* blood. They are the closest thing I've ever met to Werewolves."

"I gather you've mixed it up with one or two."

"One or two at least. It was outstanding. I suspect your accomplice Olivia falls into that category." Dad took a sip. "She had her eye on you," Dad said.

"So it was a good thing Sonny turned up."

"Good for Sonny."

"You think I missed something."

"For sure, that."

"Looks like I've turned conservative," I suggested. "Comes with being a father."

"What!" I had never seen Dad's jaw drop with surprise before. "Linda?"

"So Sonny tells me."

"You meshugena," Dad said. "Really?"

CHAPTER XXIII

As everything turned out, that interlude in Havana was what it took to cauterize Ramon's exposure. And ours. Everything opened up for us. A wave of energy rolled into our lives we could barely cope with.

I thought it probably had something to do with the congregation of spirits that descended on our wedding. It made sense to put the actual ceremony off until the beginning of October, when everybody could be sure that the worst of the blanketing heat and chronic hurricane scares of late summer were behind us and Dad wasn't scheduled to be jumping around the country pushing his Keynes biography. The pre-reviews were euphoric, and all the late-fall festivals and book fairs were clamoring to ink him into their schedules.

If Rabbi Ginsburg thought Wendy's wedding in Coral Gables pushed intercultural accommodation to the breaking point, I found myself wondering what she was going to make of our wedding. We held it at the principal reform temple in St. Petersburg. Rabbi Ginsburg and Linda's mother, Sakwa, conducted the ceremony jointly. Sakwa's accomplishments as a medicine woman gave her a standing among the Comanches equal to a tongue speaker in the Native American Church, eligible to oversee ceremonies or conduct a vision quest.

Along with the dovening and the readings from the Pentateuch and the V'Yistadal, our wedding was highlighted by a sun dance on the side lawn. Rabbi Ginsburg had anticipated no problem with that, and didn't begin to panic until she and Angela McCarthy happened upon a brave – naked to the waist in buckskin leggings, wooden skewers woven in and out beneath the flesh and muscle of his chest and connected by long rawhide thongs to the top of a cottonwood center pole hauled in from Lawton. The moment the ceremony ended, the brave launched into his high-stepping gyrations around the trembling ridgepole, a propitiation of the sun spirits executed against the throb of tom-toms.

"I know we're supposed to represent the liberal wing of Judaism," Rabbi Ginsburg cornered my father to insist during the reception in the synagogue's atrium afterwards, "But, Bube, your family keeps pushing out the mothering limits."

"Wait 'til you meet the Hutu maiden my nephew's got his eye on," Dad said. "We're all trying very hard to get her to give up cannibalism. Between missionaries. She is especially susceptible to people of the cloth. They're so well cared for, and plump. Meticulous about depilating themselves. Toothsome!"

"Sylvan, you are essentially a mumser. I think you should consider applying for membership in another congregation."

"I've thought of that," Dad said. "But I'm smitten with you."

It was a mixed lot. Linda's father had made the trip. Tall, friendly if a little taciturn, he had the preoccupied look much of the time of a Randolph Scott/Gary Cooper-style lawman who missed his six-guns. I saw where Sonny got a lot of his duende.

Sonny himself showed up with — of all people – Olivia. She watched the proceedings with no small amusement. "Did you bring your pistol?" Dad stage-whispered to her when he got the chance.

"Natuerlich."

"Please don't shoot anybody until I give you the heads-up. I've got a list."

Wendy brought little Carlos, already a handful. I had the feeling Ramon might not have attended our wedding, except that he wanted badly to have a look at his new-born grandson. Ramon seemed less jittery if a lot older. Actually, Dad and Ramon had been back and forth more often over the course of the previous summer than during the heyday of the hedge fund. Dad was advising Ramon on securities. On Dad's advice Ramon had liquidated his riskier assets before the market tanked and paid off his looming Mafia stakeholders. Ramon listened to Dad when stocks cratered and had also moved in and bought several hundred thousand shares each of Ford and Oshkosh. Somebody from Dad's prep school had an inside track with the important military suppliers around the Middle West and tipped him off that Oshkosh was on the cusp of a big Pentagon contract.

Both stocks turned into ten-baggers, as market parlance has it; the gains made Ramon whole again. He wouldn't require our capital. The next spring Rick and Wendy relocated to Coral Gables so that – between martial arts tournaments – Rick could apply his freshly acquired financial management degree to reinvigorating Ramon's Sunrise Medical Ventures.

Ramon was pleased. High-strung and instinctively refined – his family had originated as nobility in Segovia – Ramon always made an effort with Wendy, although her brash style and easy-going manners keep Ramon on edge. At feeding time she had a way of flopping out a bub in front of anybody and everybody and nourishing the hell out of hungry little Carlos.

Some people let you down, and some people keep showing you more and more. St. Petersburg is an invigorating hodge-podge of colleges and trade schools and universities, art galleries and theater groups and grab-bag cultural smorgasbords like Bob Devin Jones' 620 club, where action painting meets soul music meets open-speaker poetry night on wide-open turf everybody around town seems to be pawing the ground to claim.

Legitimized by marriage, Linda wanted it all. Without giving up her new department-manager slot at Walmart she enrolled in night courses. I think she worries a lot about Sonny, who spent a long night a week before Osama Bin Laden got taken out mapping the exits and guard positions inside that bristling Pakistani compound. Sonny assured his sister that he had prepared for this ordeal by fasting until the thunder beings came to him in a vision and helped him prepare his spirit. Now Linda worries less.

She herself is definitely settling in. She destroyed all opposition in neighborhood eight-ball tournaments. Most important, as the months passed, Linda discovered classical music. Mother took her to a Shostakovich concert at the Mahaffey, and halfway through the first violin concerto Linda erupted in tears. Linda needed music, badly. After that the two never missed a performance of the Florida Symphony.

For Christmas in 2008 I gave Linda her first violin and a year of lessons. Having been a prodigy as a pow-wow dancer, I suppose the concentration and instinct for rhythm came naturally to her. Her teacher was amazed, and by the time baby

Sylvan came along in January Linda could play the little rascal a tolerable cadenza.

Sylvan Ten Bears Landau. Trips off the tongue. Ten Bears was Linda's father's Indian name, although I never heard him addressed as anything but Sam. At three our son keeps reminding me of Sonny – willowy, easily alarmed and inherently skeptical, touchy and inclined to sulk if things don't go his way, magnetic and irresistibly handsome. Already, he is very much in charge every time his half-brother Carl visits. He can dominate with a gesture. If something or somebody offends little Sylvan his eyes narrow, just like Sonny's.

Left alone five minutes he will attempt to ride Penelope around the living room of our bungalow in the Pink Streets. He has a good touch with the colicky little Chinese orphan Carol and Buckley adopted. Two months after she arrived Carol turned up pregnant, but Lin Kee still owns them both.

Dad keeps it to himself, but I can see that Ten Bears is primus inter pares among his proliferating grandchildren. Both of them are skeptics, they argue, each betrays a deep if carefully hedged commitment to life. To Mother's delight, Dad was selected to occupy a visiting chair at Oxford for a semester recently. Every time he called his first question was: "How's that dratted papoose?"

So things are settling down. My law practice is flourishing – after running Muldavey Court for years I understand troubled property; to have it bruited around town that I have a good hand when it comes to stalling foreclosures in the Age of Obama hasn't hurt one bit. I'm deeply in love. Mother is on top of her immunities. I can tolerate Dad.

It could be a lot worse.

Acknowledgements

A number of literary people have now read and responded to *The Hedge Fund*. Let me now indicate a few whose comments seemed most germane and useful. First – he deserves a paragraph of his own – I want to thank the inimitable George Pequignot for his discerning and unmatched help with our publishing ventures over what is now decades. An original and powerful writer himself, his legerdemain all around the universe of computer composition and printing details has been genuinely indispensable.

Several individuals were especially useful while I was pulling together the background information that fed this book. Francis Sing, herself for years a prominent Comanche pow-wow dancer, sparked a lot of what animated my narrative. The exquisite Sylvia Grijalva brought her to the front cover. Professor Carolyn Johnston of Eckerd College and Chief Billy Cypress put me on the trail of a great deal of Native American sociology, which I used freely. Many of the financial details that drive this story were vetted by the expert Michael Miller. Ray Hinst, the impresario of Haslam's internationally famous bookstore, supplied a lot of the ballistic and intelligence background I needed from time to time. My brother-in-law, James Eiseman, Jr., explained the niceties of the light-rail system around Philadelphia. Cheryl Bradley put Drago through his paces. Drago is the world's most alert Boxer.

I actually read quite widely into the literature of the Native American experience. Two books come to mind among the many. *The Seminole and Miccosukee Tribes of Southern Florida* by Patsy West was very helpful. I couldn't have done without *Sanapia, Comanche Medicine Woman* by David E. Jones.

A number of friends and literary personalities have been kind enough to read and respond to my text. They include Kay and Mike Barnes, Charles Gaines, Hunter Hague, David Kranes, Rich Rice, Ron Satlof, Liz Smith, James Wightman. Many thanks, much appreciated.

Burton Hersh, March 2014

113600043R00144